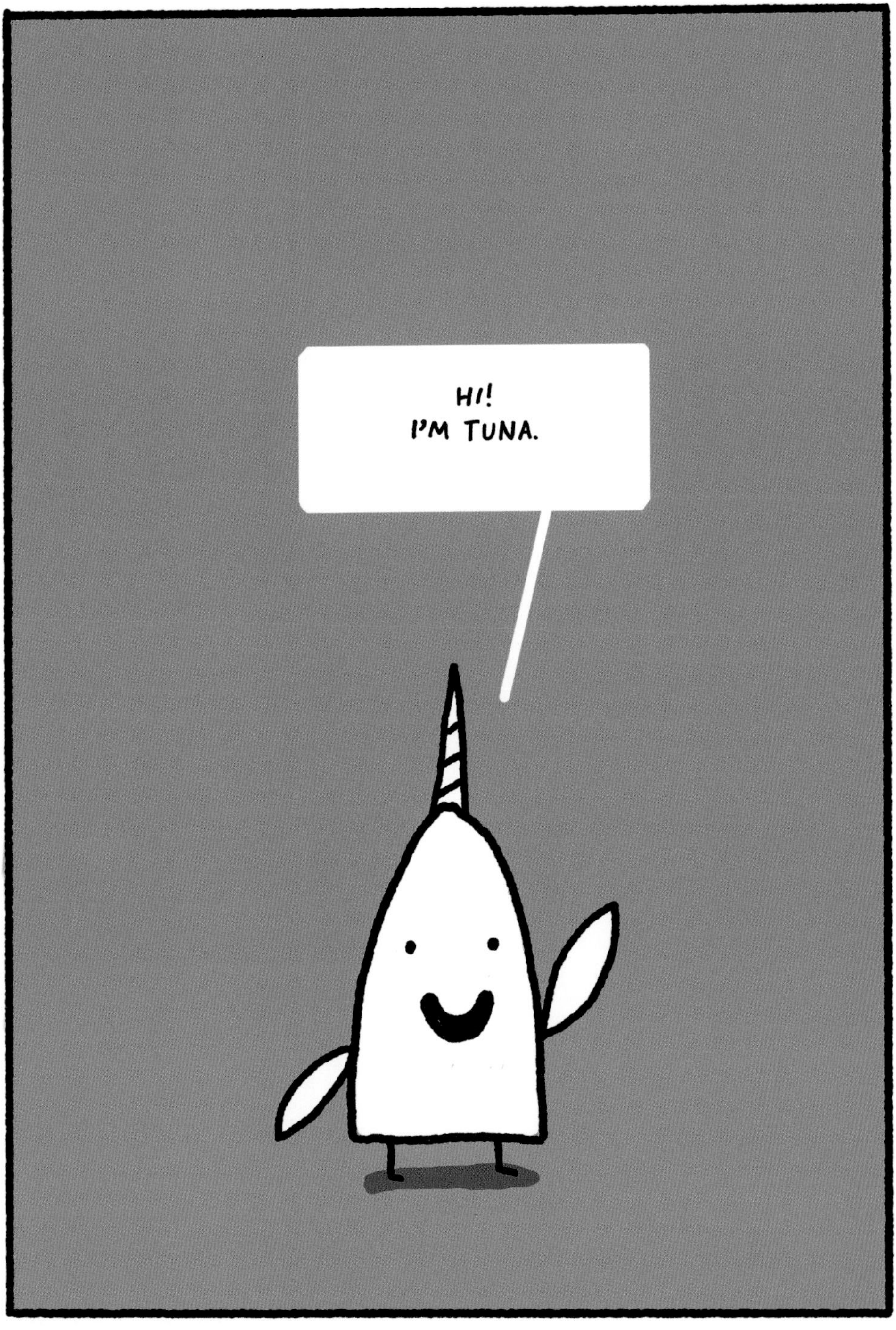
HI!
I'M TUNA.

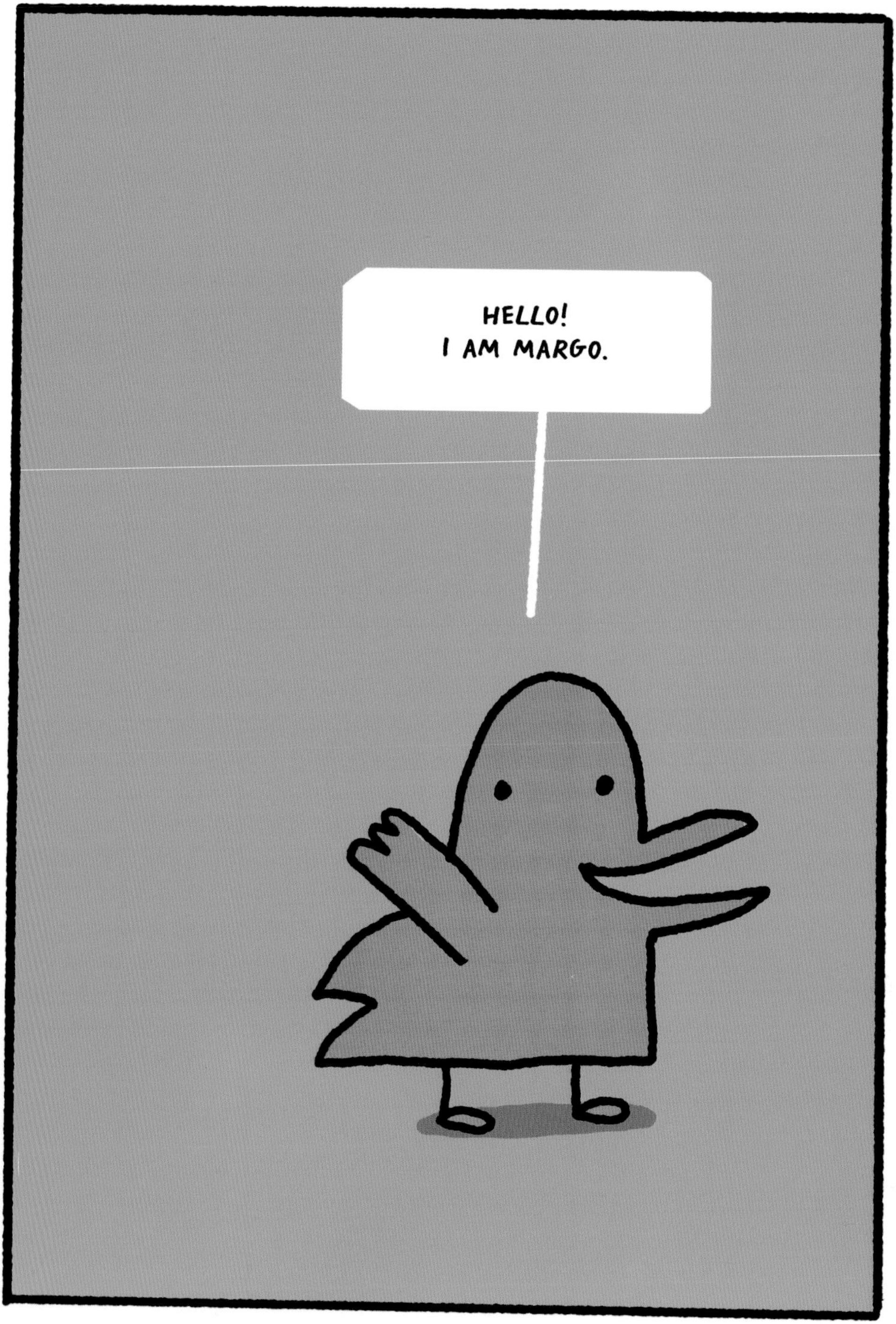
HELLO!
I AM MARGO.

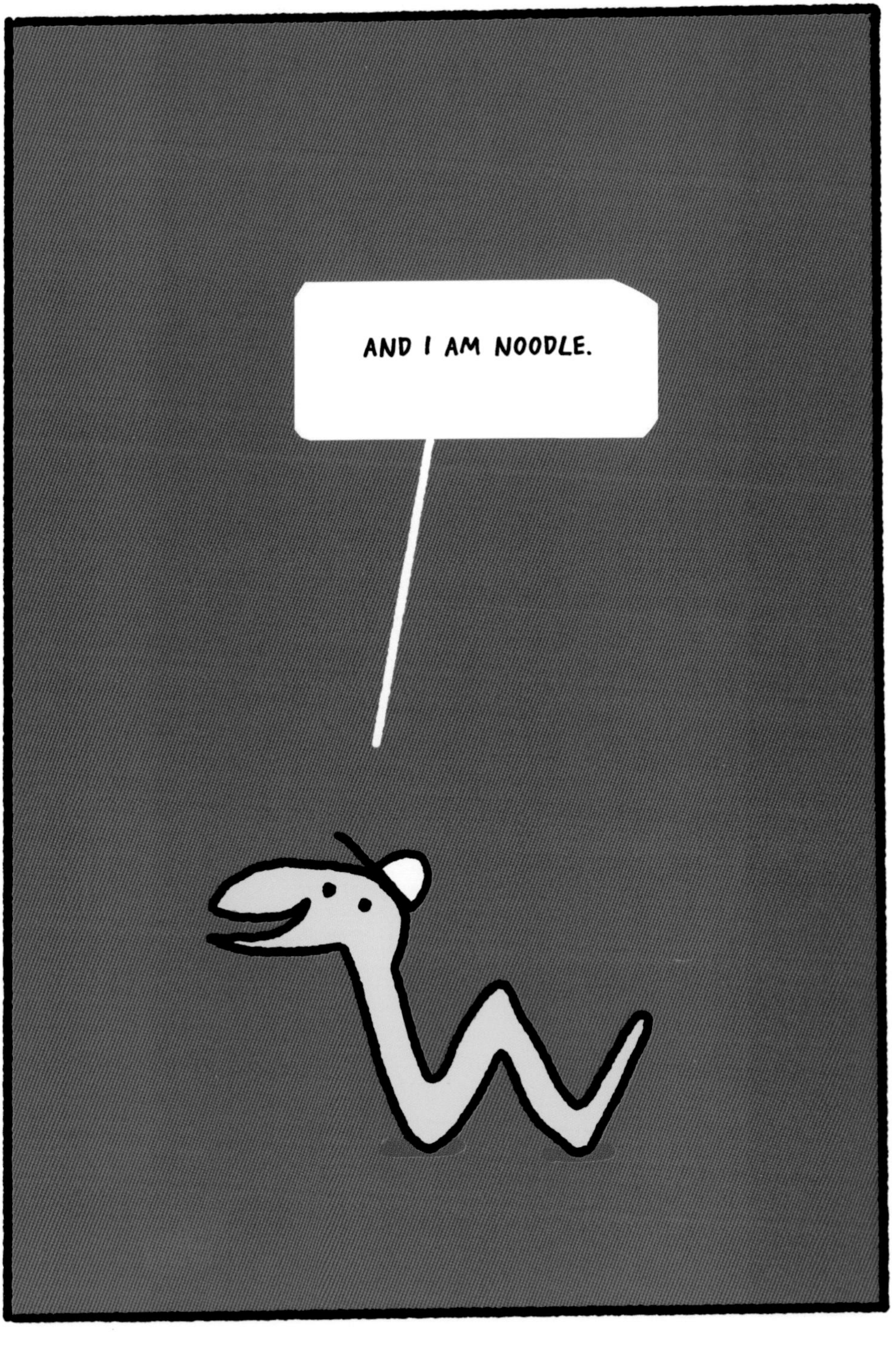
AND I AM NOODLE.

Cataloging-in-Publication Data has been applied for
and may be obtained from the Library of Congress.

ISBN 978-1-4197-5273-5

Text and illustrations © 2021 Frank W. Dormer
Book design by Heather Kelly

Published in 2021 by Amulet Books, an imprint of ABRAMS.
Printed and bound in China

10 9 8 7 6 5 4 3 2 1

Amulet Books® is a registered trademark of Harry N. Abrams, Inc.

ABRAMS The Art of Books
195 Broadway, New York, NY 10007
abramsbooks.com

WE HAVE A

PLAYDATE

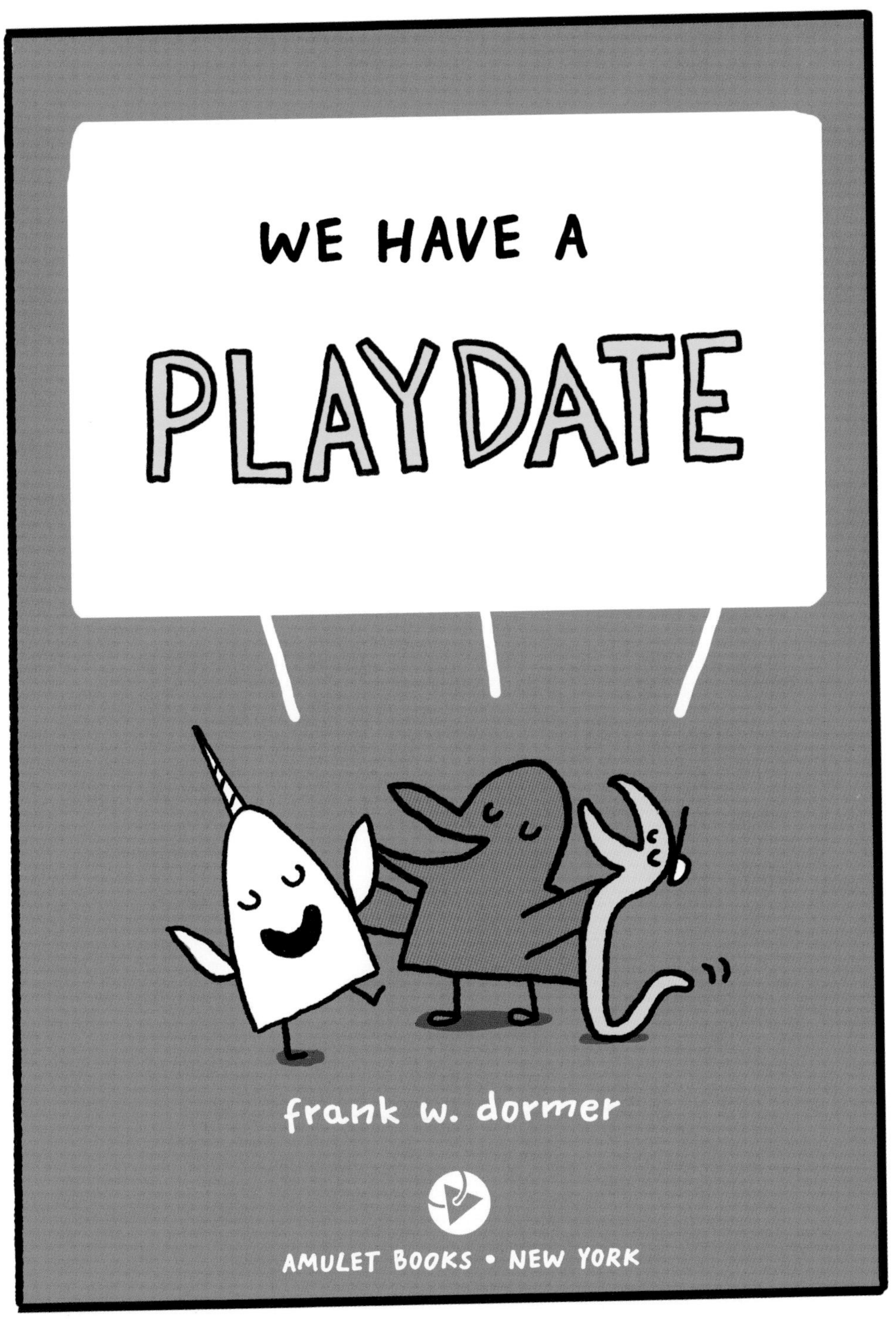

frank w. dormer

AMULET BOOKS • NEW YORK

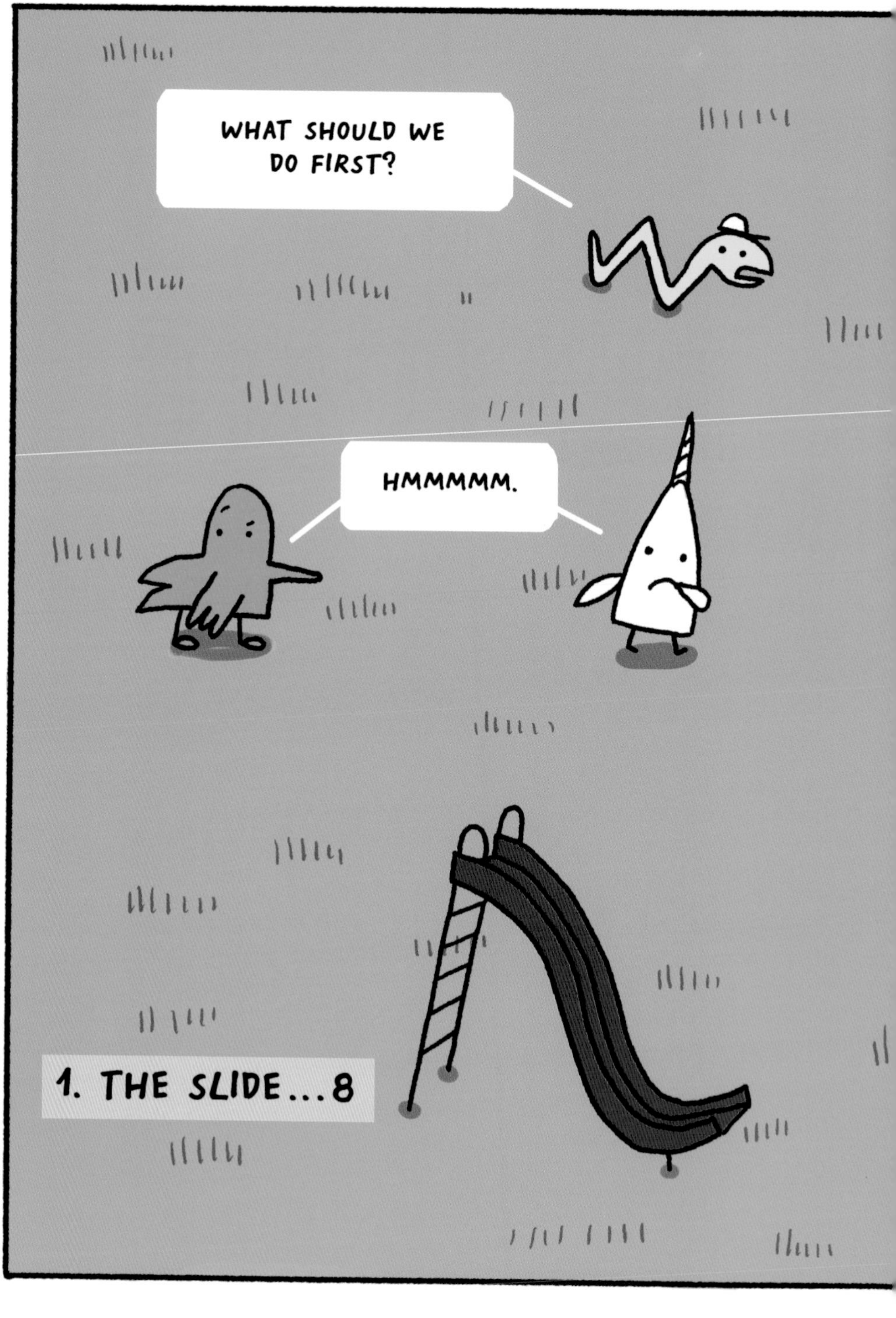
WHAT SHOULD WE DO FIRST?
HMMMMM.
1. THE SLIDE...8

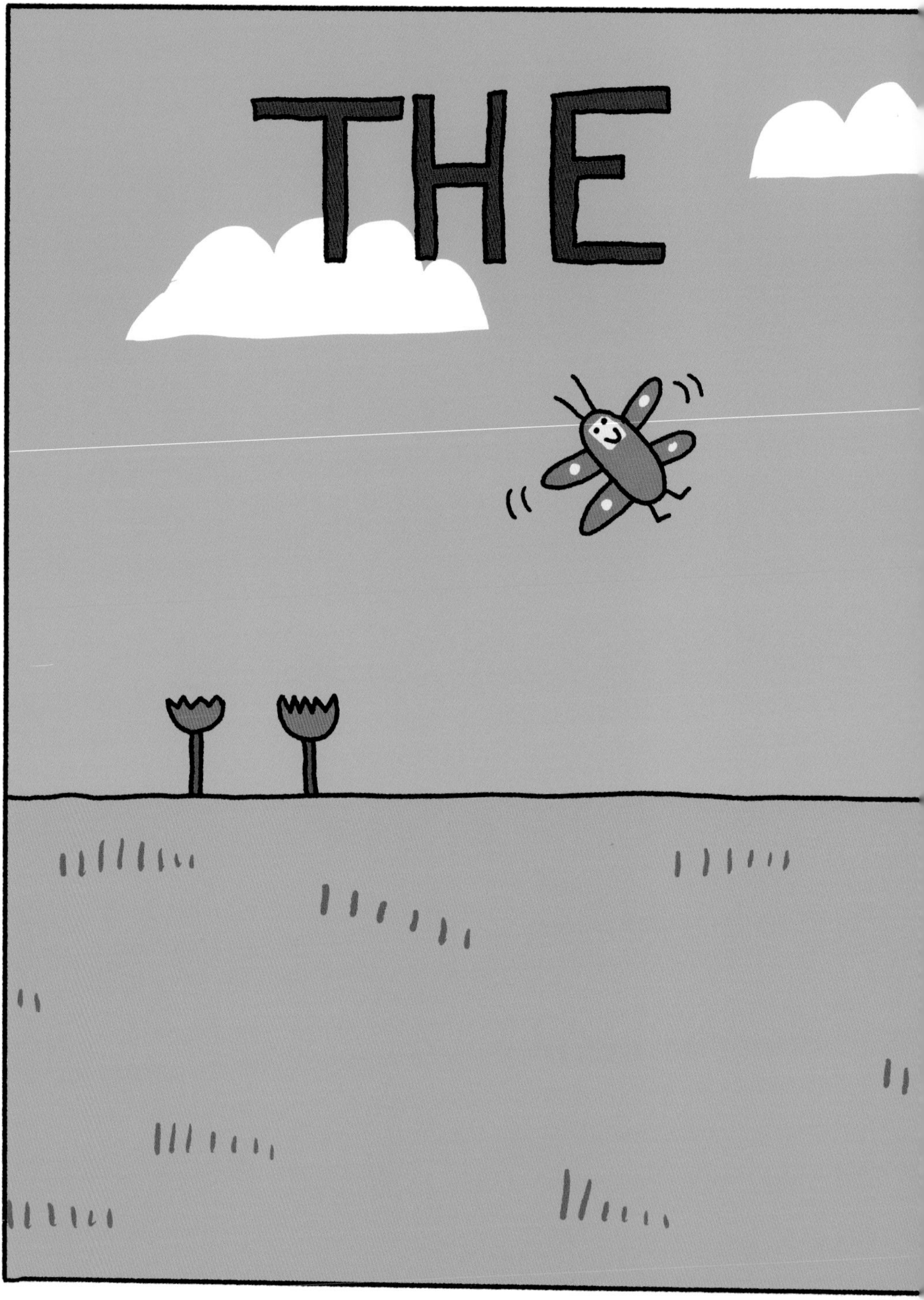
THE

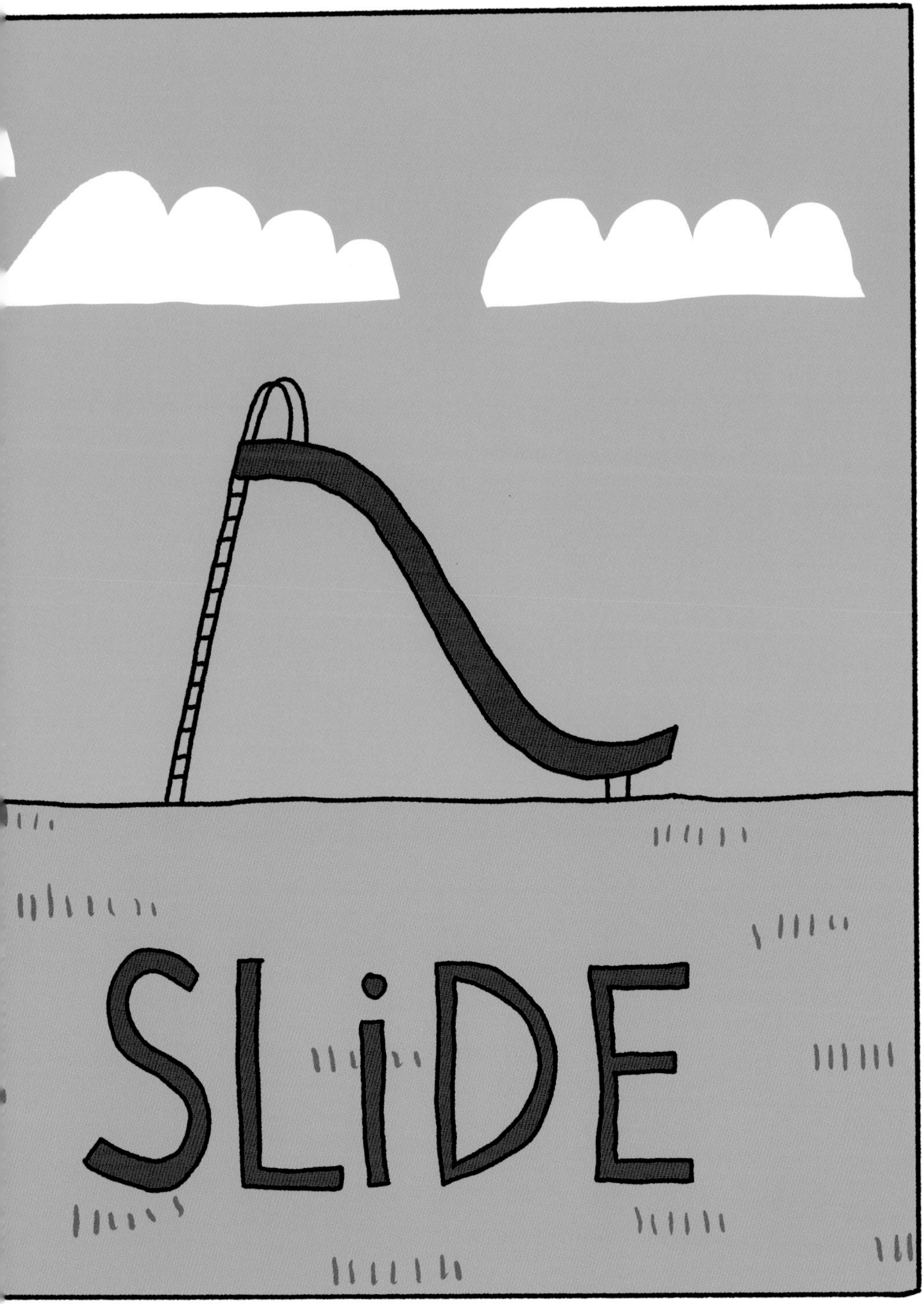
SLiDE

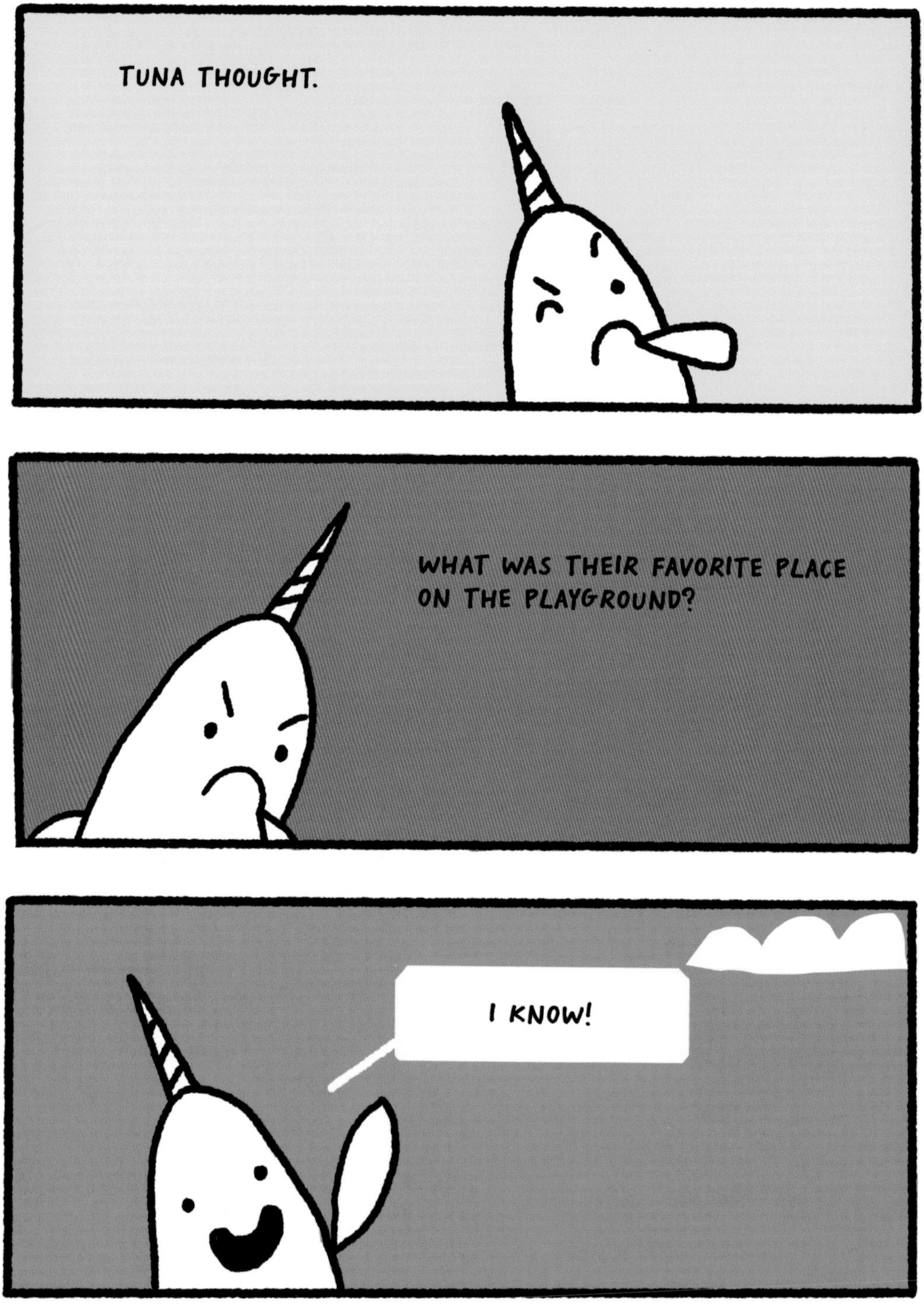
TUNA THOUGHT.
WHAT WAS THEIR FAVORITE PLACE ON THE PLAYGROUND?
I KNOW!

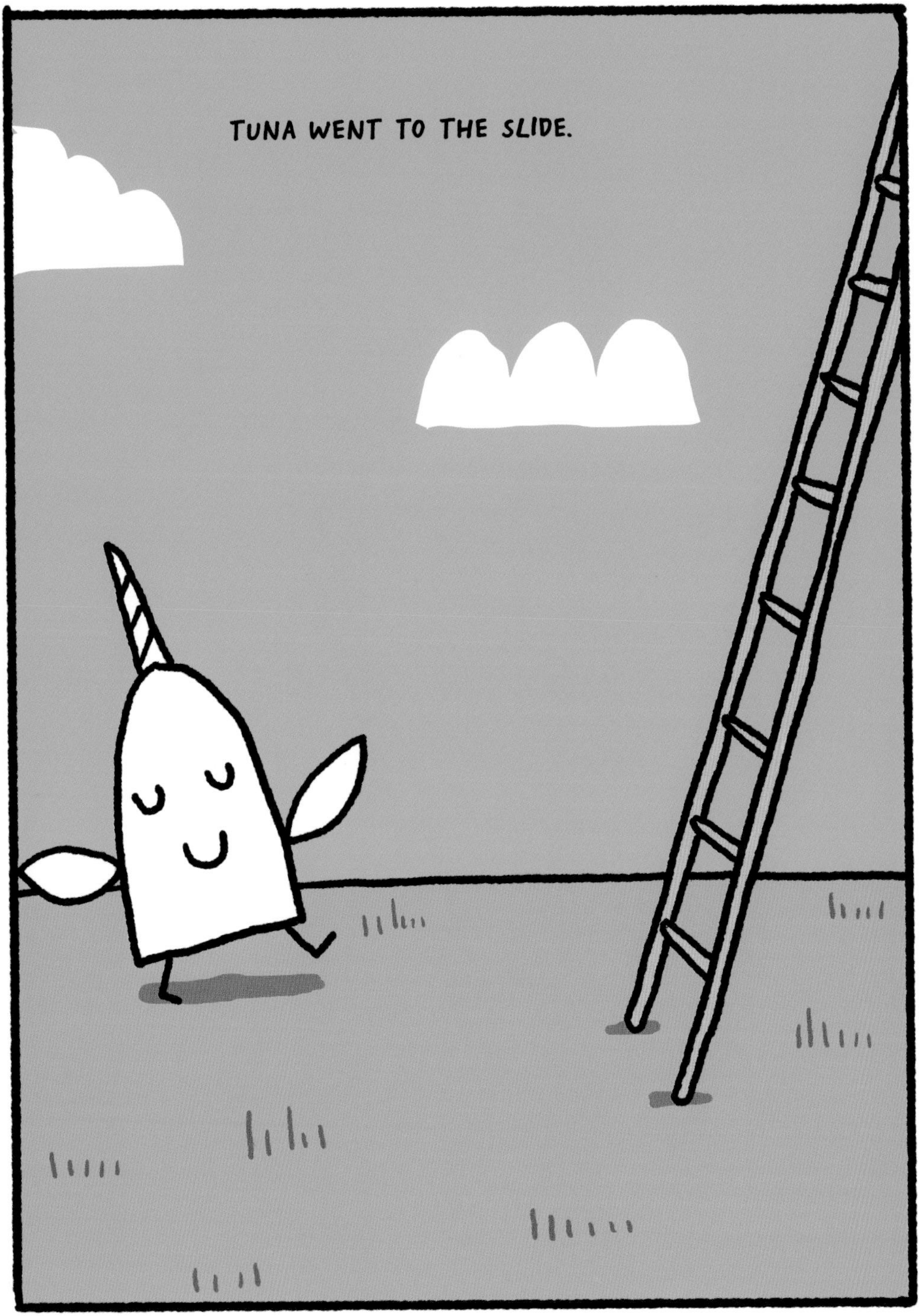
TUNA WENT TO THE SLIDE.

THERE WAS A BEAR ON THE SLIDE.

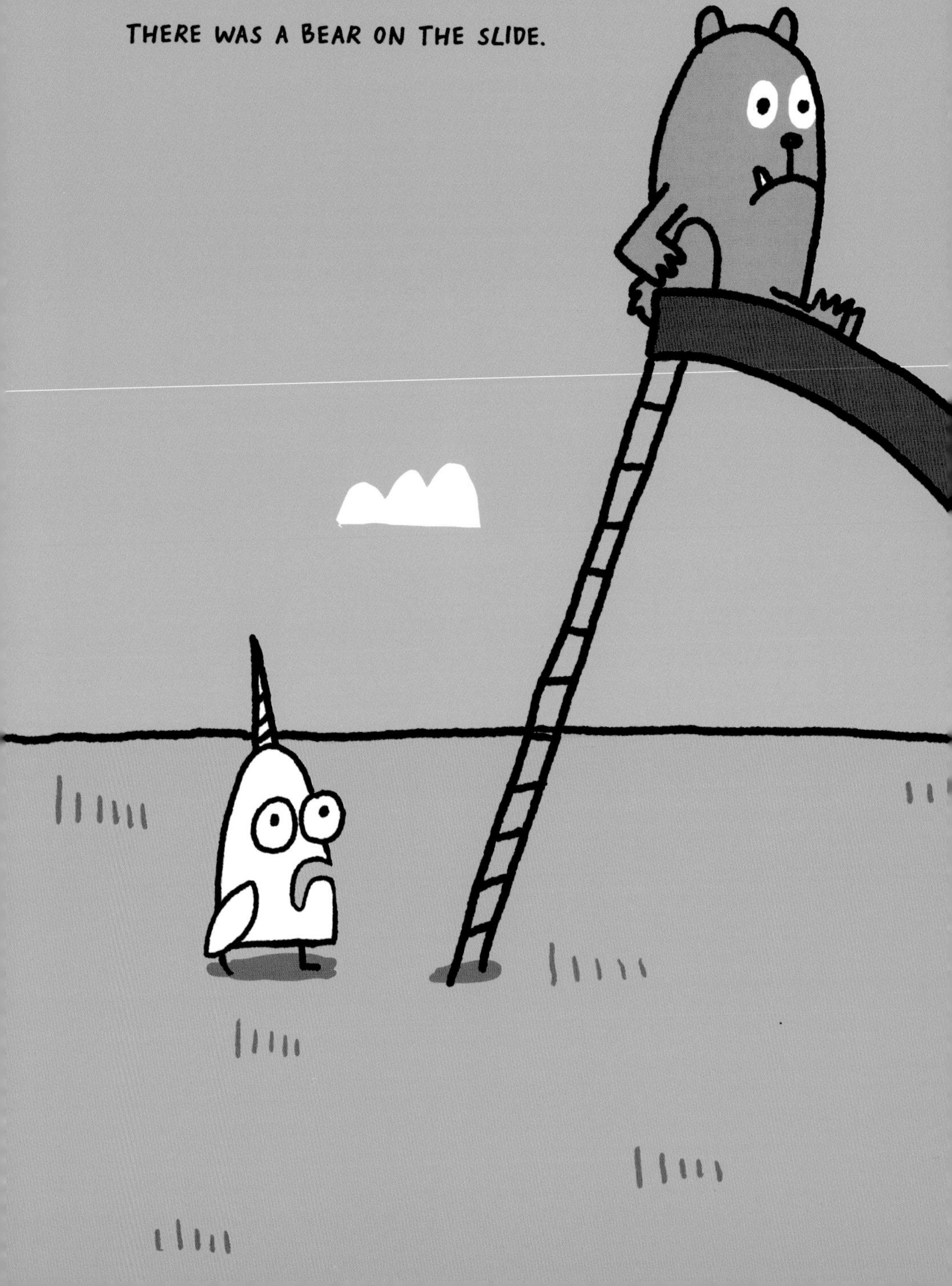

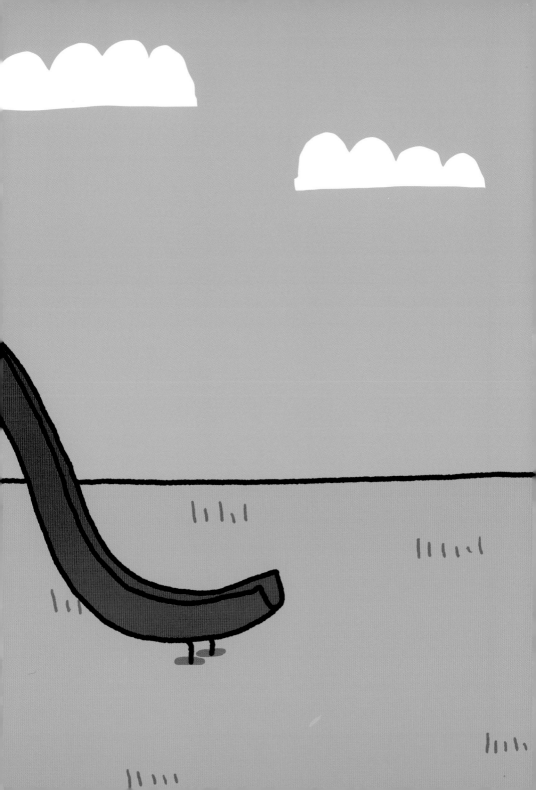

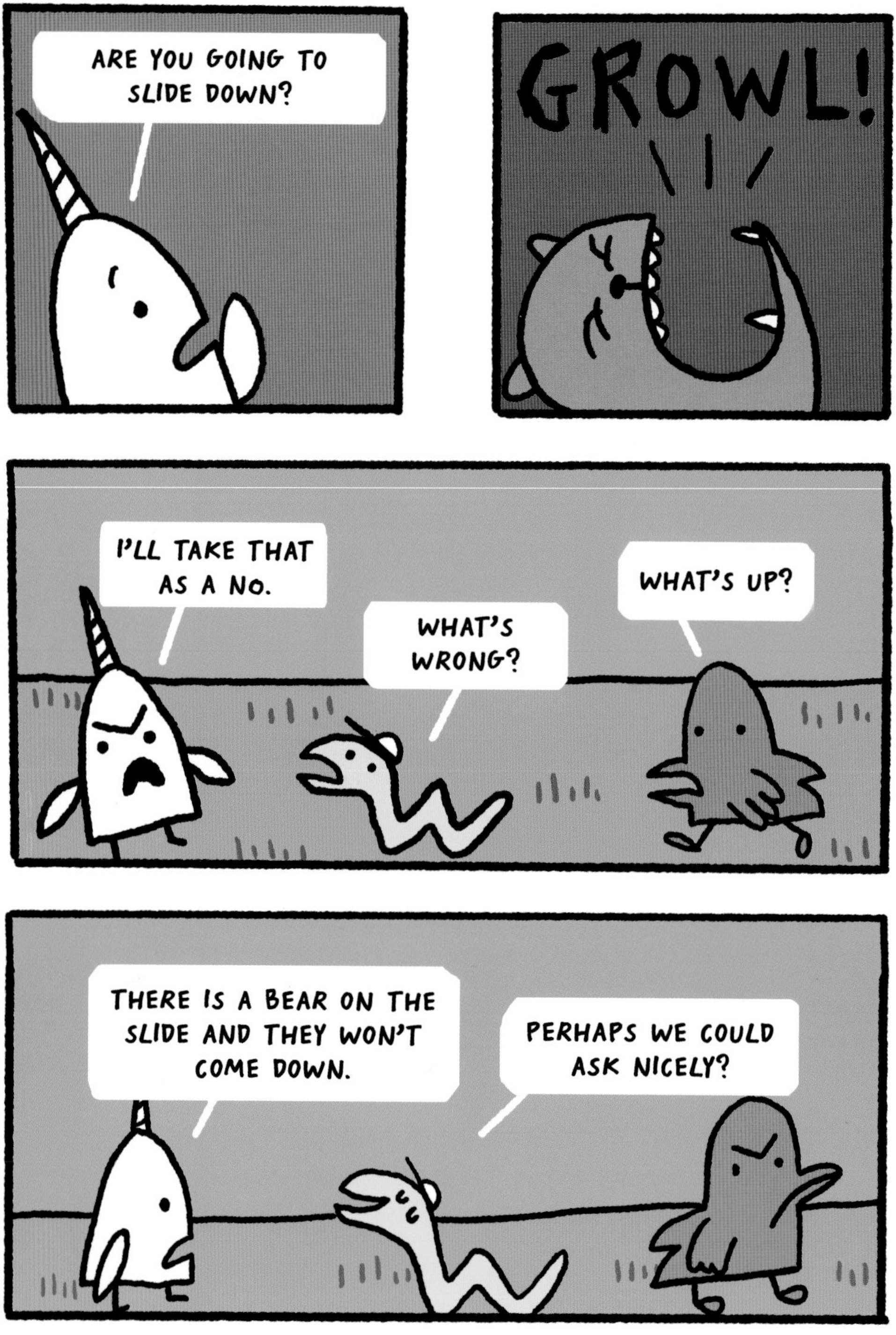
ARE YOU GOING TO SLIDE DOWN?
GROWL!
I'LL TAKE THAT AS A NO.
WHAT'S WRONG?
WHAT'S UP?
THERE IS A BEAR ON THE SLIDE AND THEY WON'T COME DOWN.
PERHAPS WE COULD ASK NICELY?

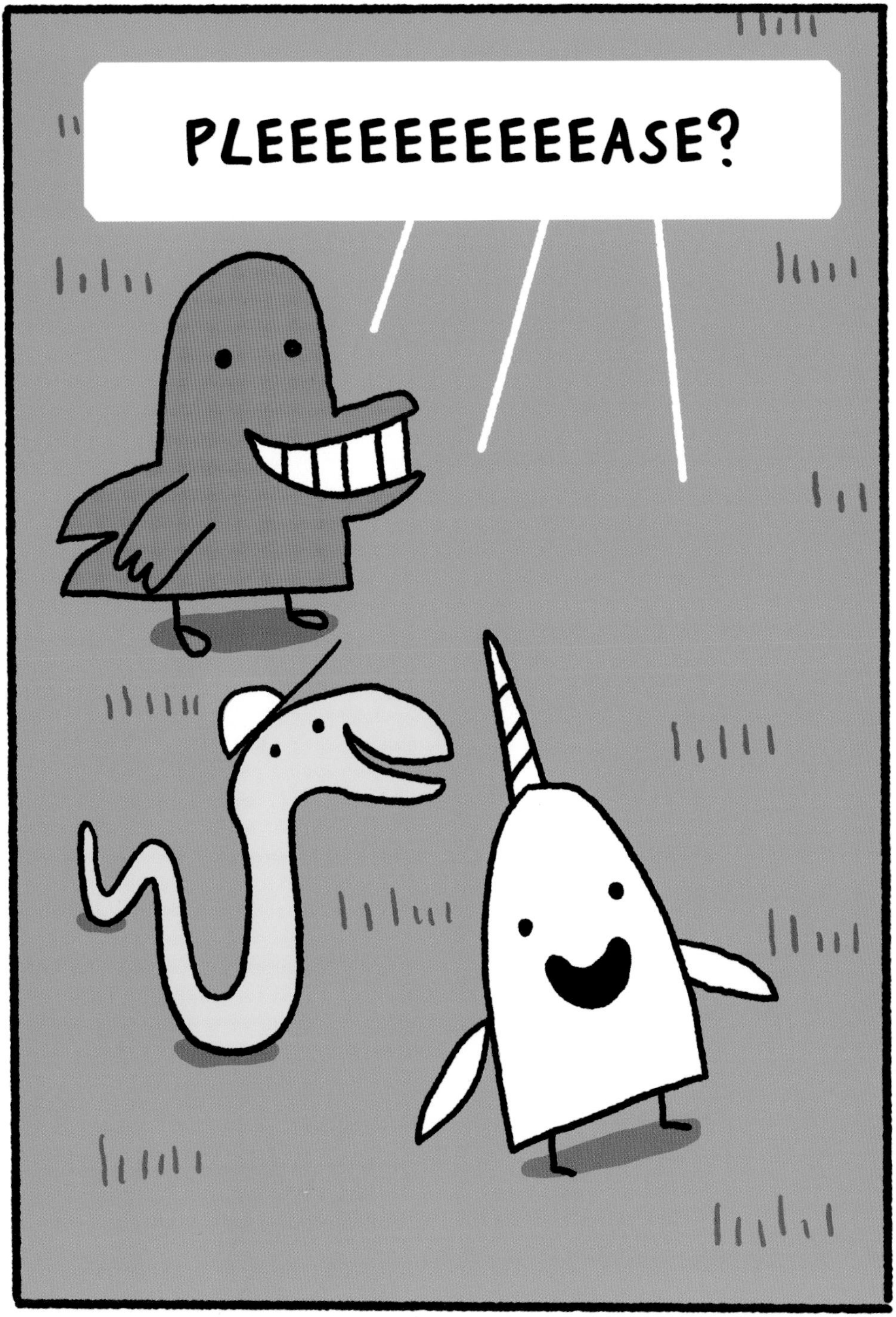
PLEEEEEEEEEEEEASE?

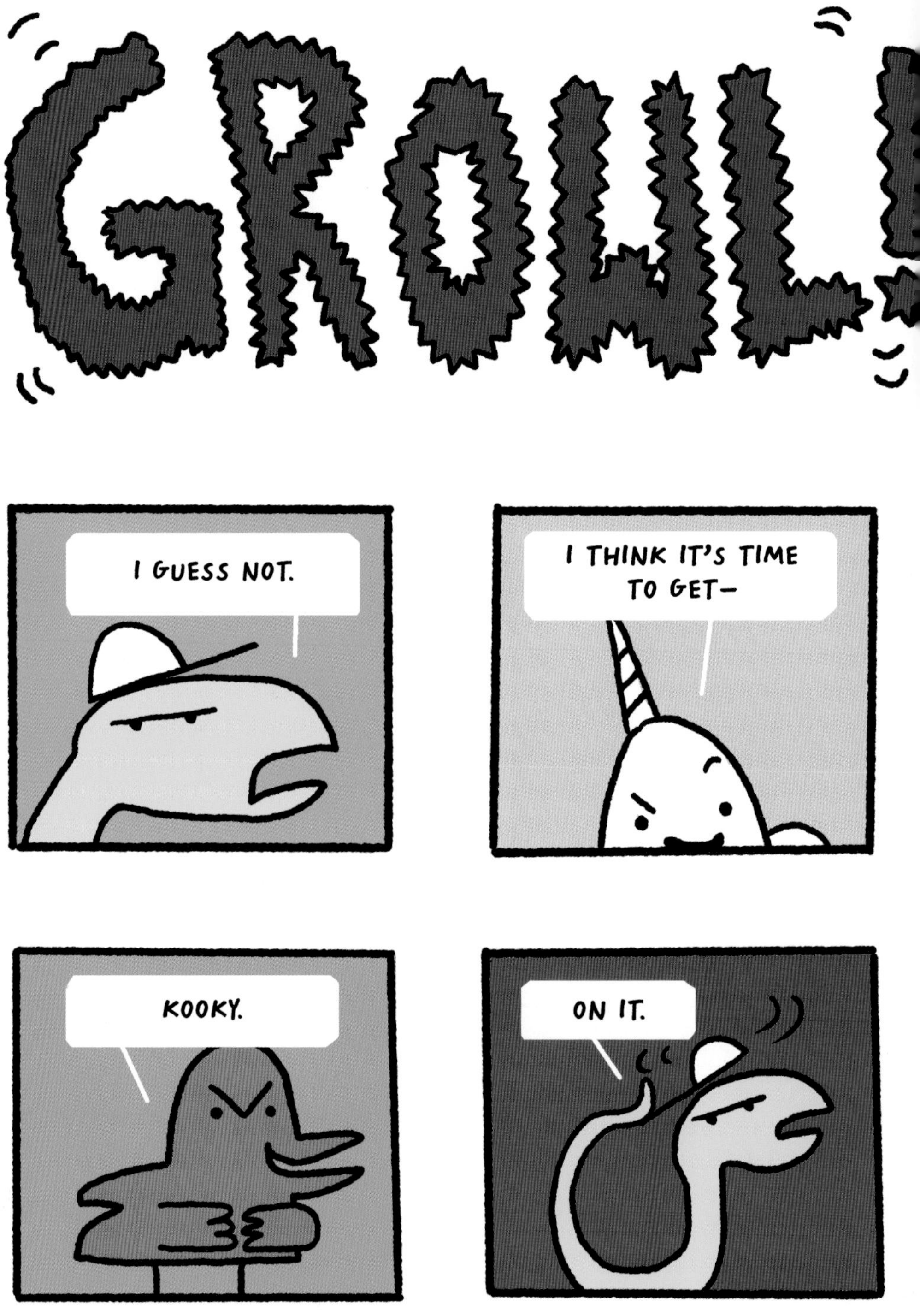
GROWL!
I GUESS NOT.
I THINK IT'S TIME TO GET–
KOOKY.
ON IT.

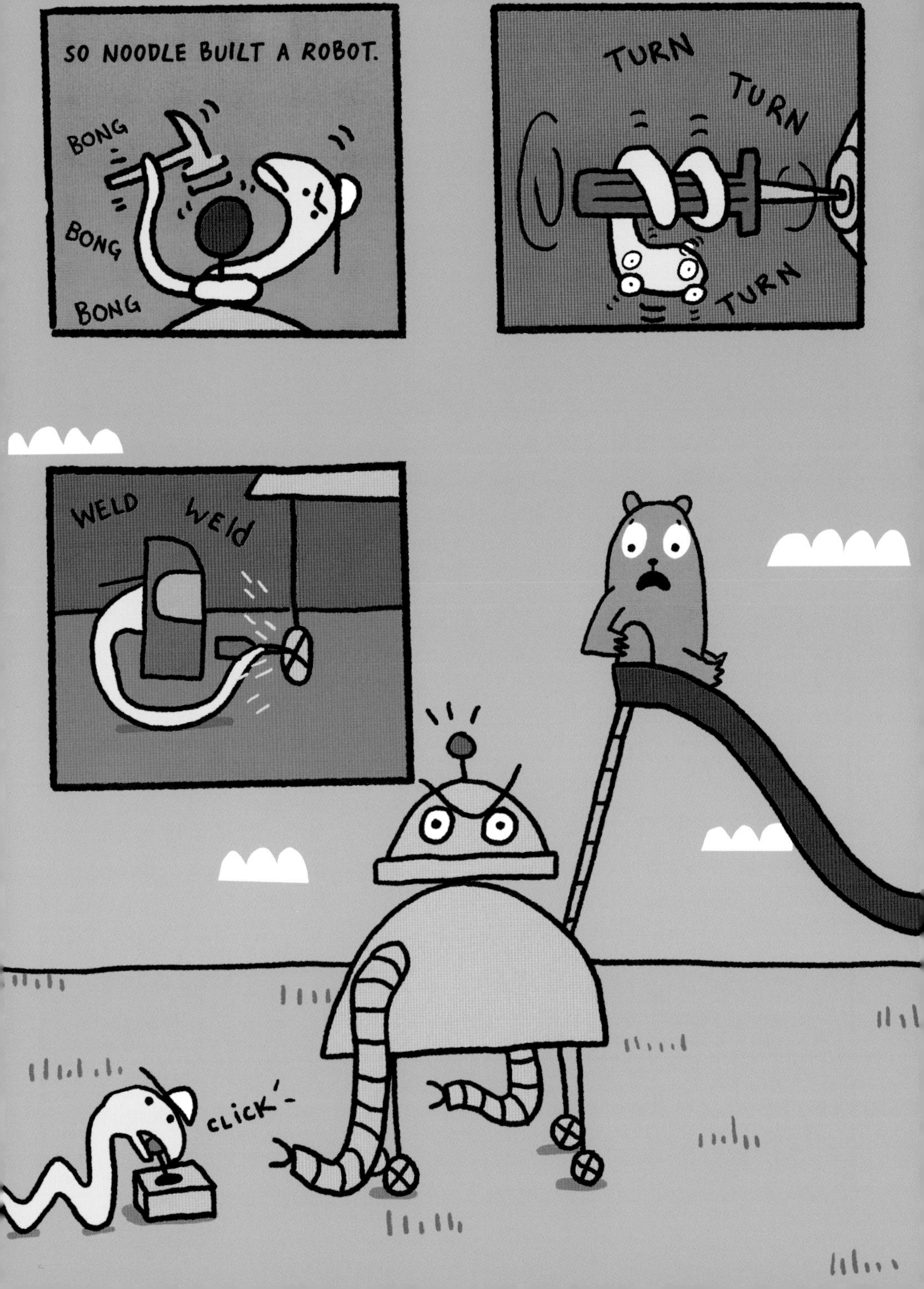
SO NOODLE BUILT A ROBOT.
BONG
BONG
BONG
TURN
TURN
TURN
WELD
WELD
CLICK

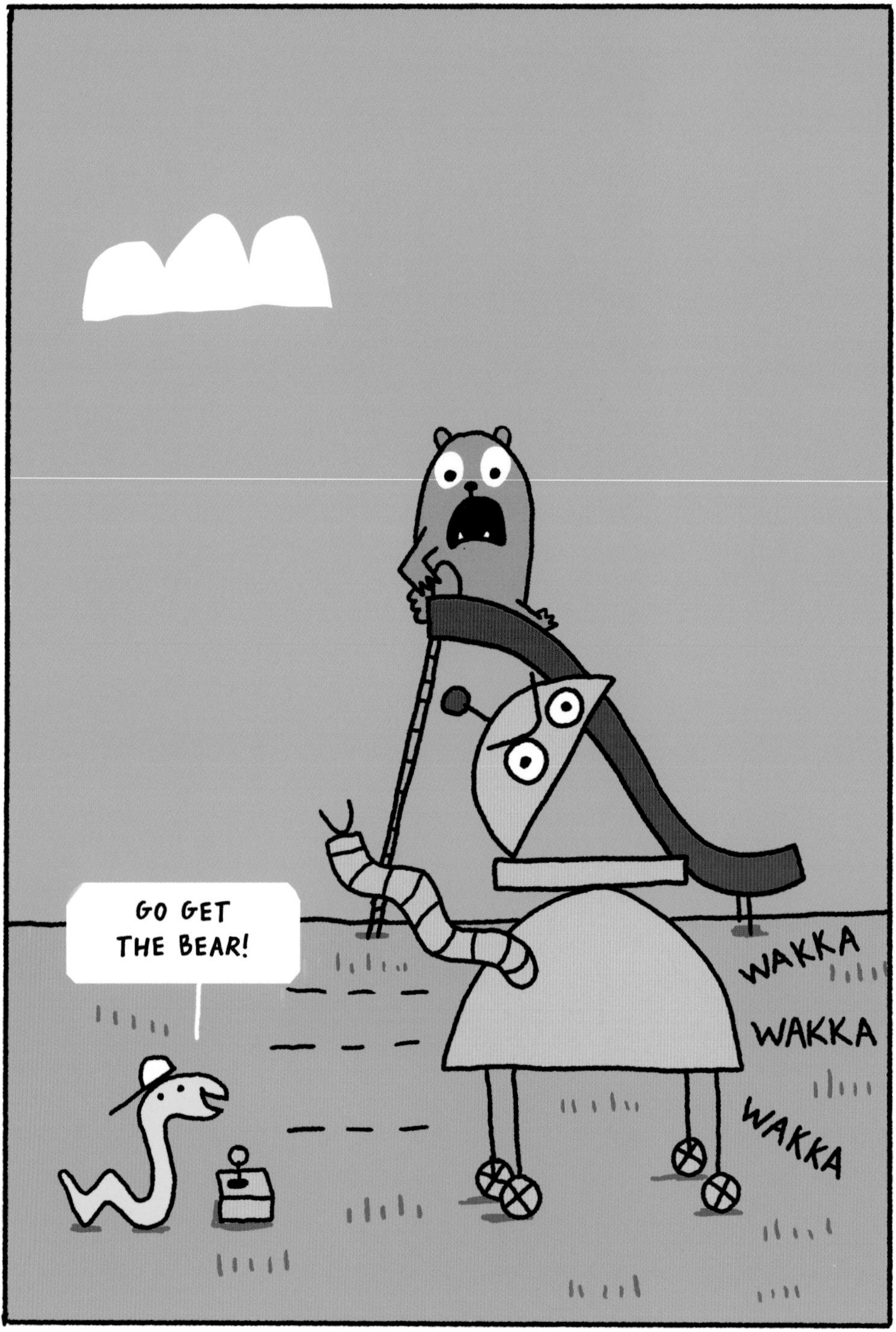
GO GET THE BEAR!
WAKKA
WAKKA
WAKKA

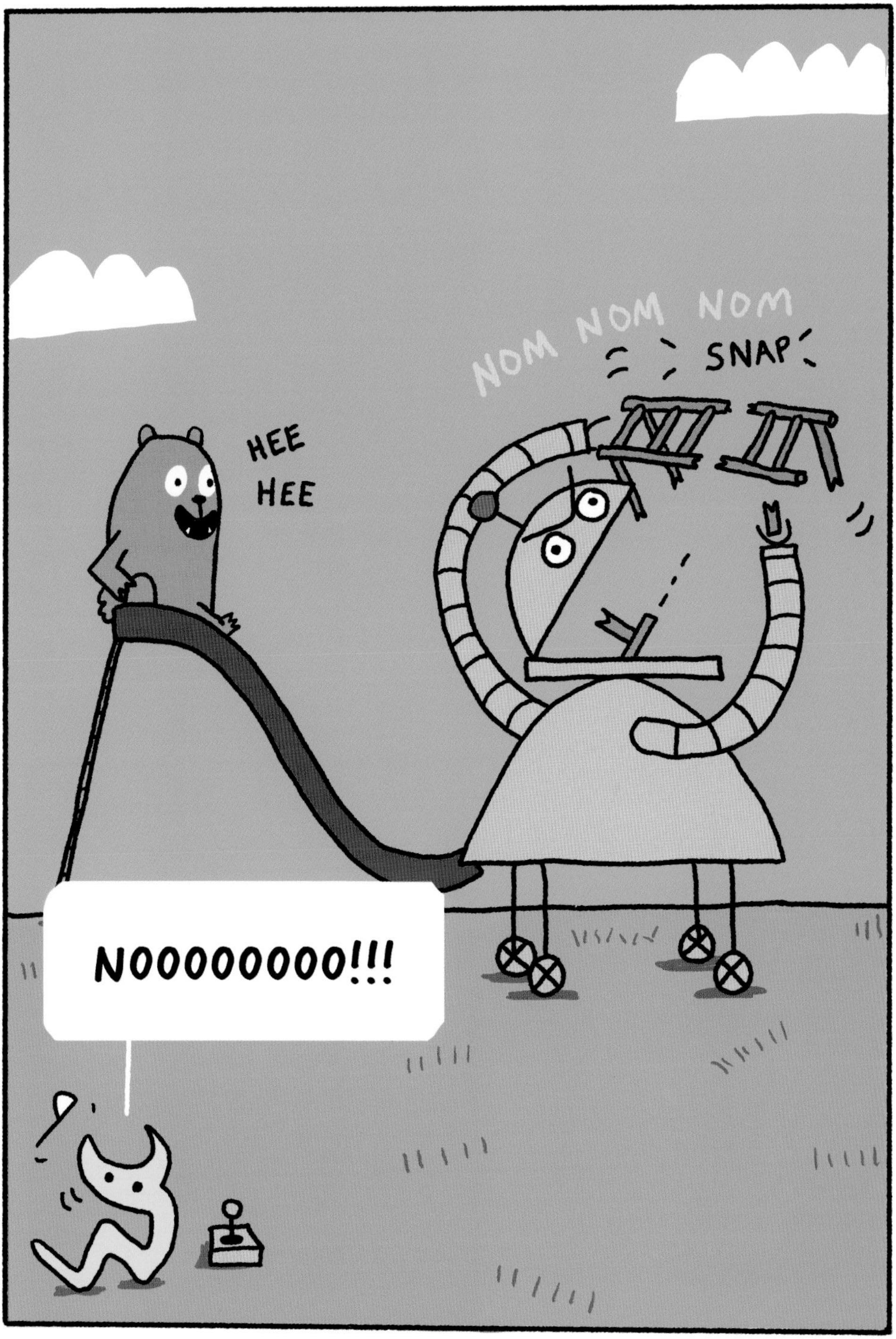
HEE
HEE
NOM NOM NOM
SNAP
NOOOOOOOO!!!

SO MARGO TRIED THEIR BEST DUCK CALLS.

THE OLD HONK.

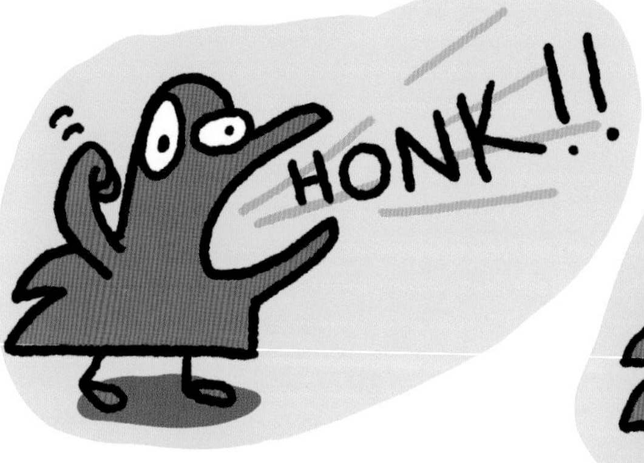
HONK!!

THE RASPBERRY.

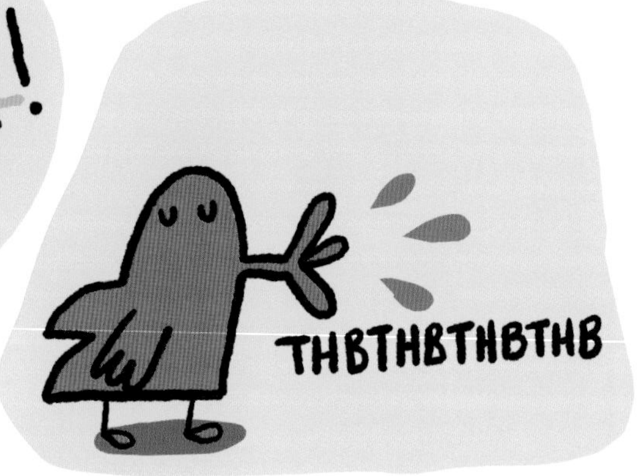
THBTHBTHBTHB

THE MOOSE.

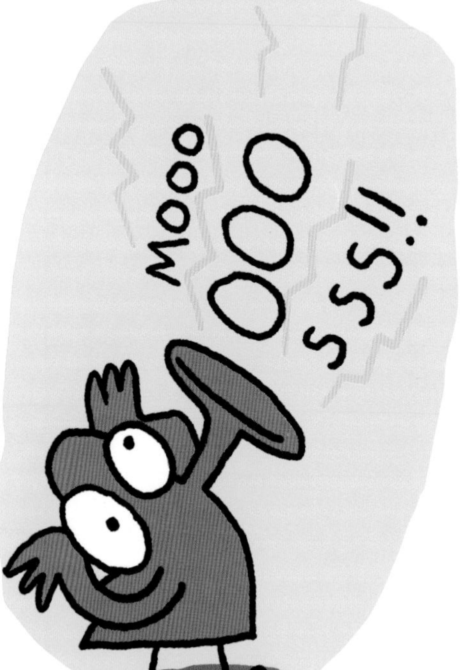
MOOOOOOOSSS!!

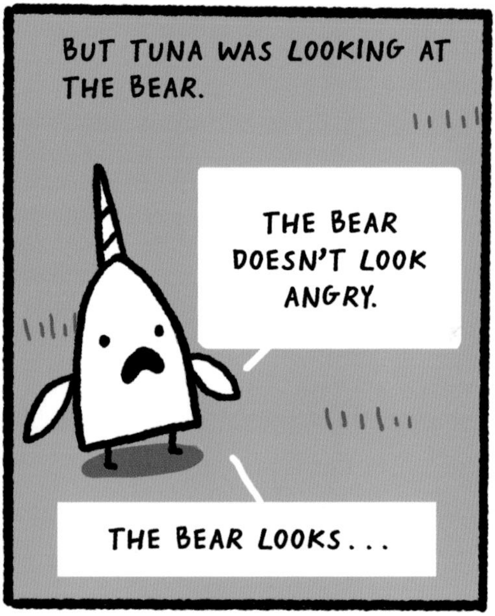
BUT TUNA WAS LOOKING AT THE BEAR.
THE BEAR DOESN'T LOOK ANGRY.
THE BEAR LOOKS . . .

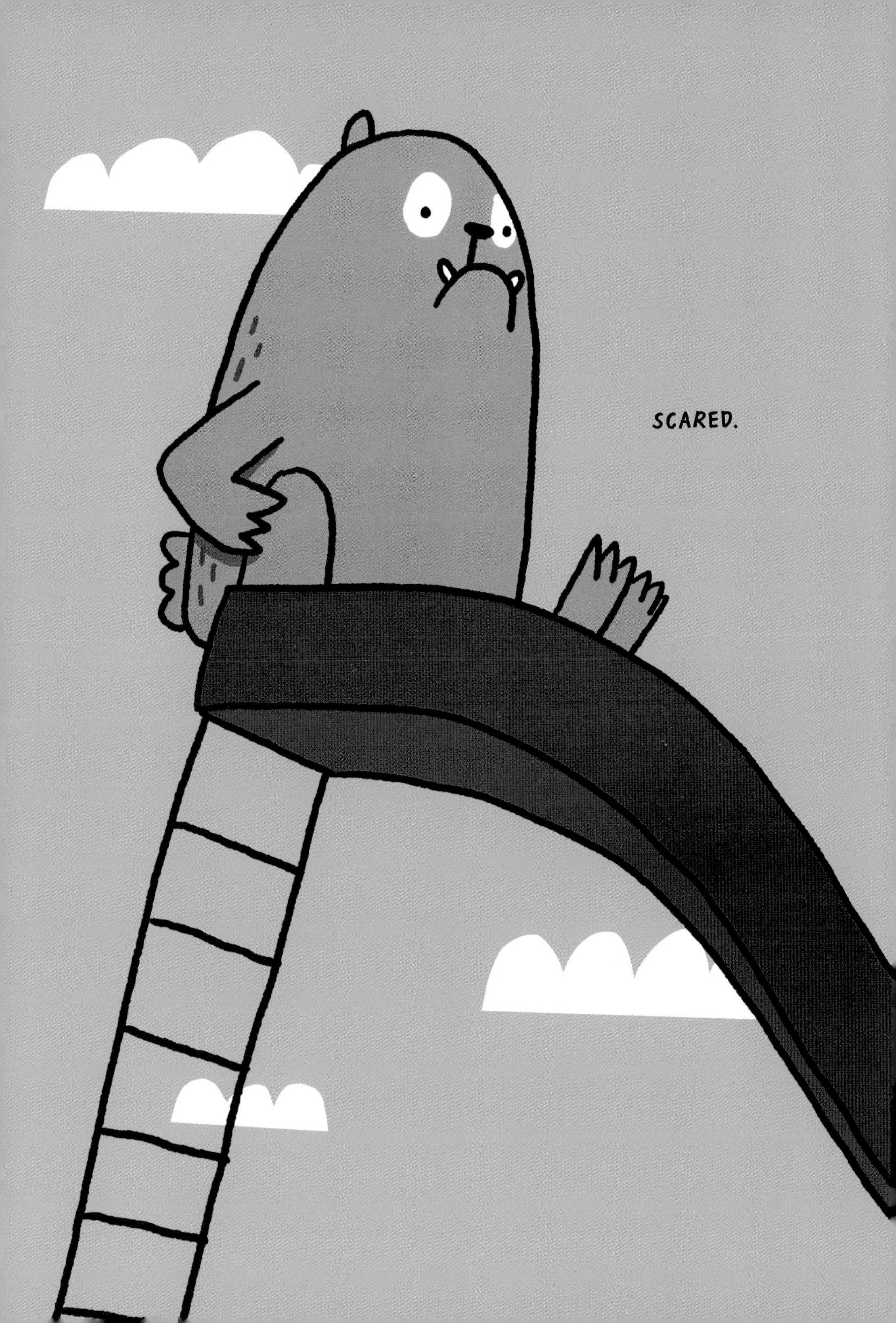

SCARED.

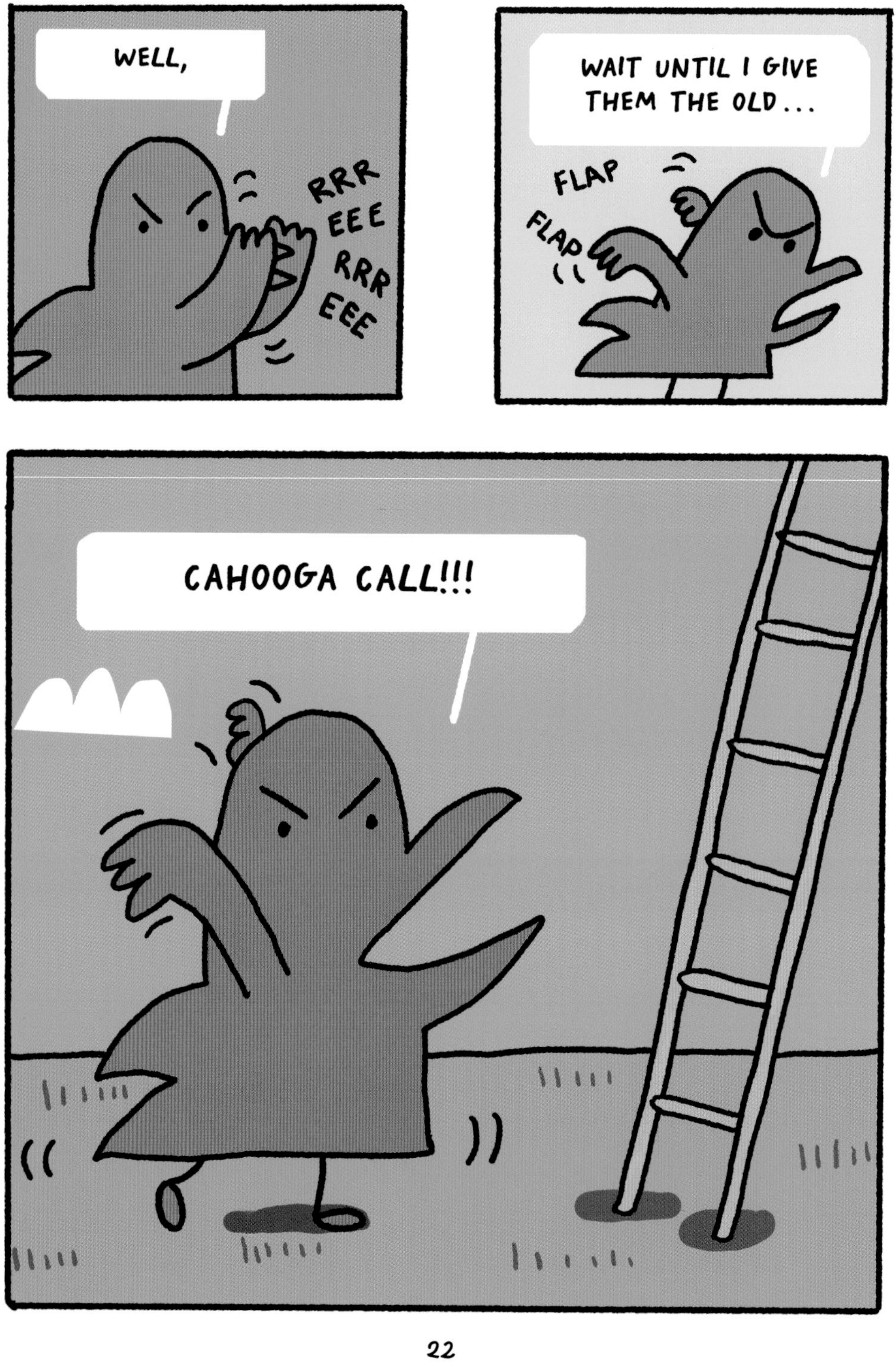
WELL,
RRR EEE RRR EEE
WAIT UNTIL I GIVE THEM THE OLD...
FLAP
FLAP
CAHOOGA CALL!!!

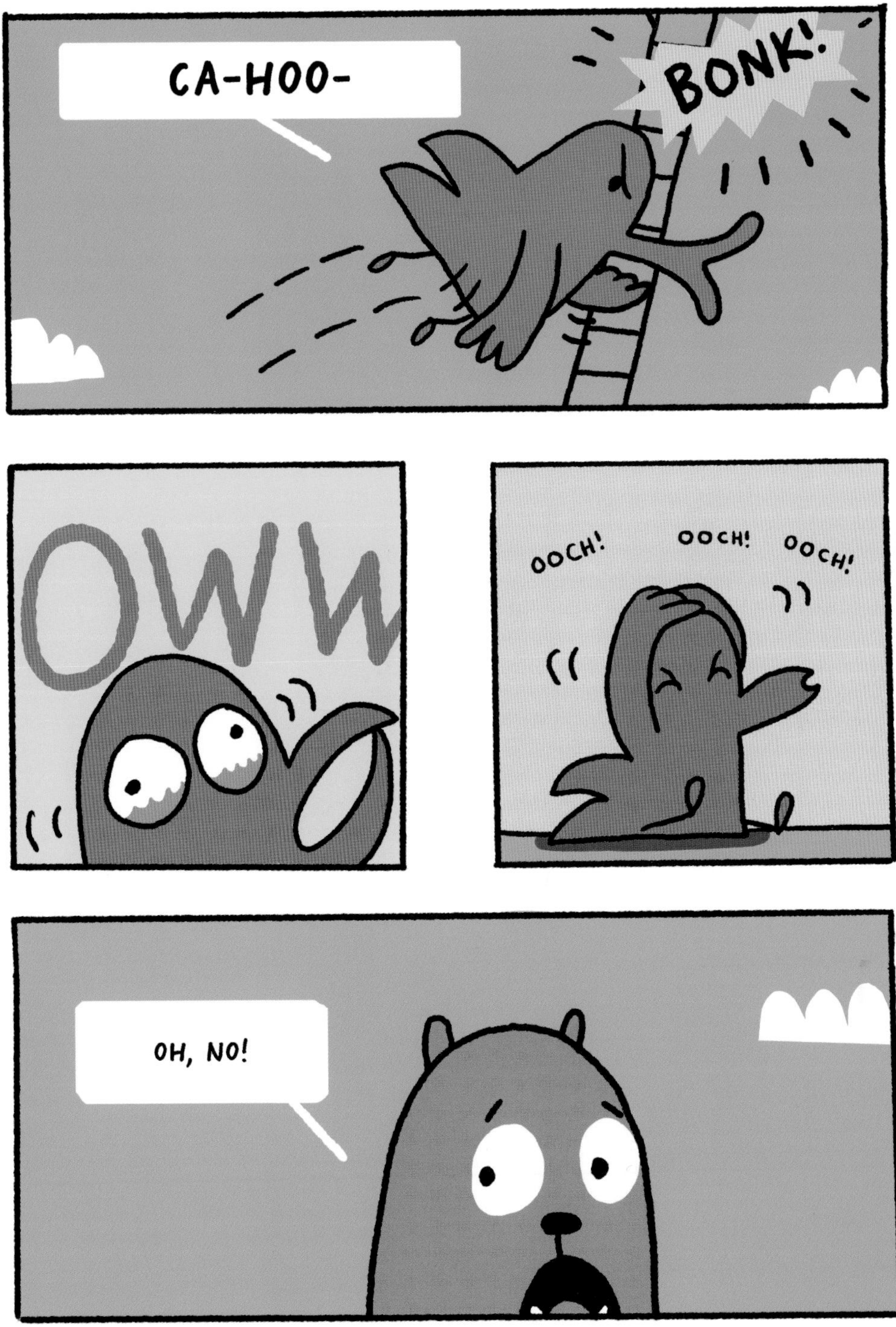
CA-HOO-
BONK!
OWW
OOCH!
OOCH!
OOCH!
OH, NO!

AND BEFORE YOU COULD SAY "NEMATODE,"

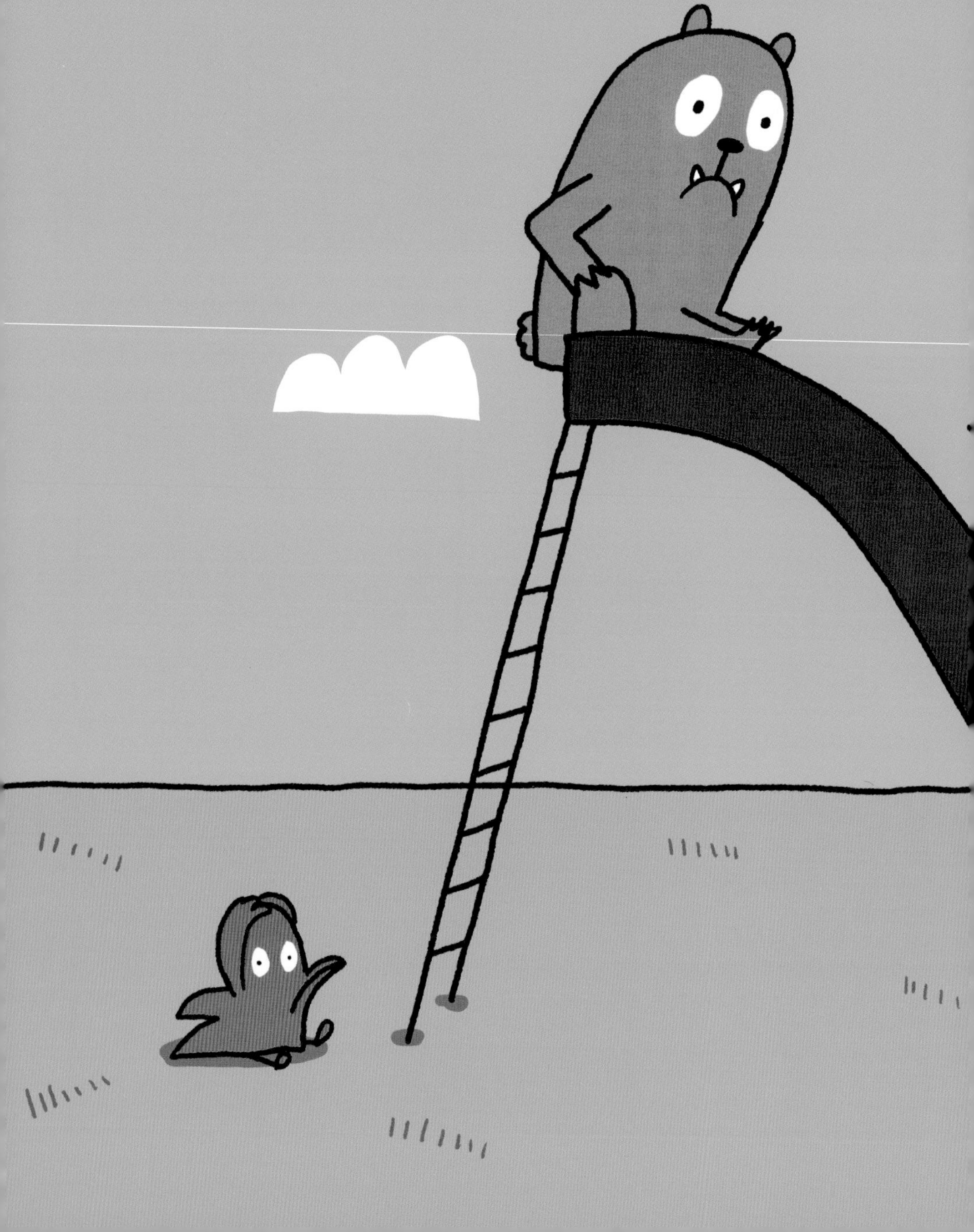

THE BEAR WENT DOWN THE SLIDE.

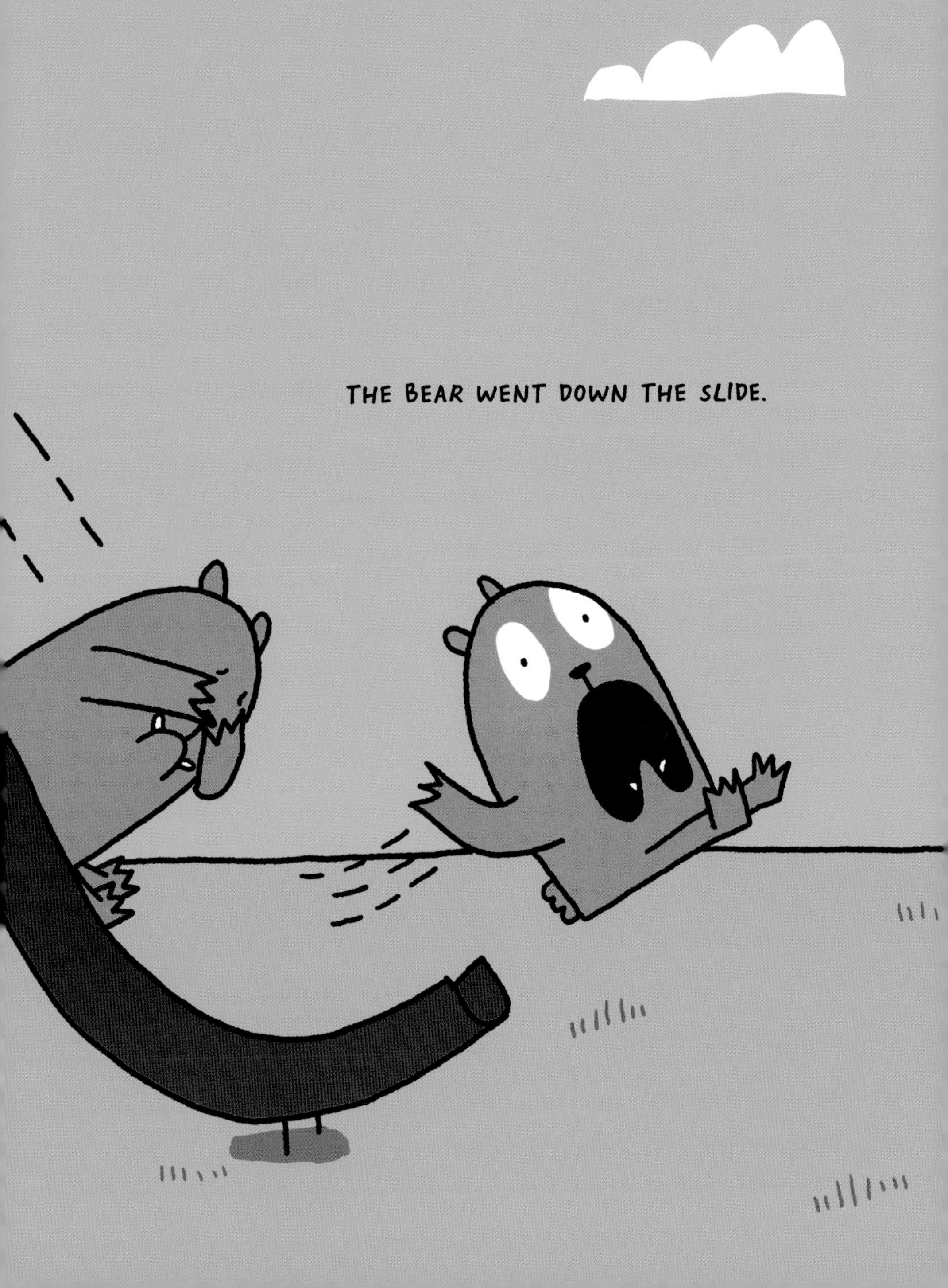

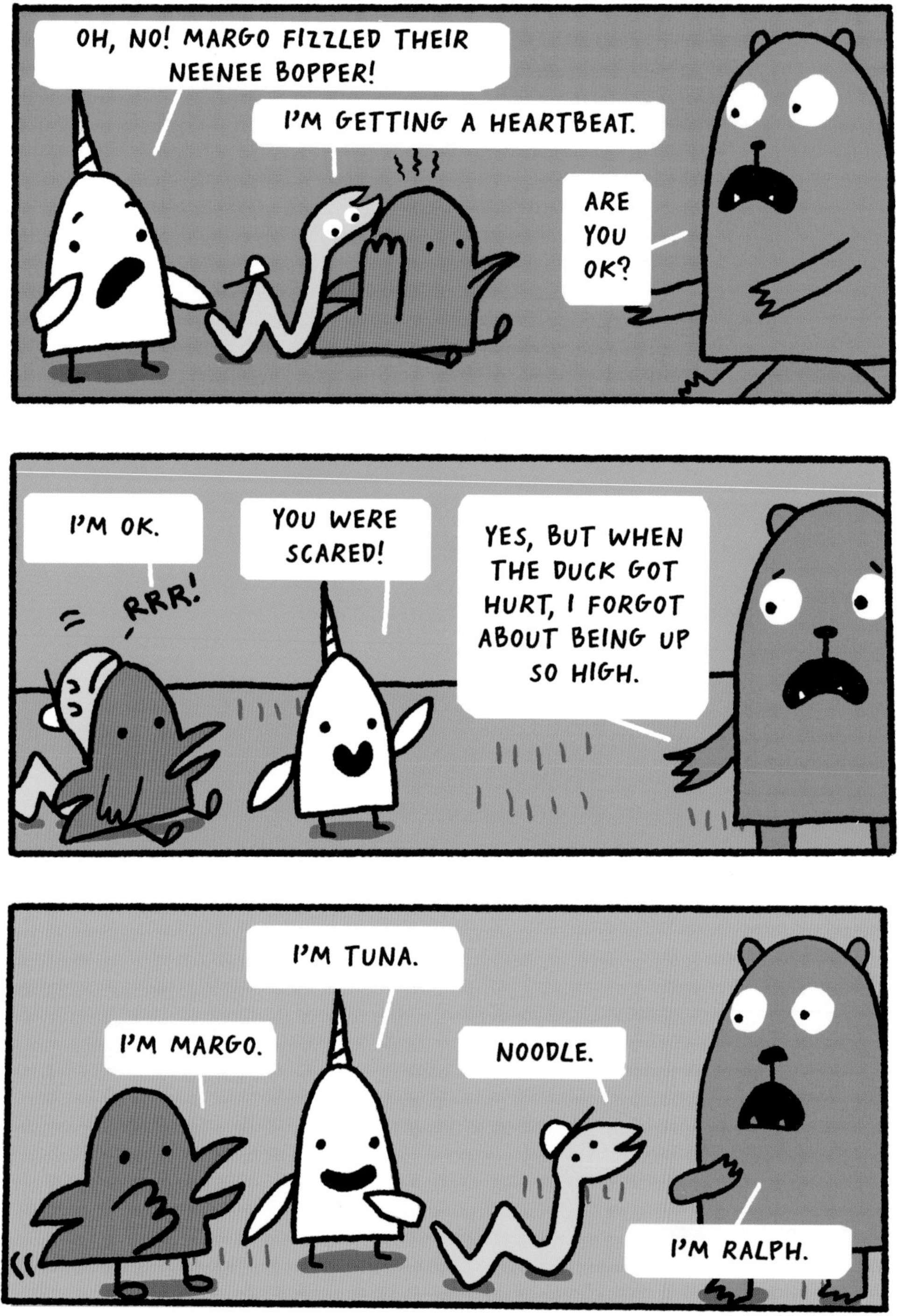
OH, NO! MARGO FIZZLED THEIR NEENEE BOPPER!
I'M GETTING A HEARTBEAT.
ARE YOU OK?
I'M OK.
RRR!
YOU WERE SCARED!
YES, BUT WHEN THE DUCK GOT HURT, I FORGOT ABOUT BEING UP SO HIGH.
I'M TUNA.
I'M MARGO.
NOODLE.
I'M RALPH.

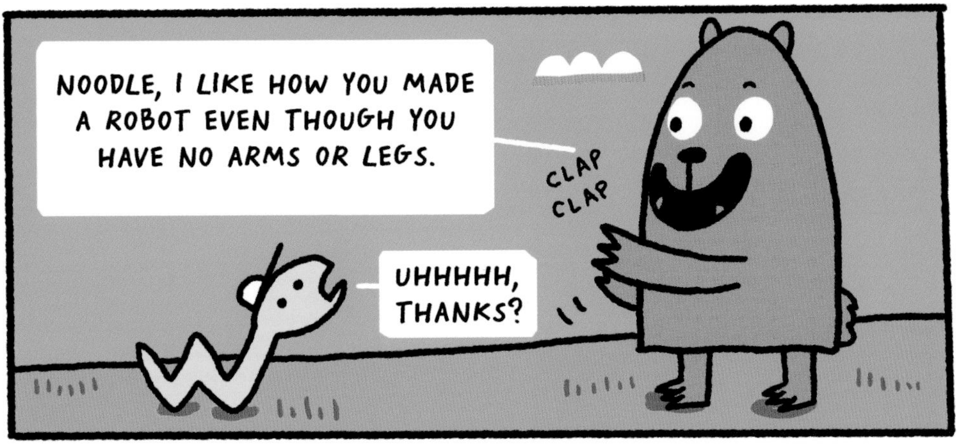
NOODLE, I LIKE HOW YOU MADE A ROBOT EVEN THOUGH YOU HAVE NO ARMS OR LEGS.
CLAP CLAP
UHHHHH, THANKS?

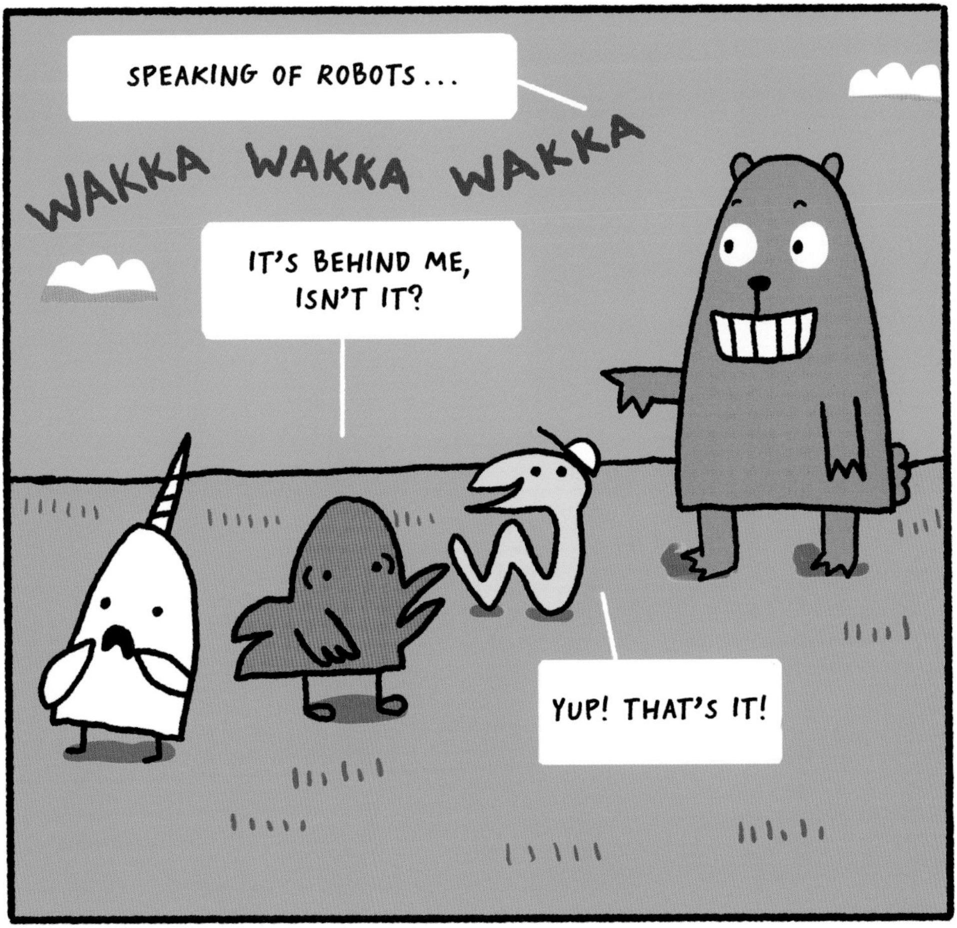
SPEAKING OF ROBOTS . . .
WAKKA WAKKA WAKKA
IT'S BEHIND ME, ISN'T IT?
YUP! THAT'S IT!

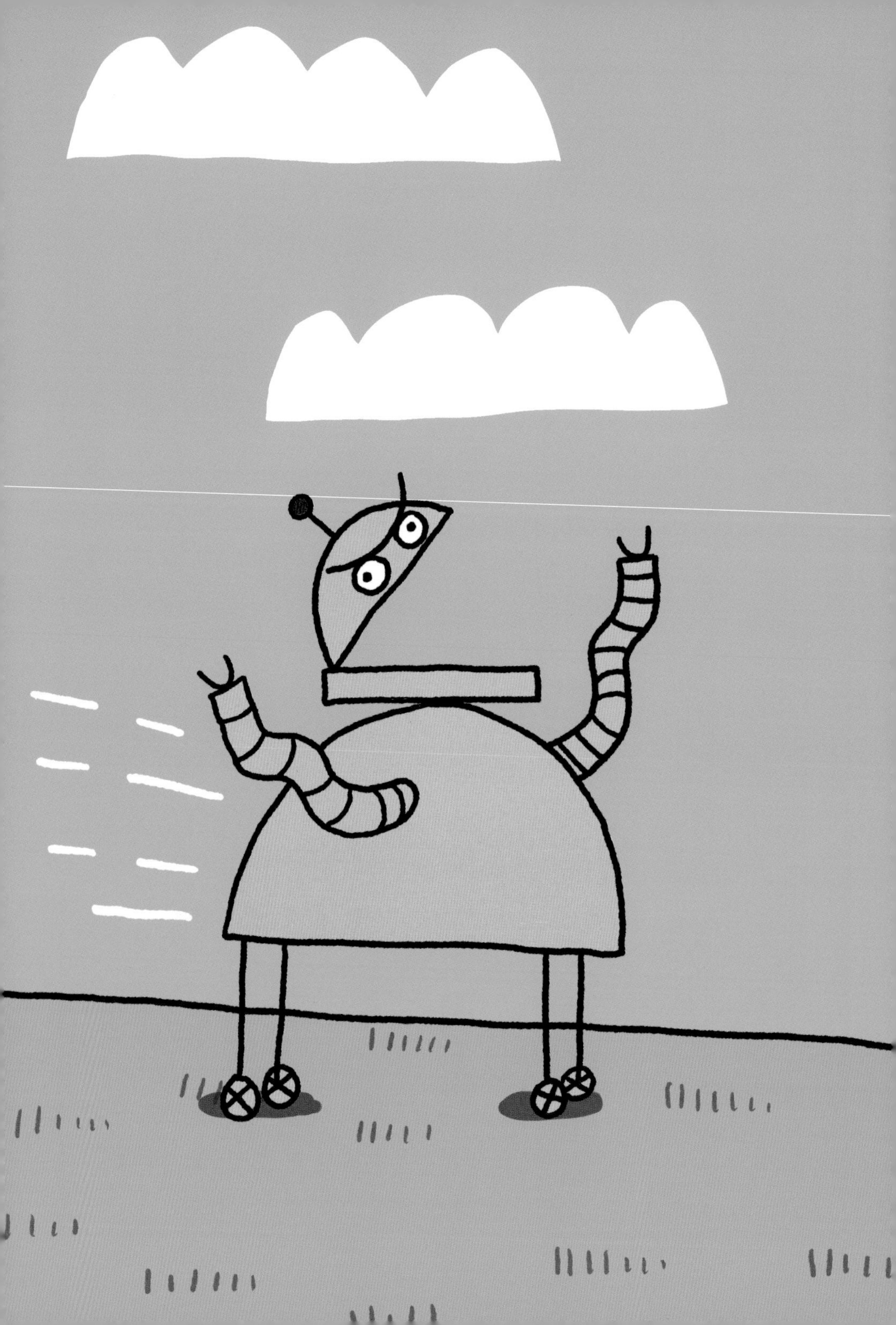

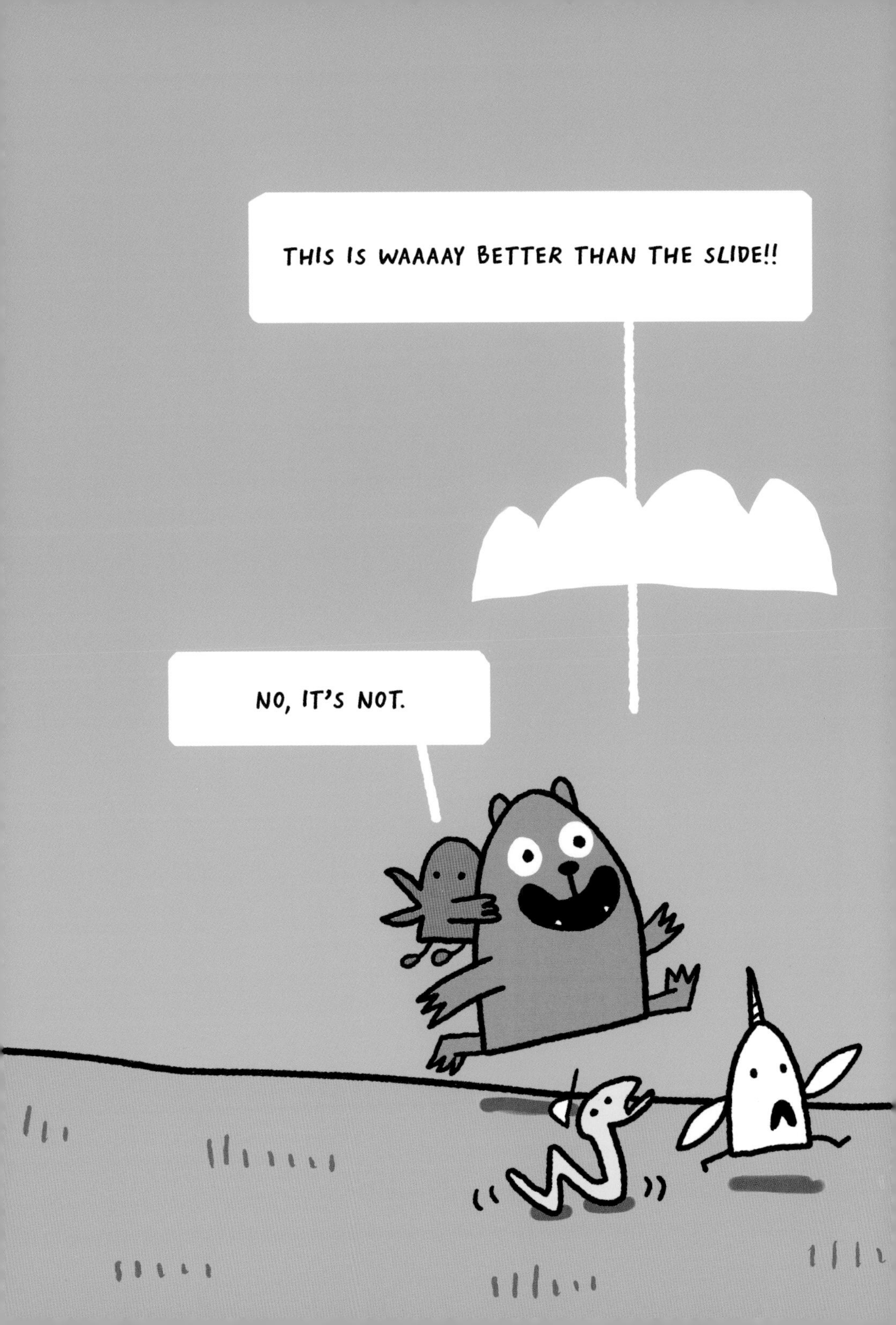
THIS IS WAAAAY BETTER THAN THE SLIDE!!
NO, IT'S NOT.

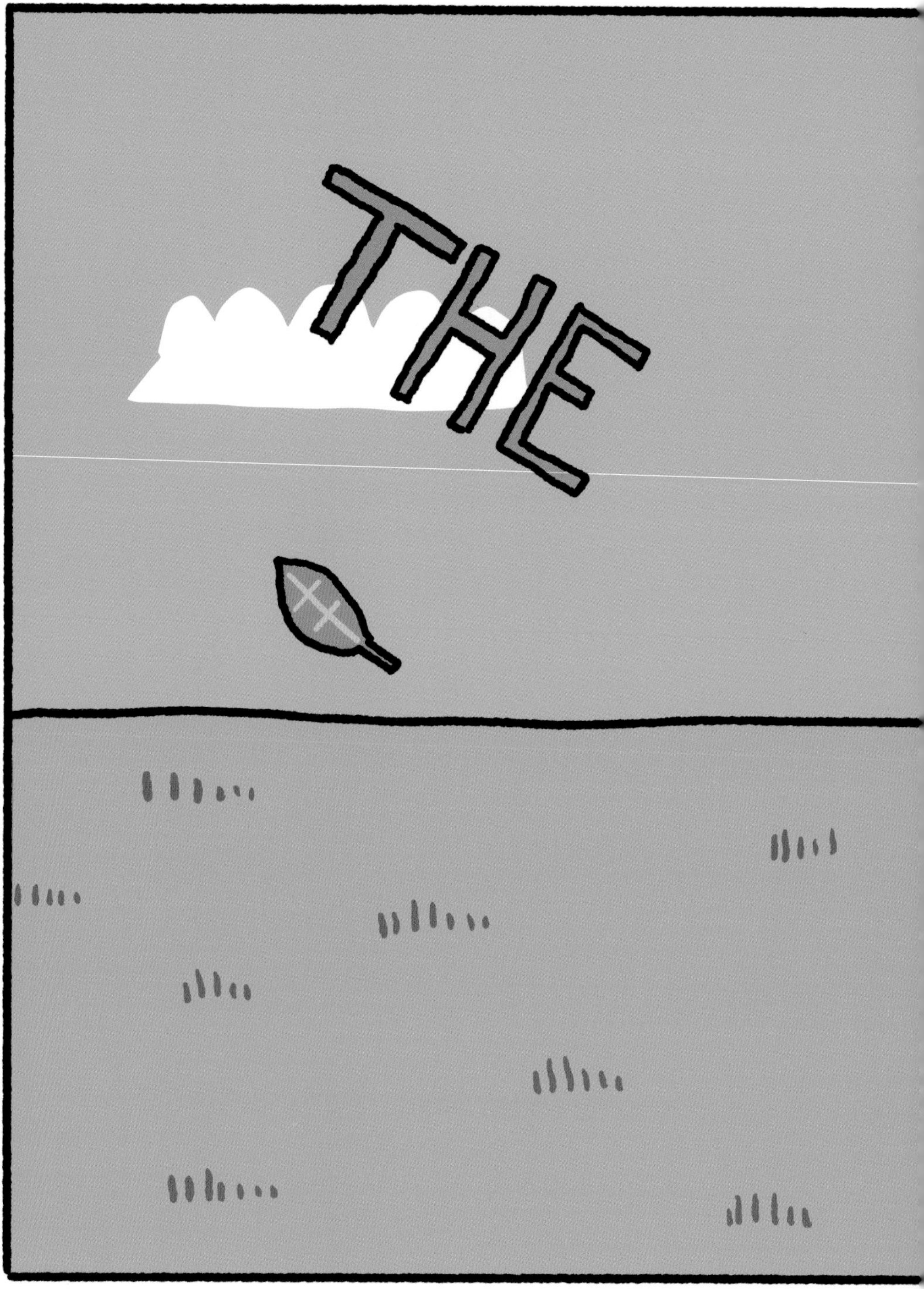
THE

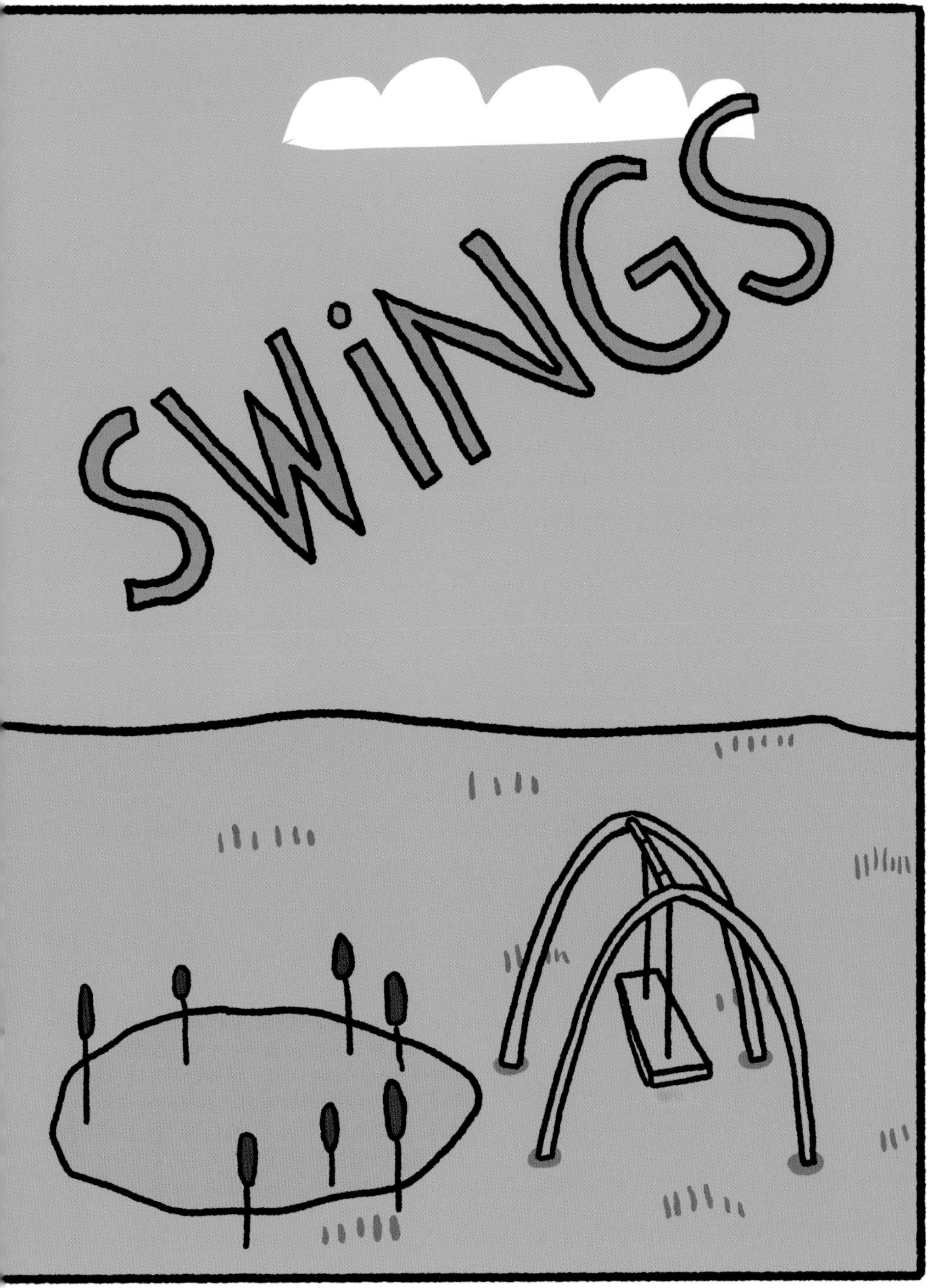
SWiNGS

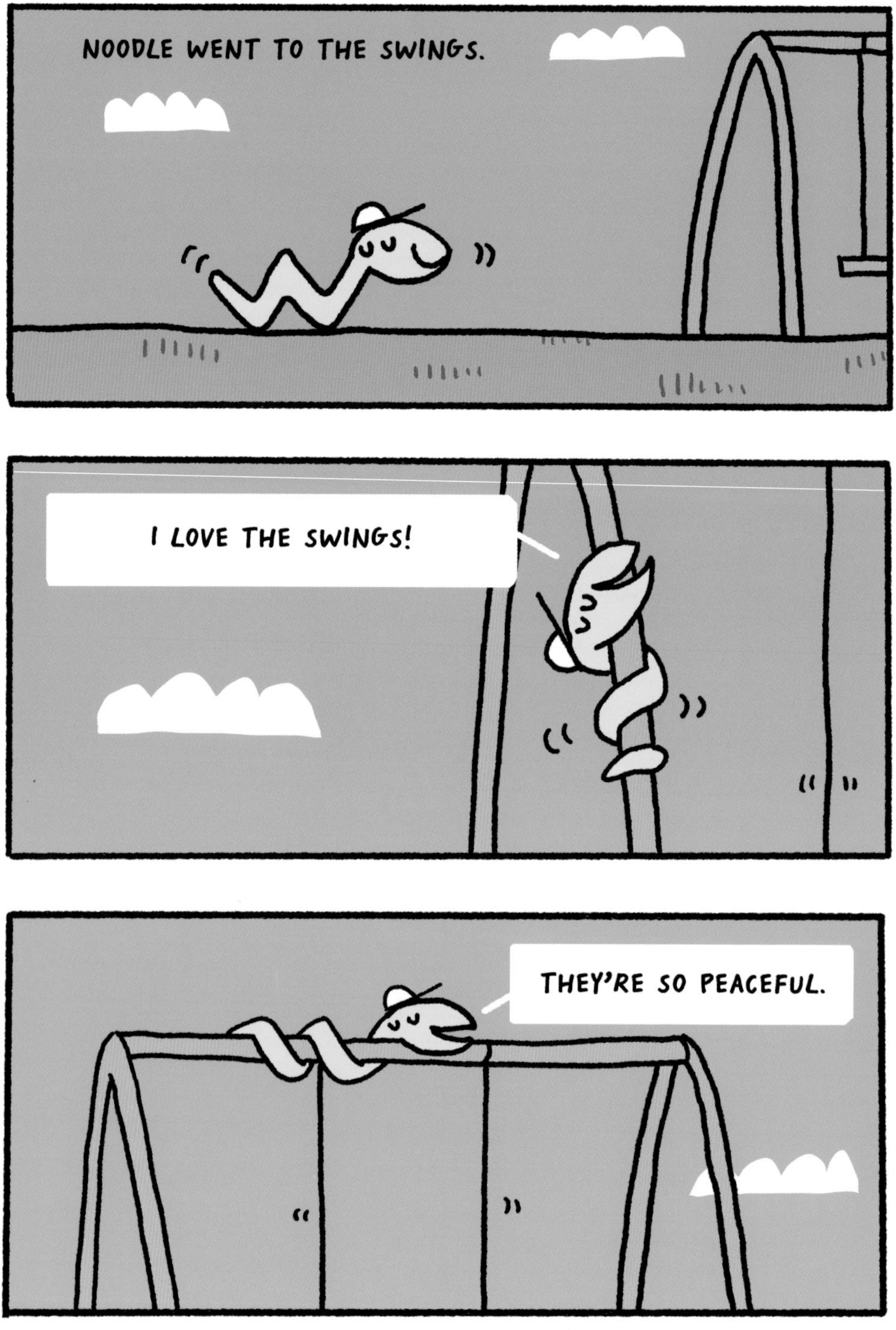
NOODLE WENT TO THE SWINGS.
I LOVE THE SWINGS!
THEY'RE SO PEACEFUL.

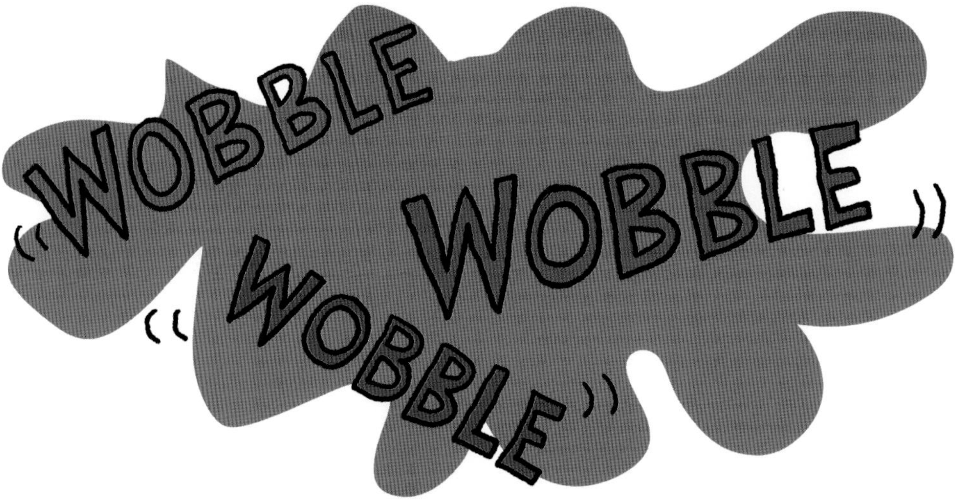
WOBBLE
WOBBLE
WOBBLE

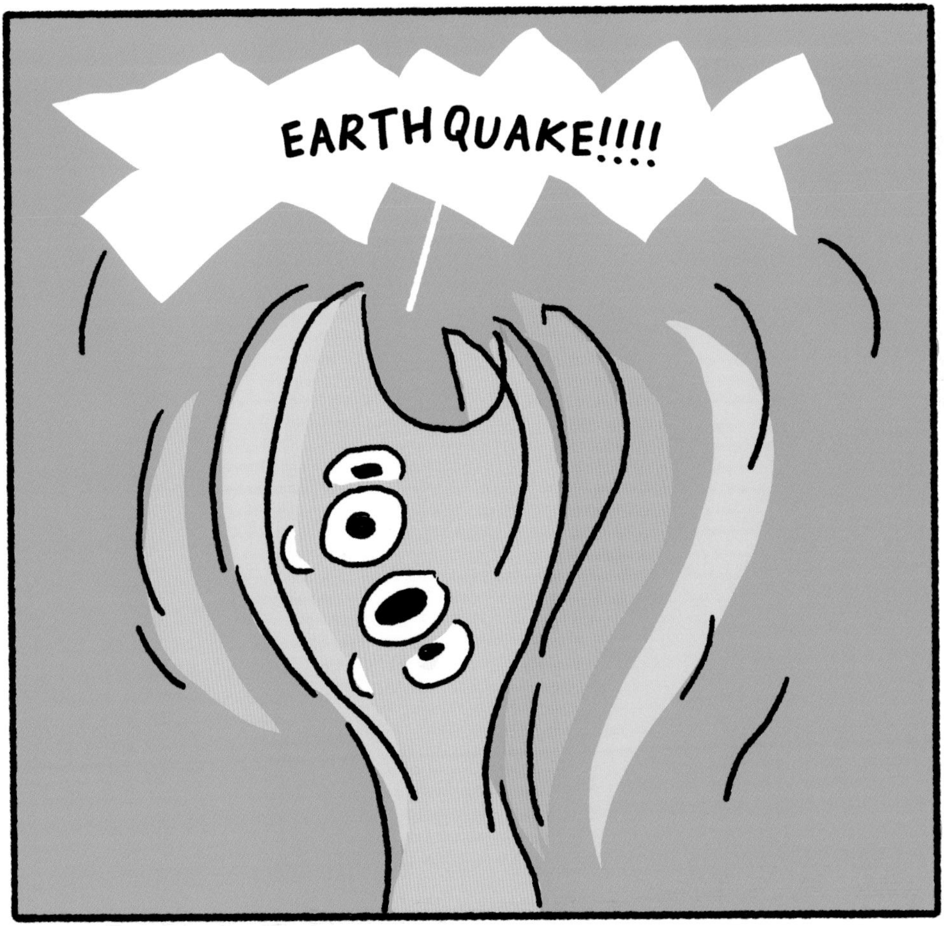
EARTHQUAKE!!!!

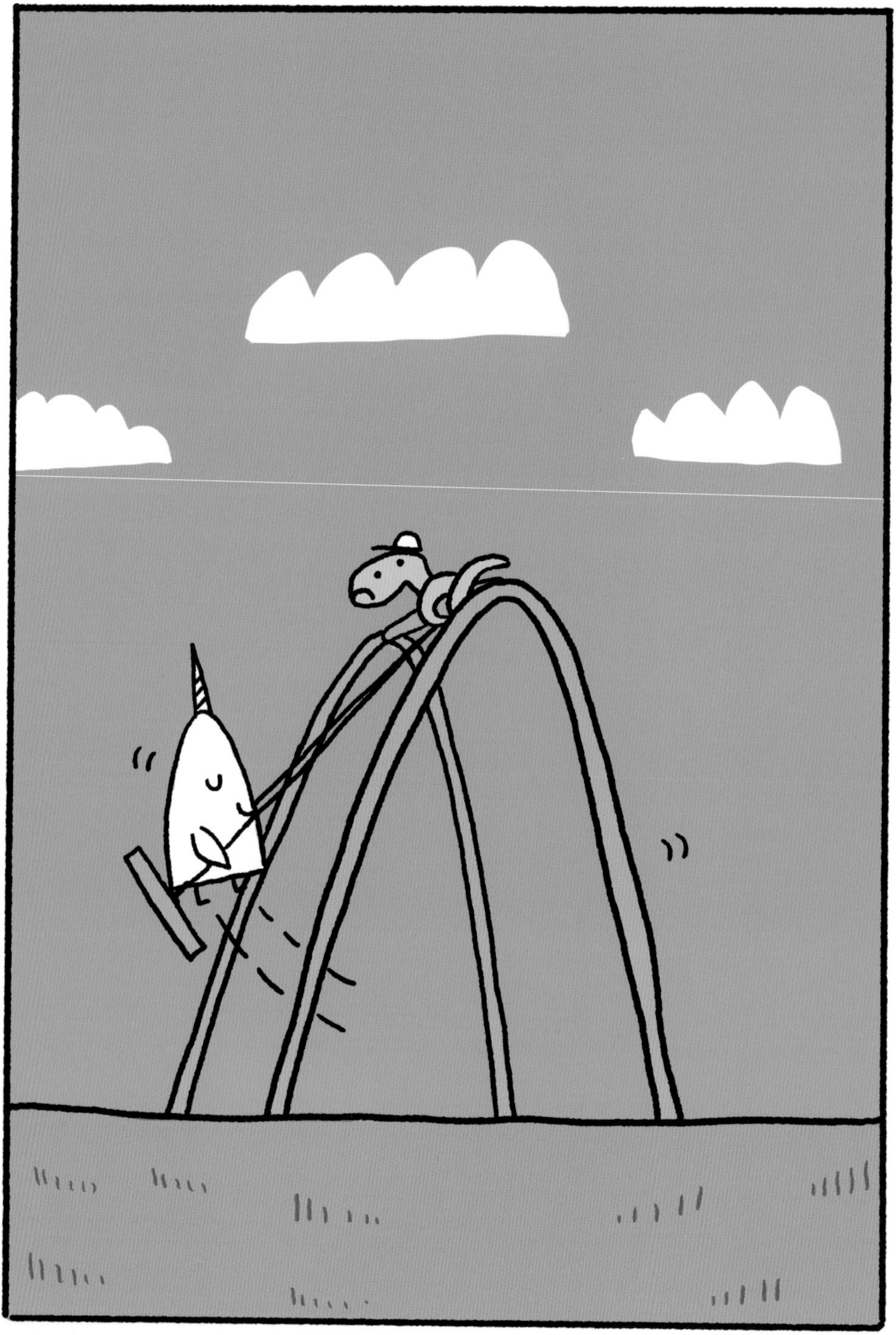

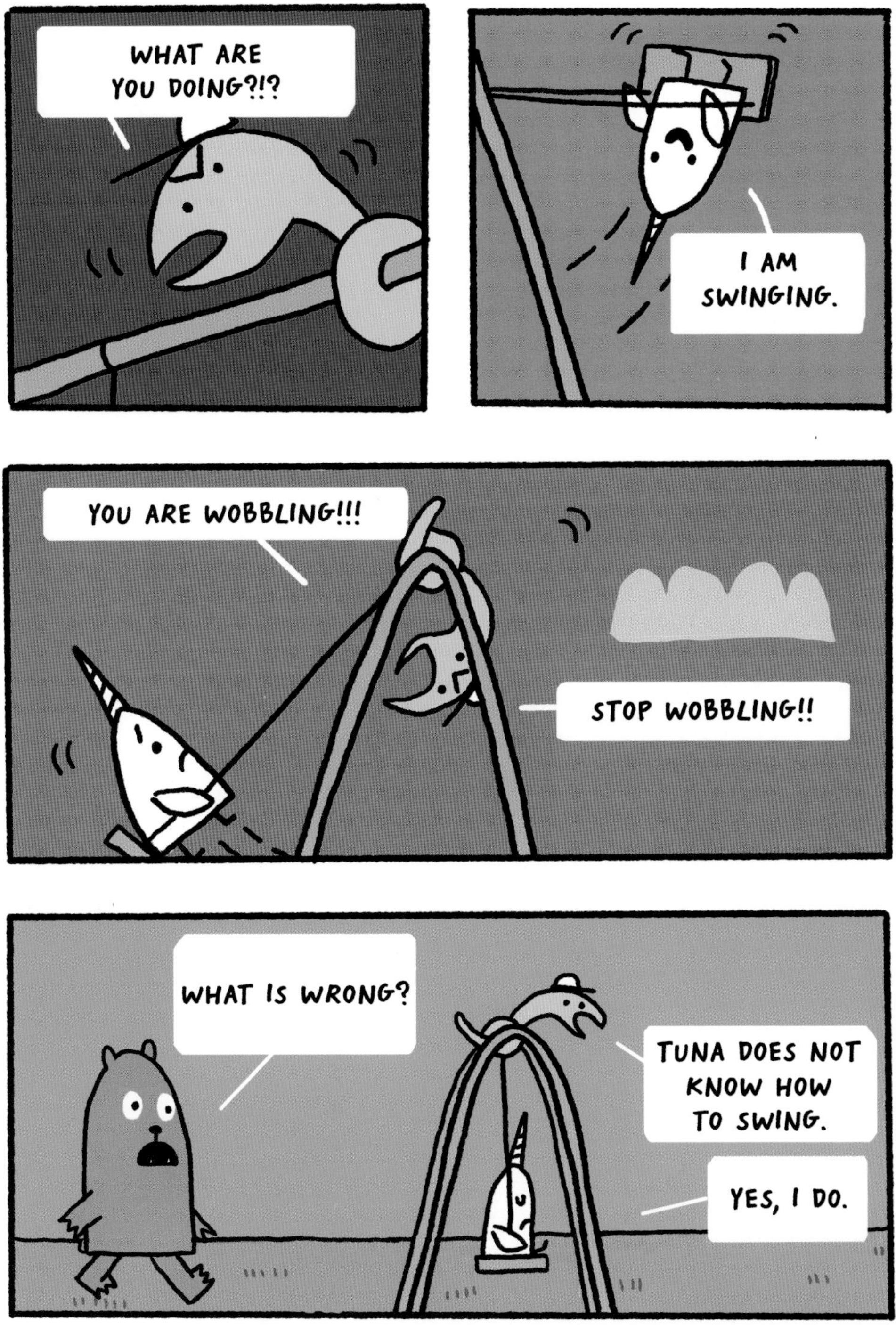
WHAT ARE YOU DOING?!?
I AM SWINGING.
YOU ARE WOBBLING!!!
STOP WOBBLING!!
WHAT IS WRONG?
TUNA DOES NOT KNOW HOW TO SWING.
YES, I DO.

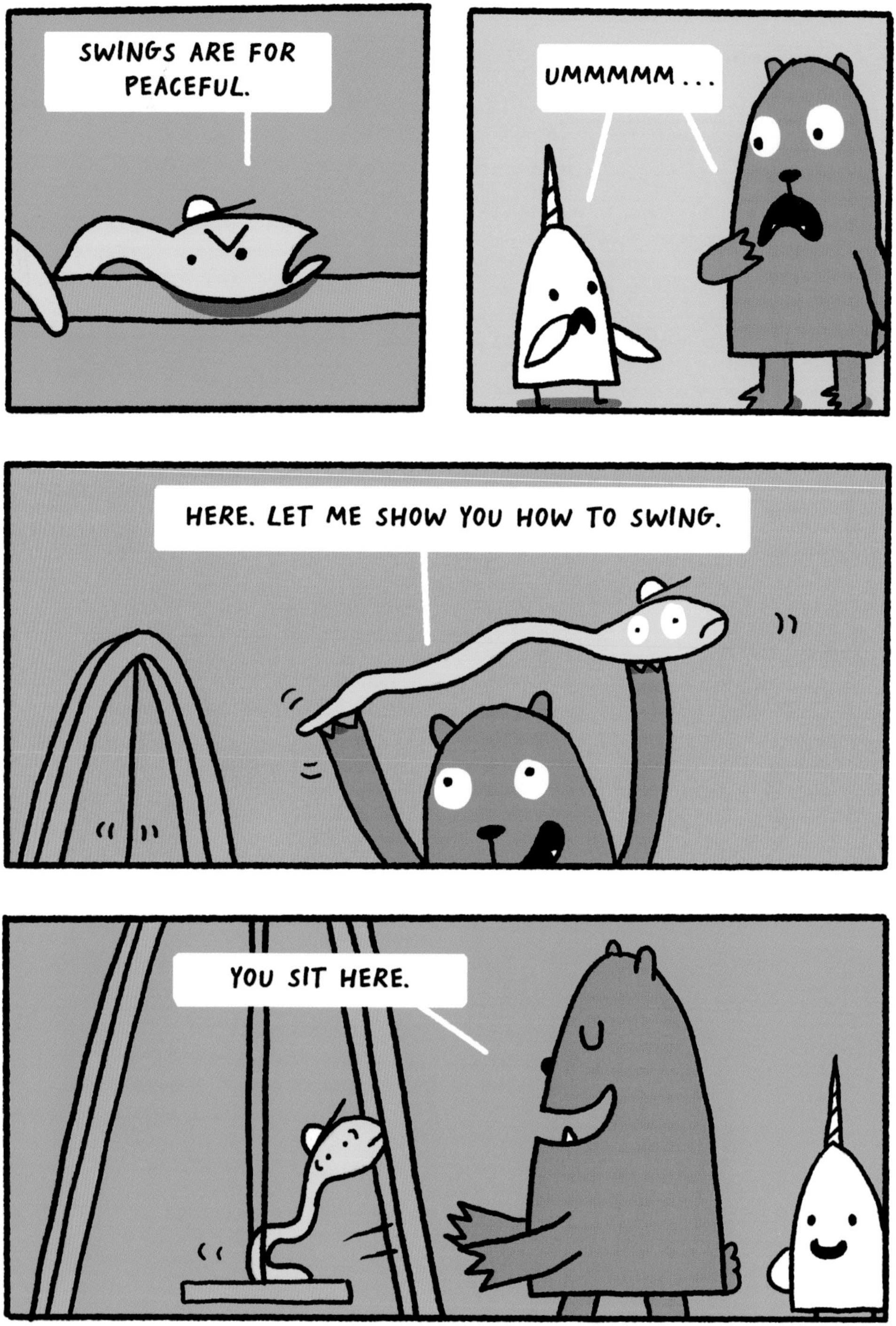
SWINGS ARE FOR PEACEFUL.
UMMMMM...
HERE. LET ME SHOW YOU HOW TO SWING.
YOU SIT HERE.

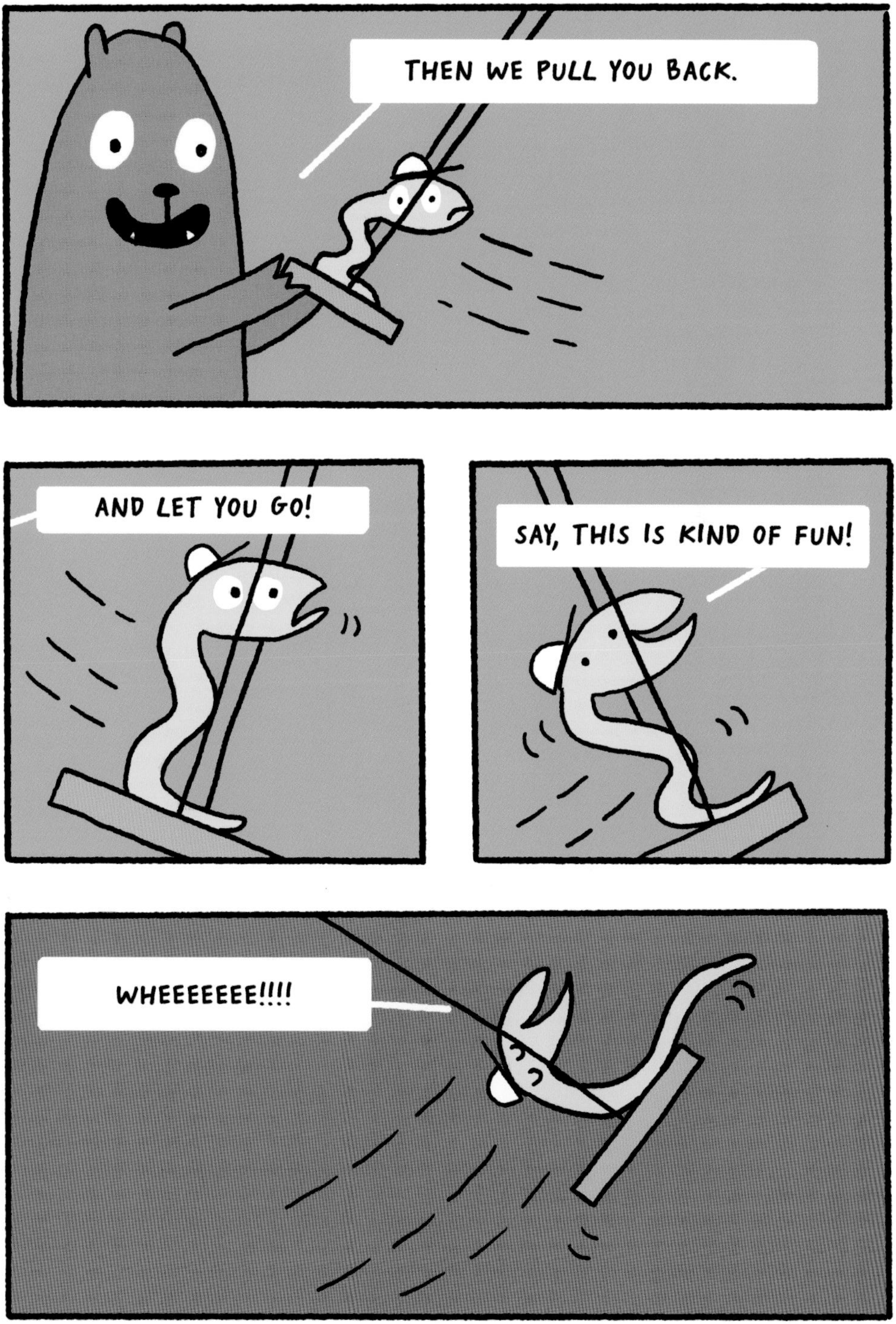
THEN WE PULL YOU BACK.
AND LET YOU GO!
SAY, THIS IS KIND OF FUN!
WHEEEEEEE!!!!

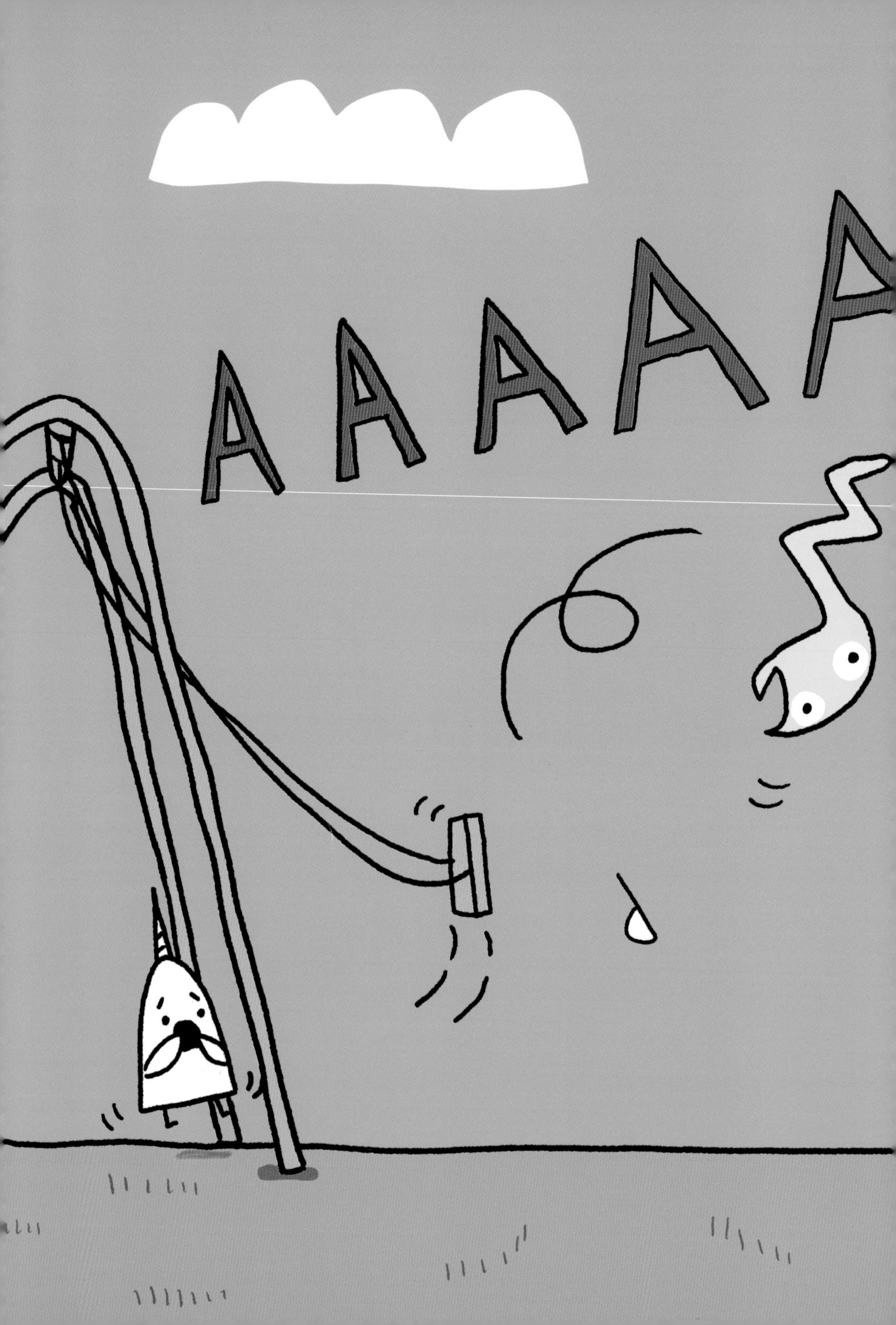
AAAAA

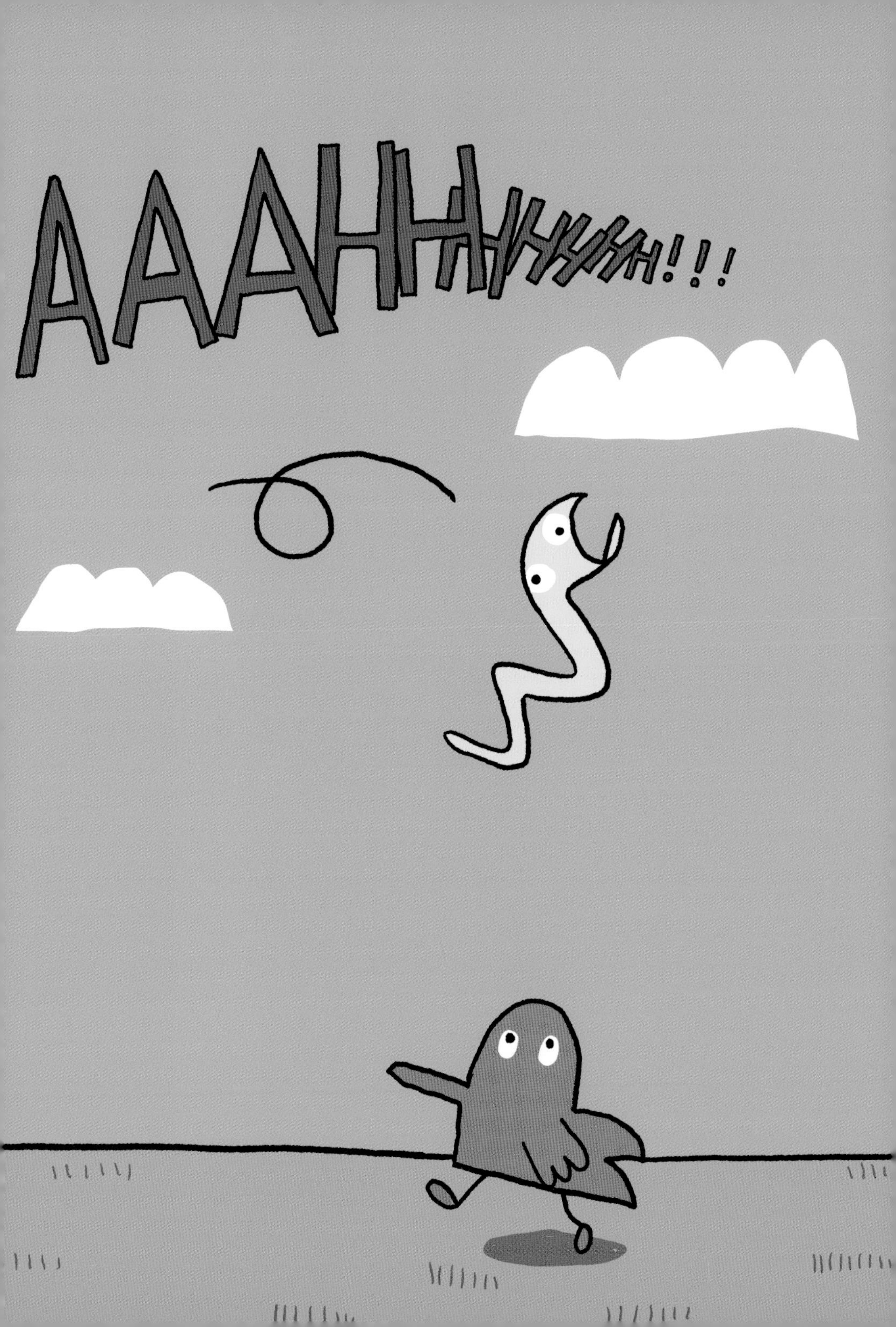
AAAHHHHHHHHH!!!

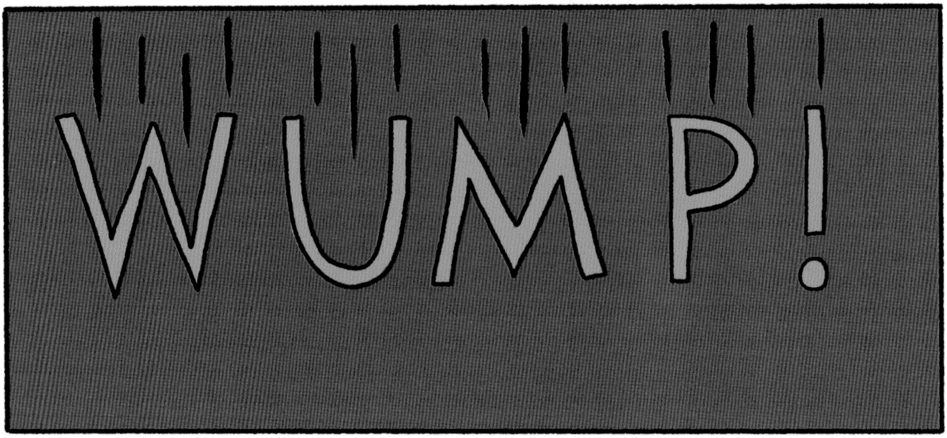
WUMP!

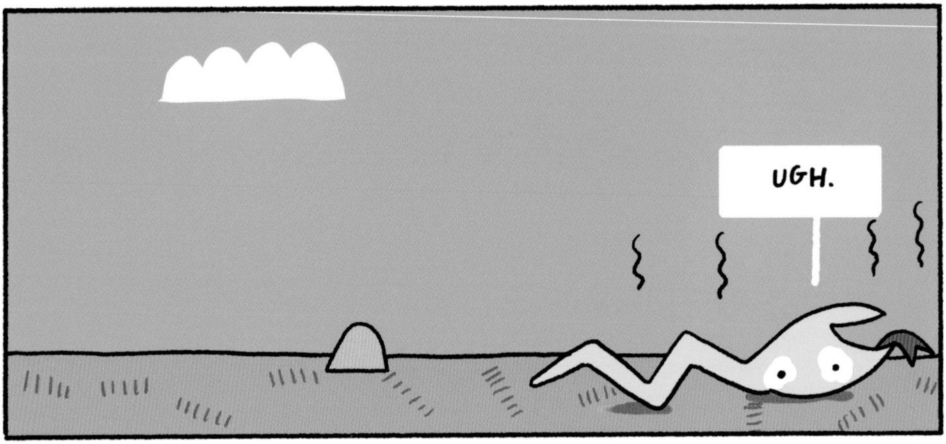
UGH.

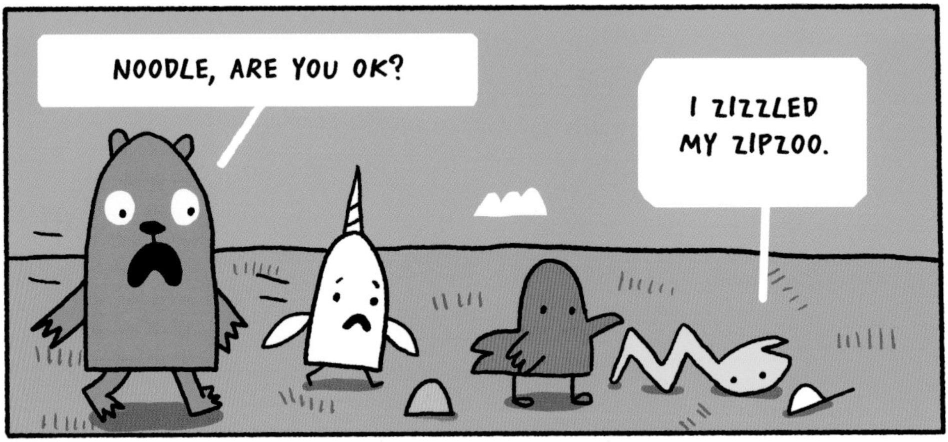
NOODLE, ARE YOU OK?
I ZIZZLED MY ZIPZOO.

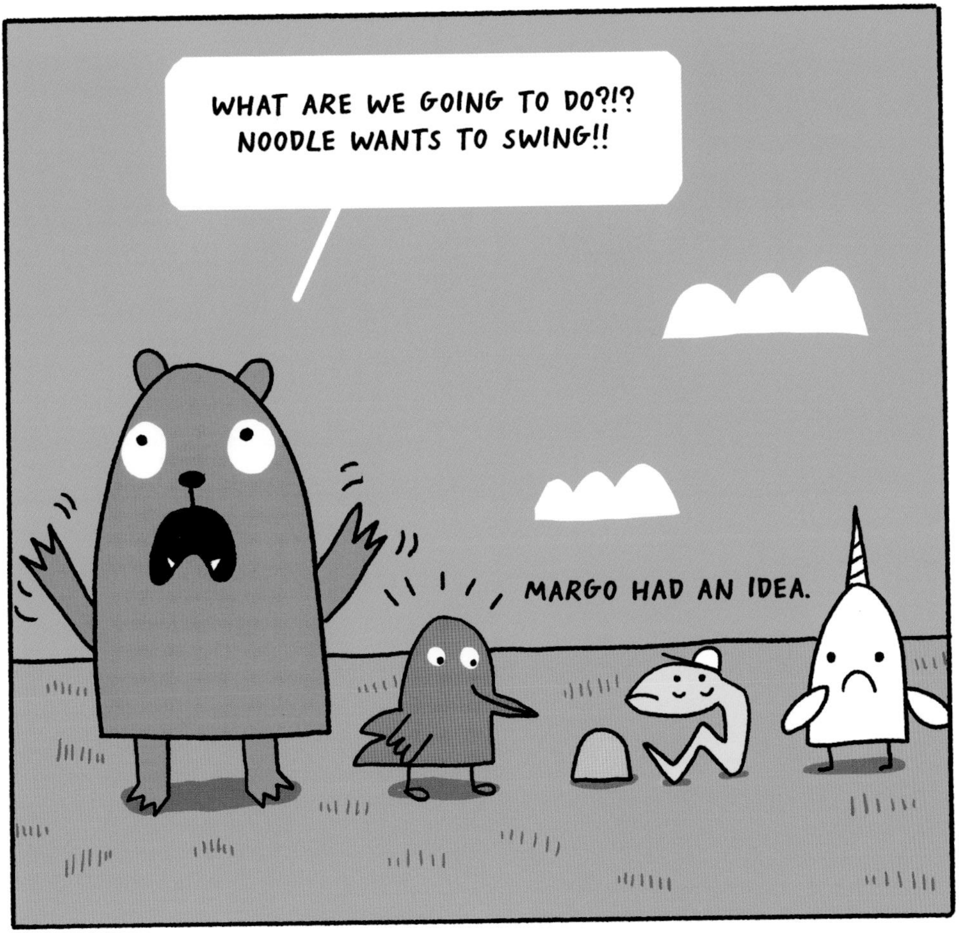
WHAT ARE WE GOING TO DO?!?
NOODLE WANTS TO SWING!!
MARGO HAD AN IDEA.

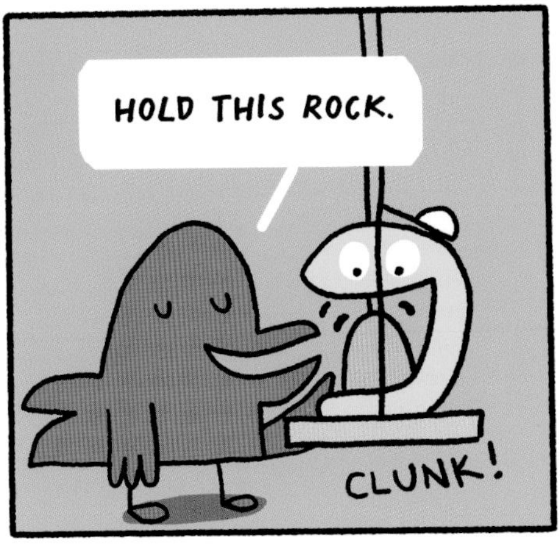
HOLD THIS ROCK.
CLUNK!

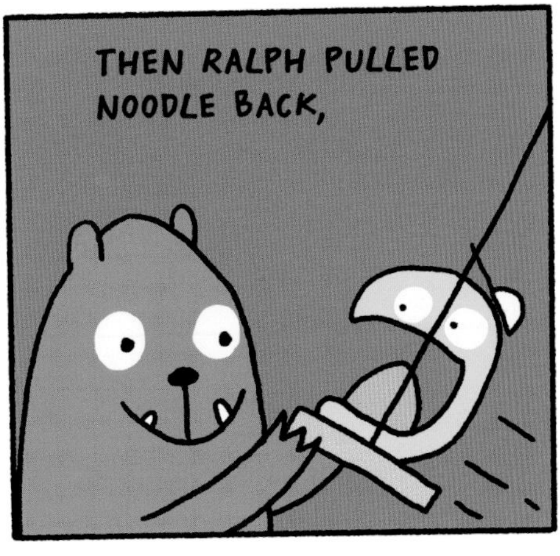
THEN RALPH PULLED NOODLE BACK,

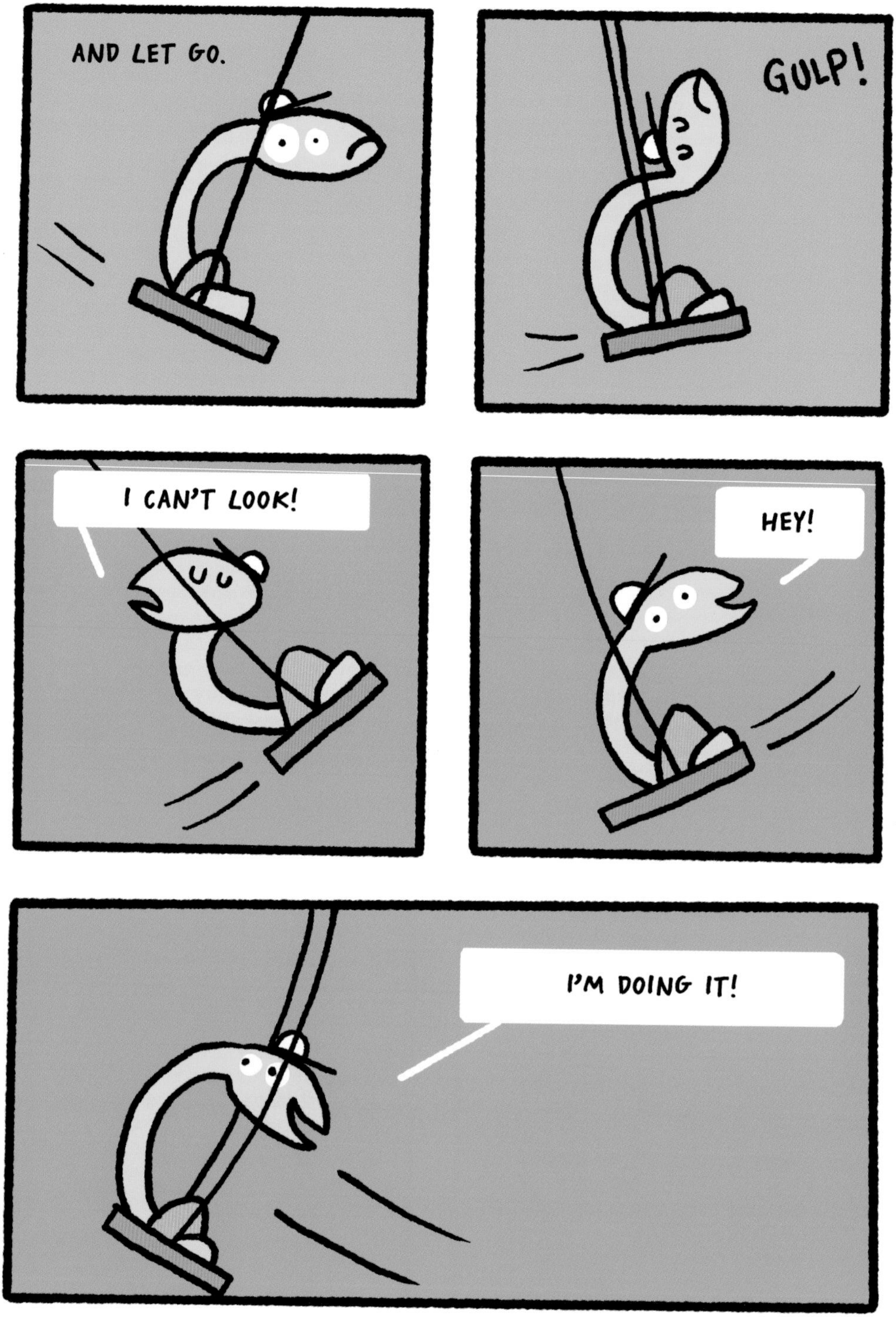
AND LET GO.
GULP!
I CAN'T LOOK!
HEY!
I'M DOING IT!

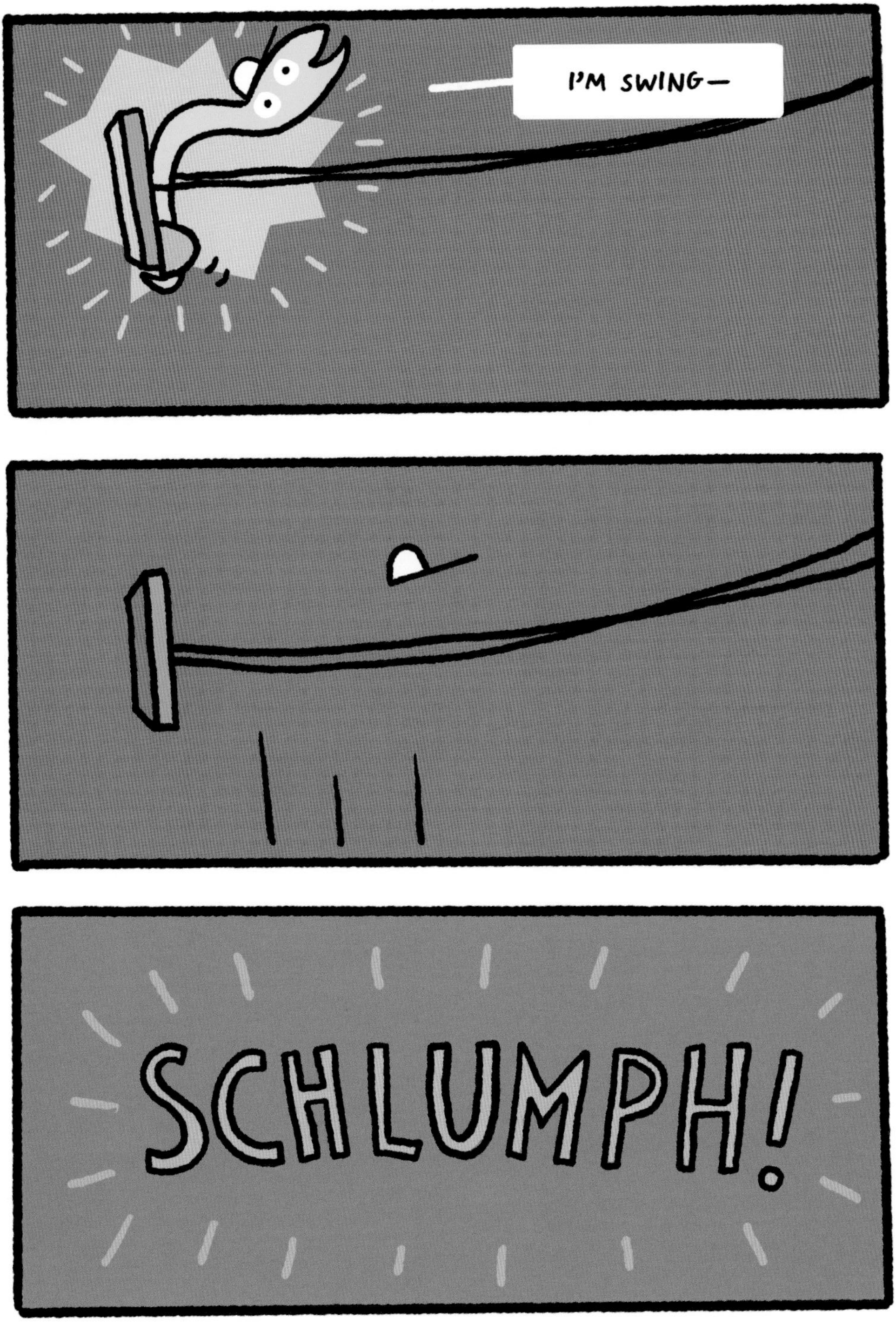
I'M SWING—
SCHLUMPH!

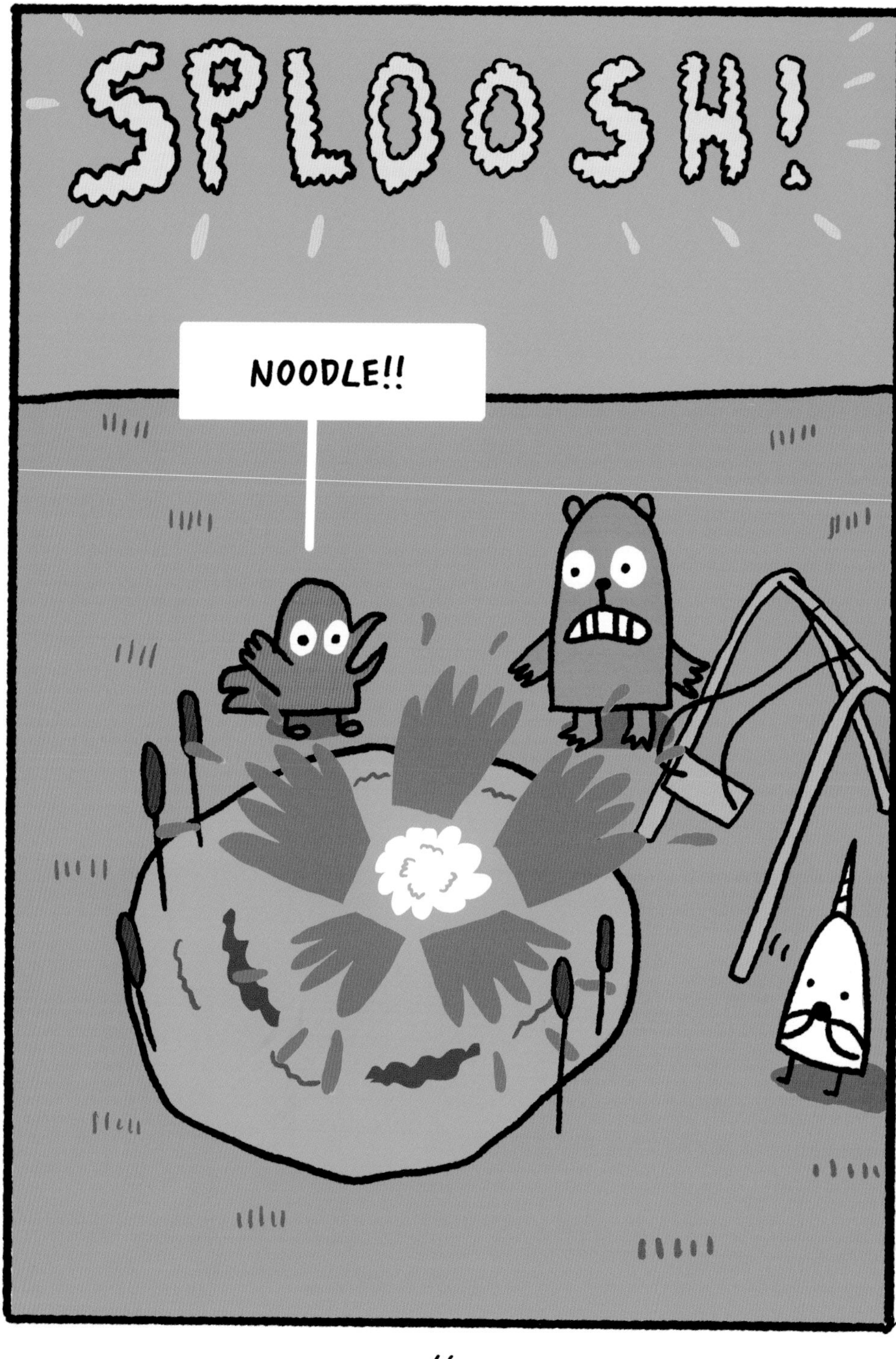
SPLOOSH!
NOODLE!!

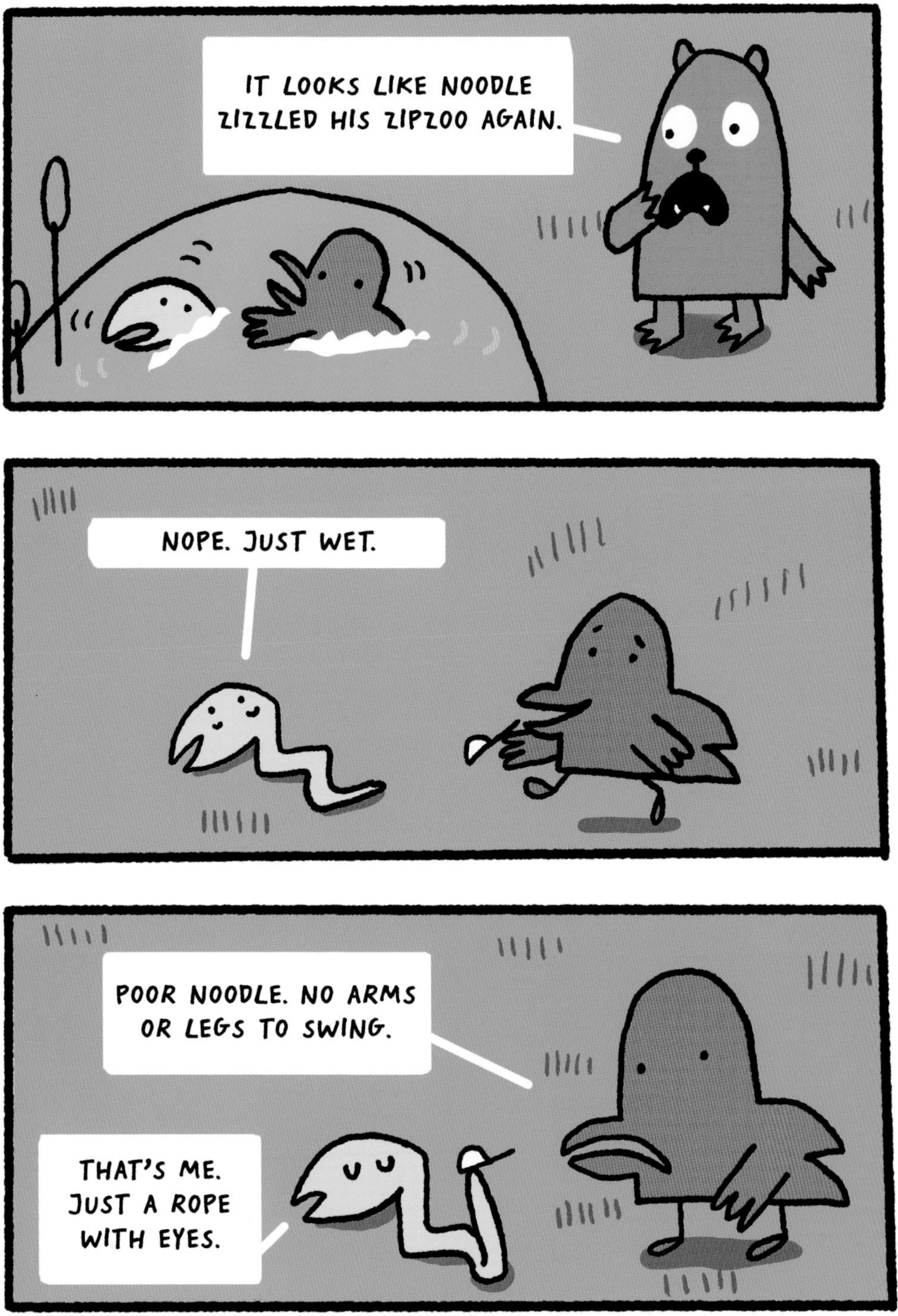
IT LOOKS LIKE NOODLE ZIZZLED HIS ZIPZOO AGAIN.
NOPE. JUST WET.
POOR NOODLE. NO ARMS OR LEGS TO SWING.
THAT'S ME. JUST A ROPE WITH EYES.

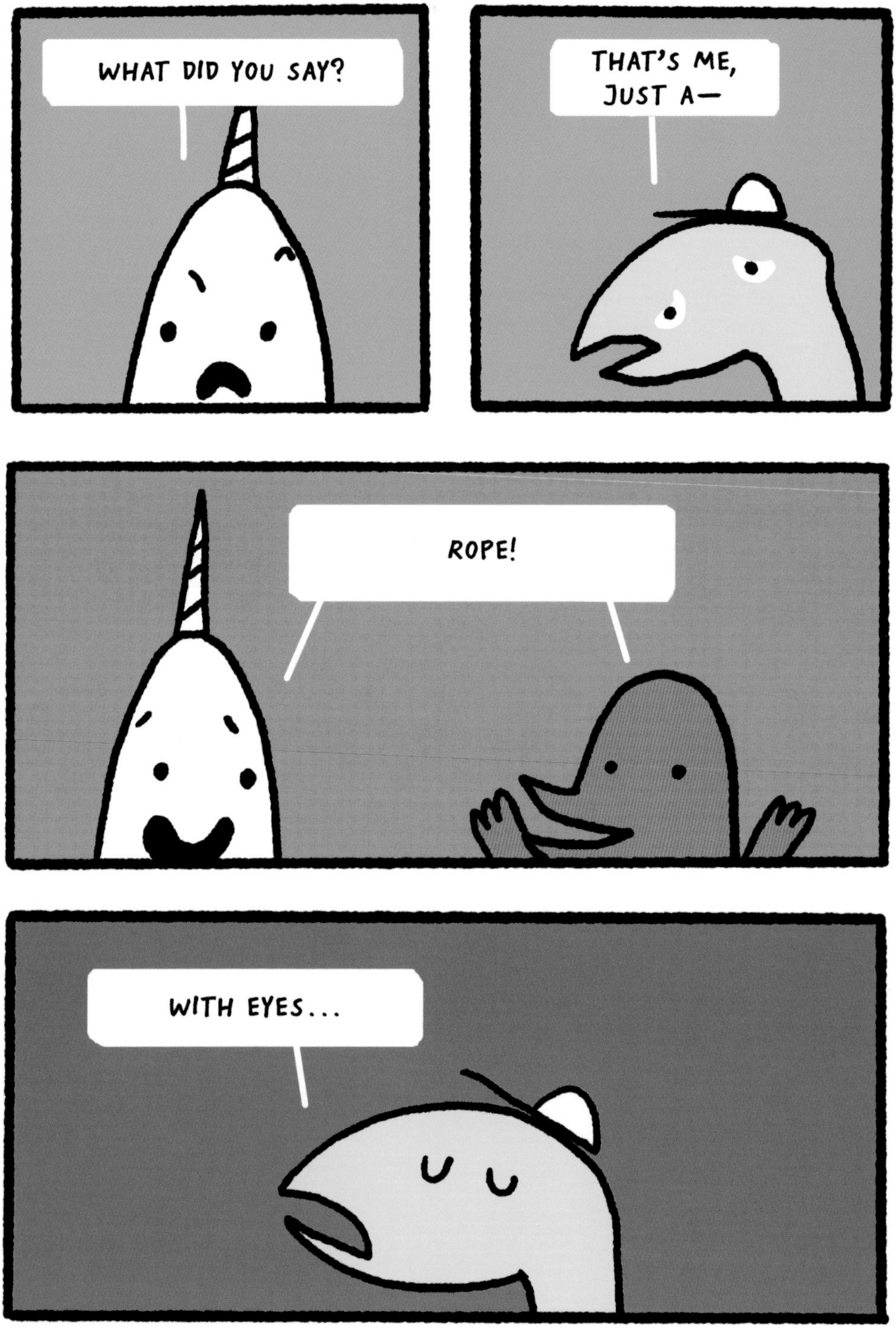
WHAT DID YOU SAY?
THAT'S ME, JUST A—
ROPE!
WITH EYES...

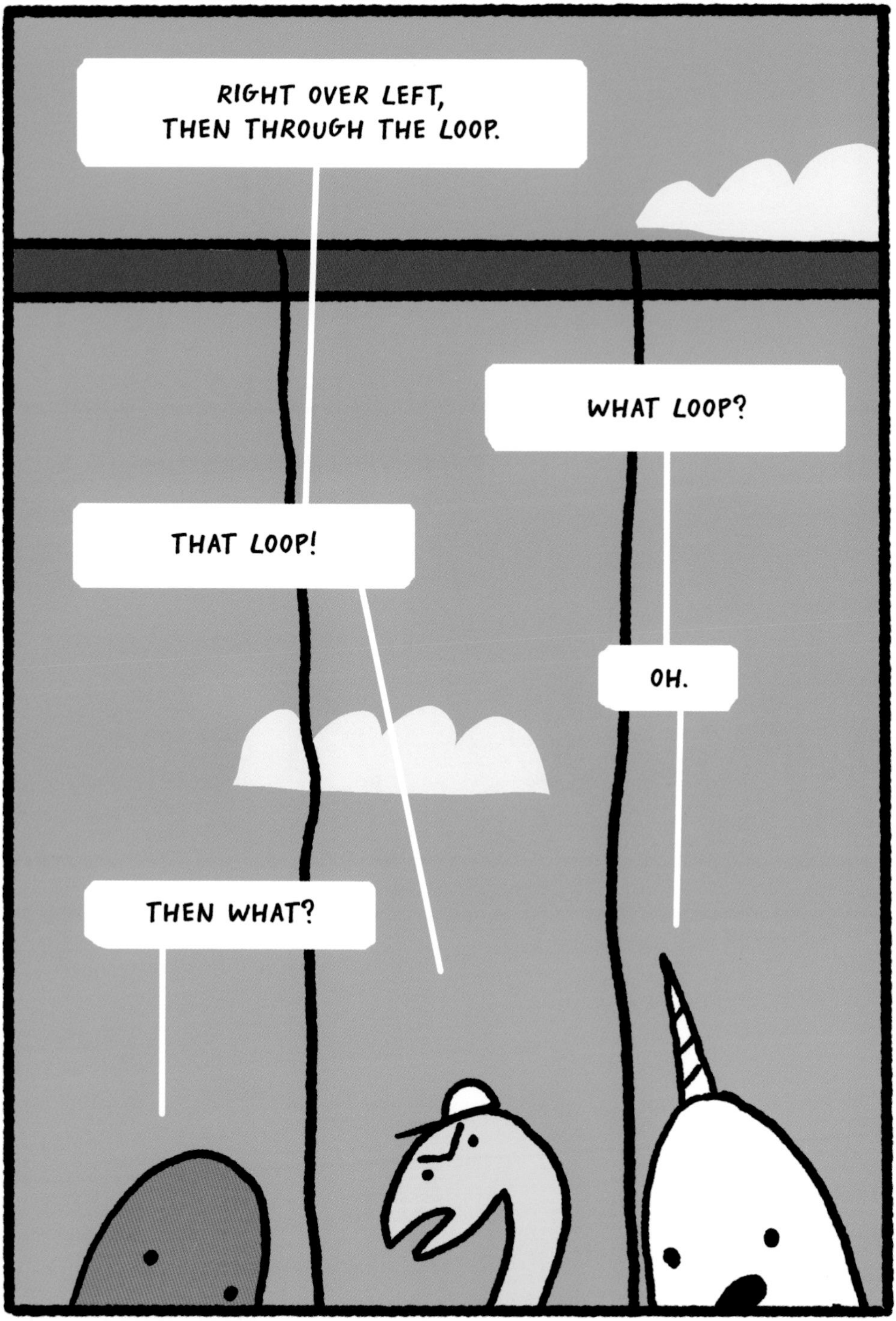
RIGHT OVER LEFT, THEN THROUGH THE LOOP.
WHAT LOOP?
THAT LOOP!
OH.
THEN WHAT?

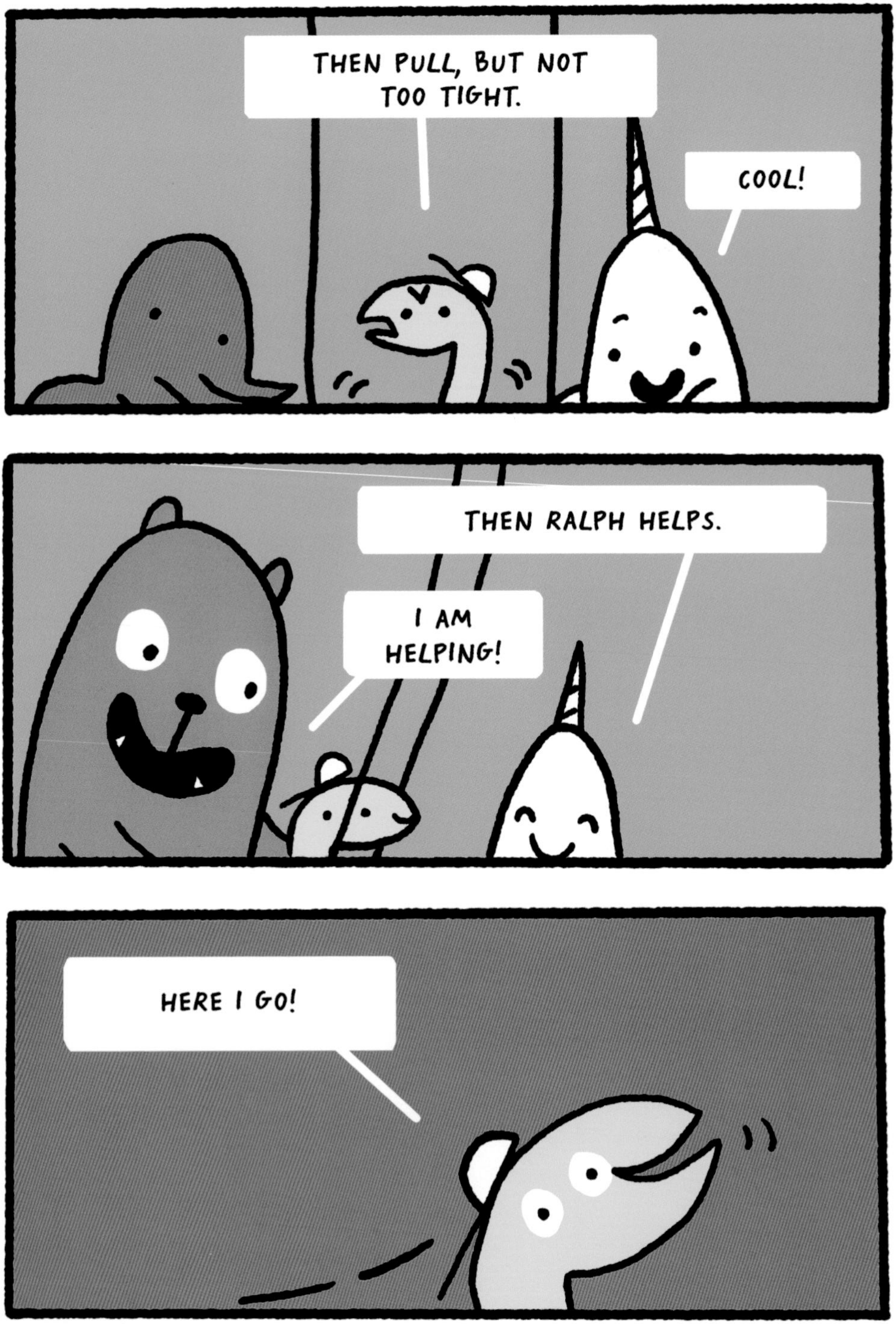
THEN PULL, BUT NOT TOO TIGHT.
COOL!
THEN RALPH HELPS.
I AM HELPING!
HERE I GO!

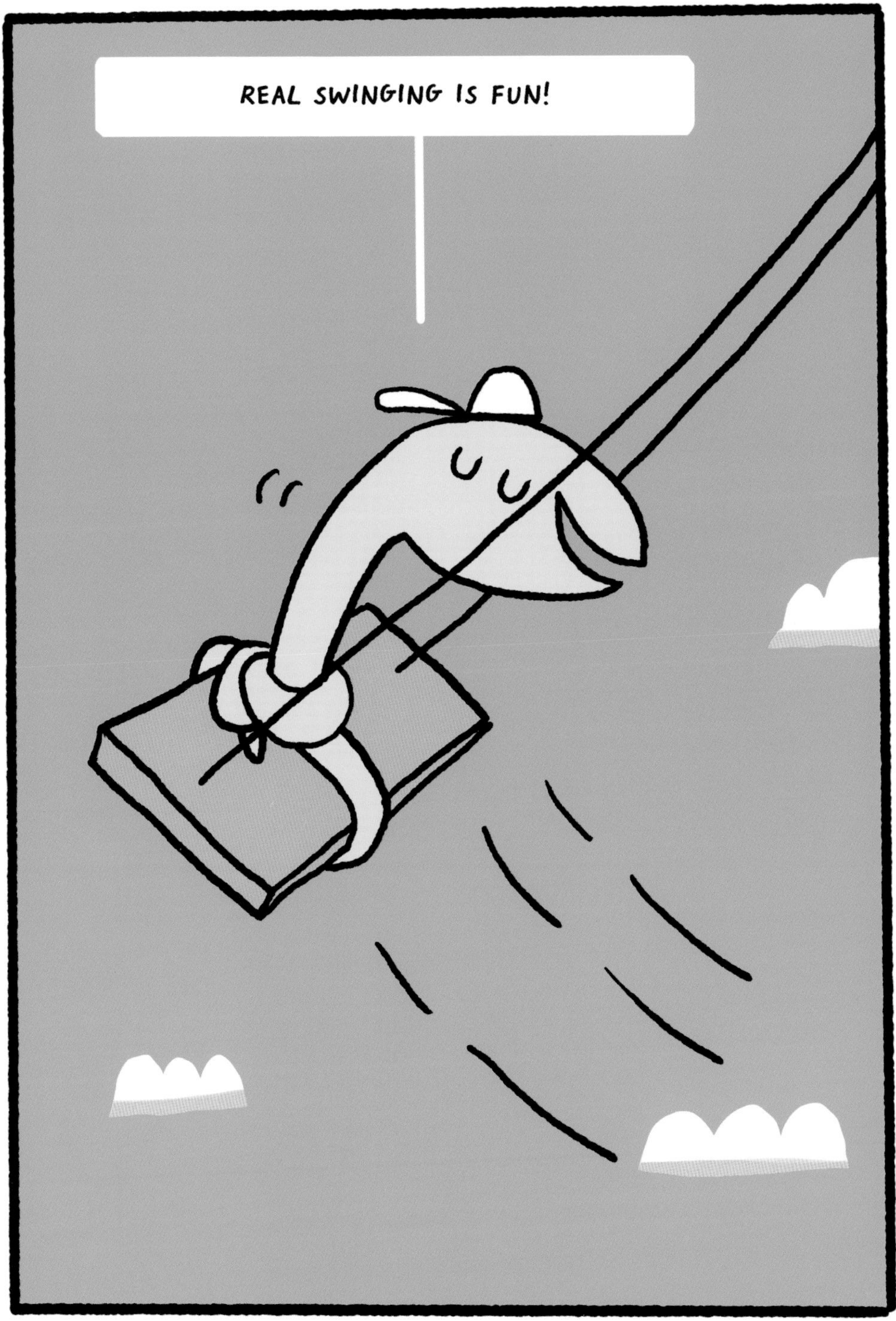
REAL SWINGING IS FUN!

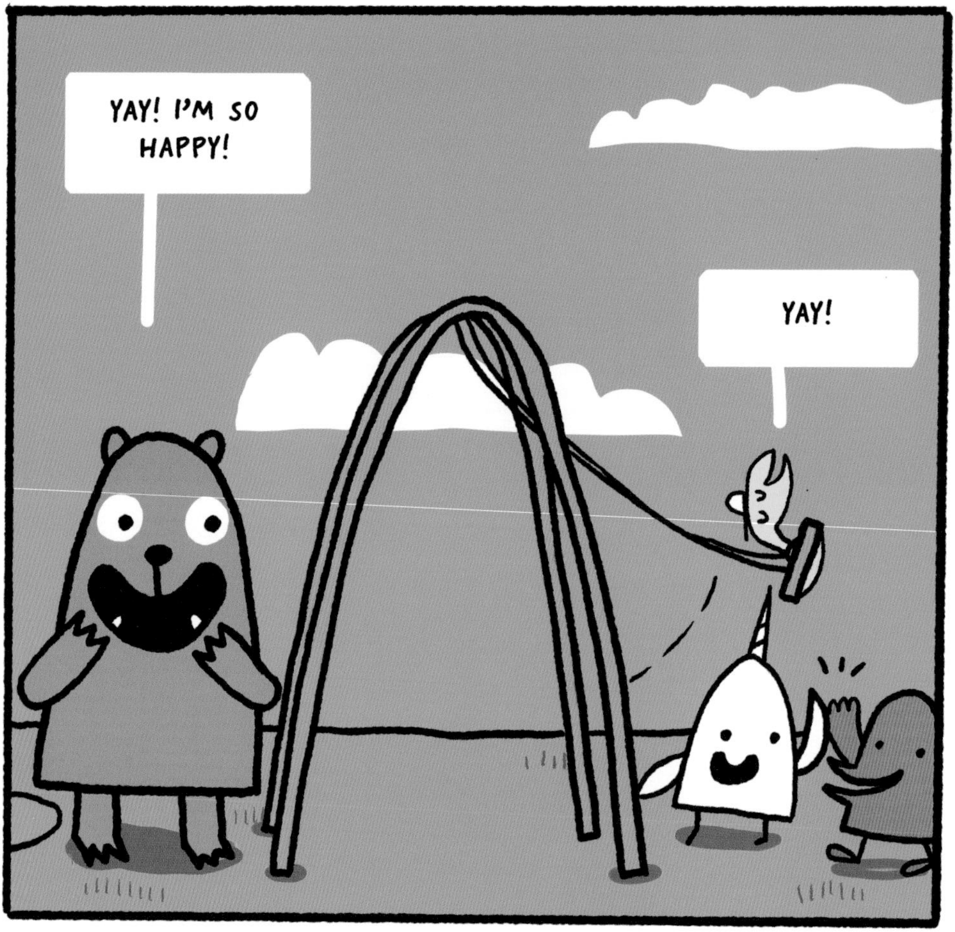
YAY! I'M SO HAPPY!
YAY!

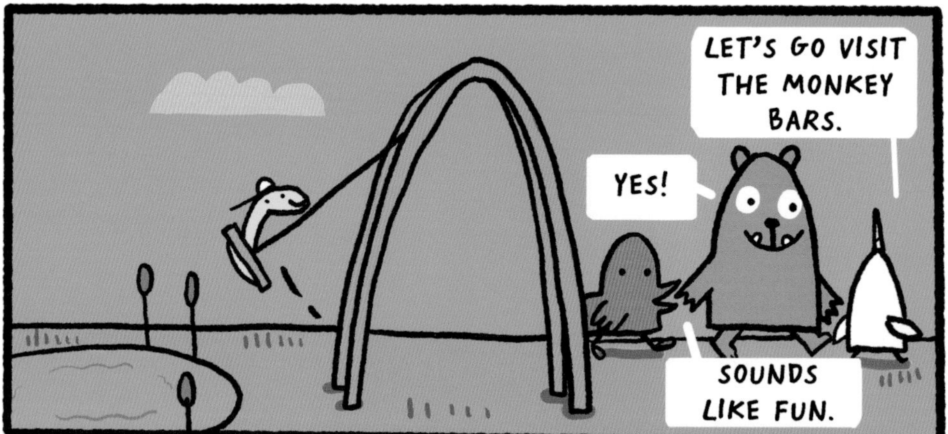
LET'S GO VISIT THE MONKEY BARS.
YES!
SOUNDS LIKE FUN.

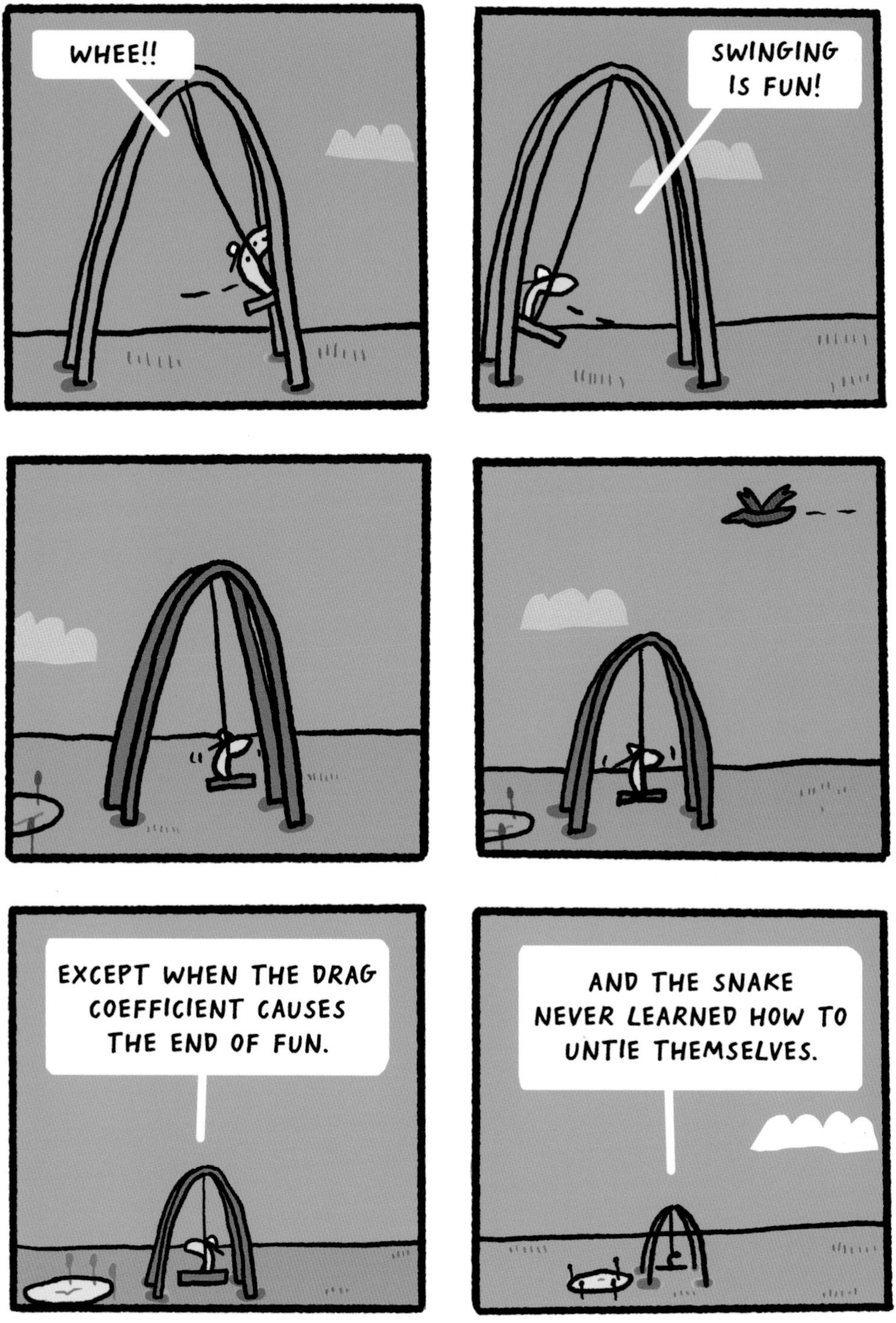
WHEE!!
SWINGING IS FUN!
EXCEPT WHEN THE DRAG COEFFICIENT CAUSES THE END OF FUN.
AND THE SNAKE NEVER LEARNED HOW TO UNTIE THEMSELVES.

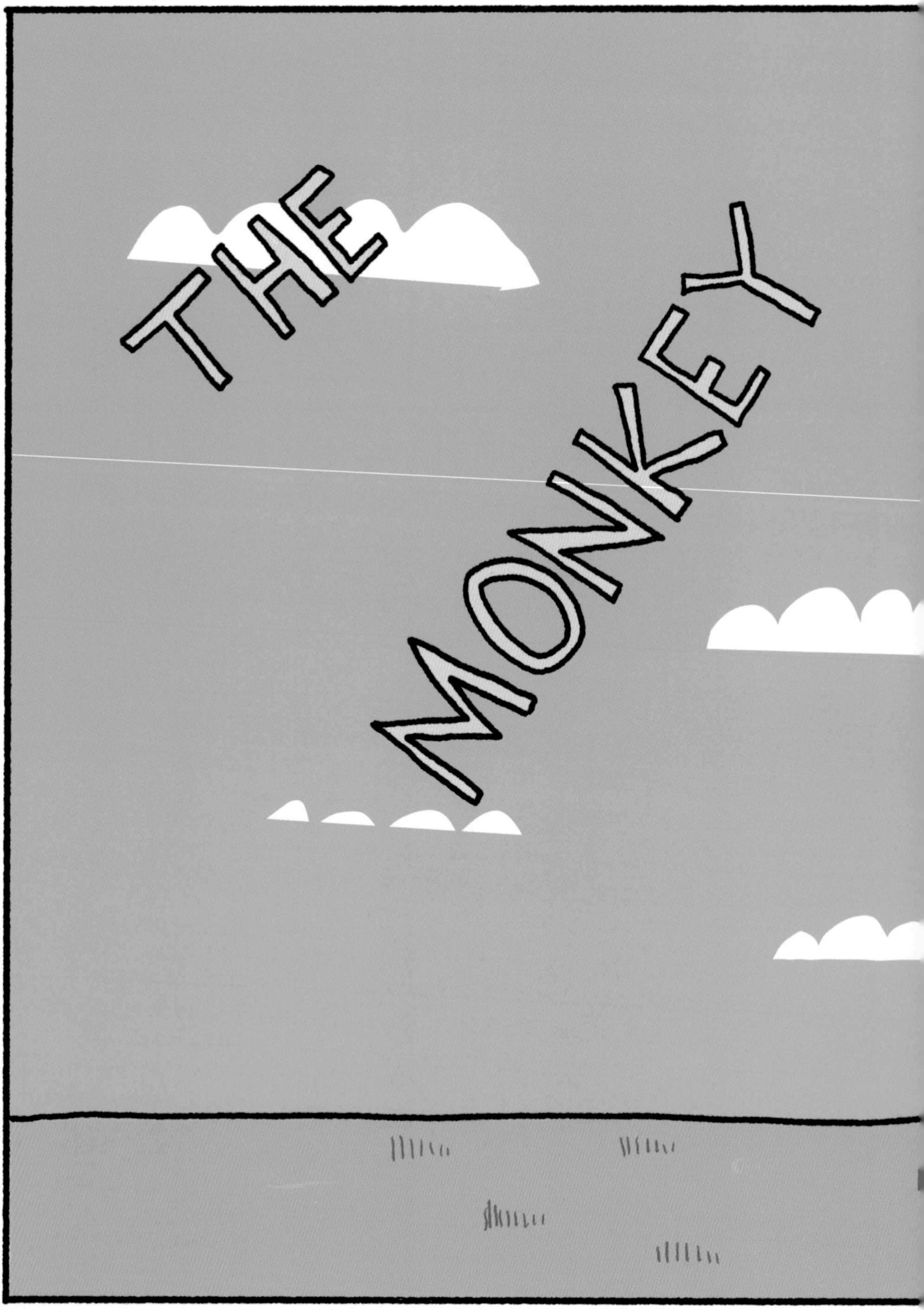
THE MONKEY

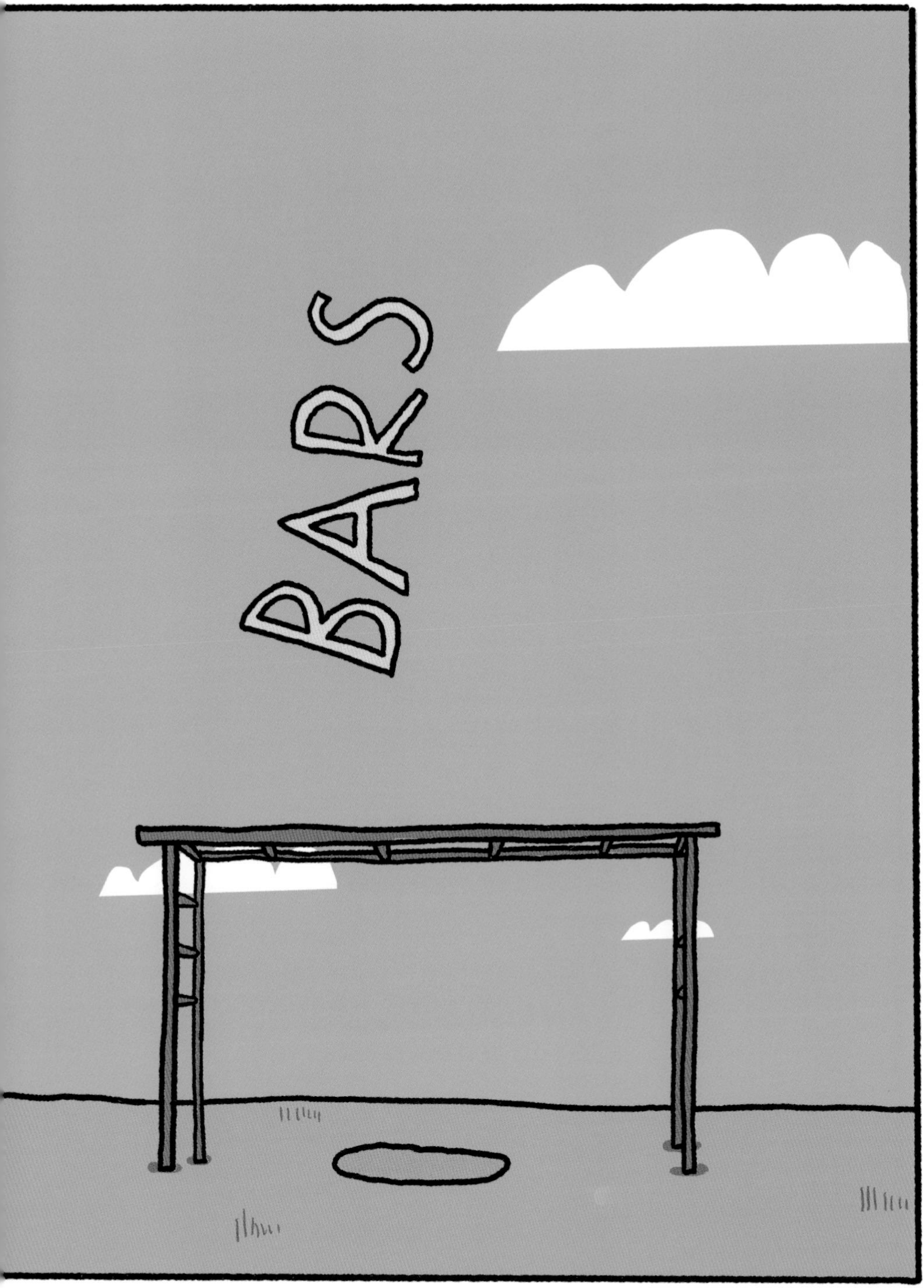
BARS

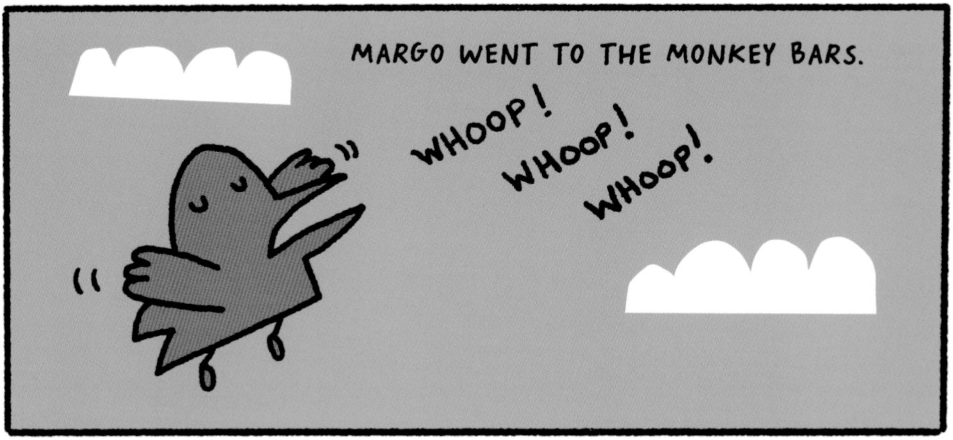
MARGO WENT TO THE MONKEY BARS.
WHOOP! WHOOP! WHOOP!

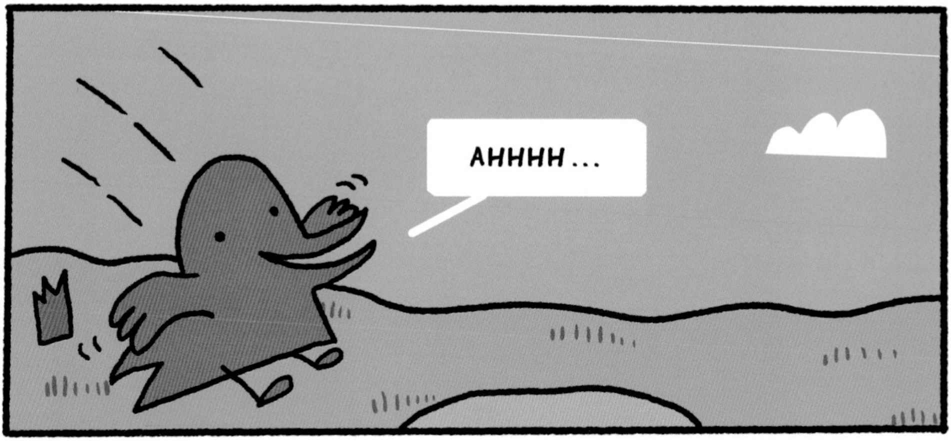
AHHHH...

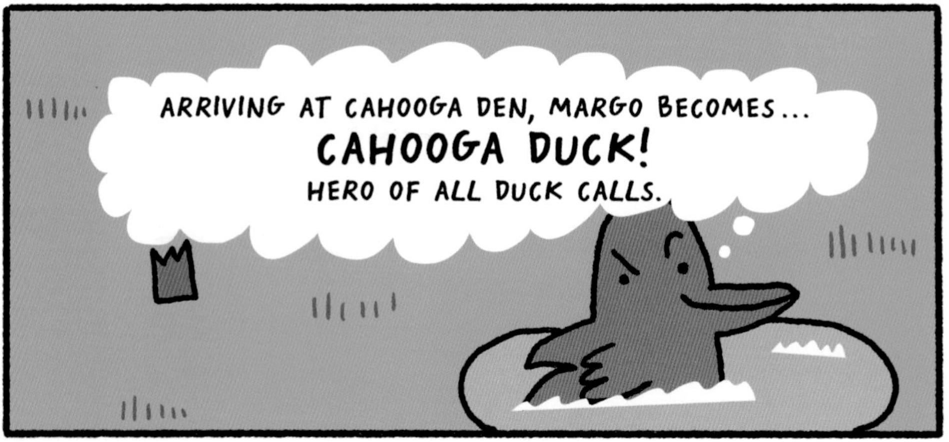
ARRIVING AT CAHOOGA DEN, MARGO BECOMES...
CAHOOGA DUCK!
HERO OF ALL DUCK CALLS.

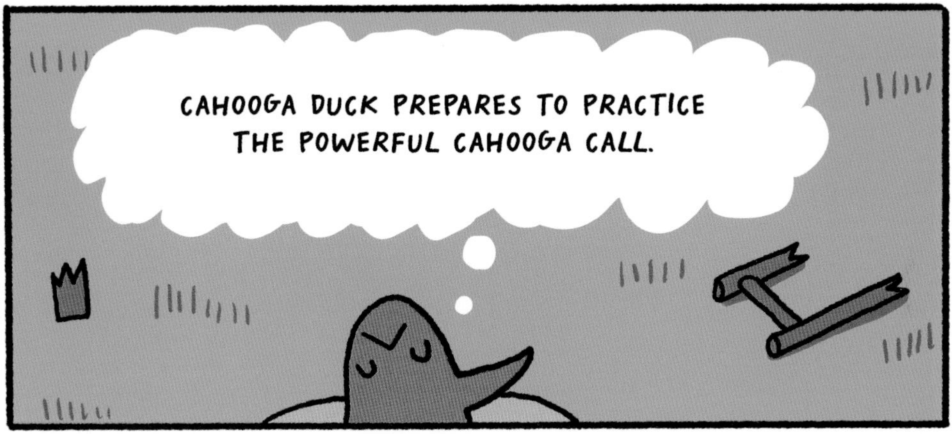
CAHOOGA DUCK PREPARES TO PRACTICE THE POWERFUL CAHOOGA CALL.

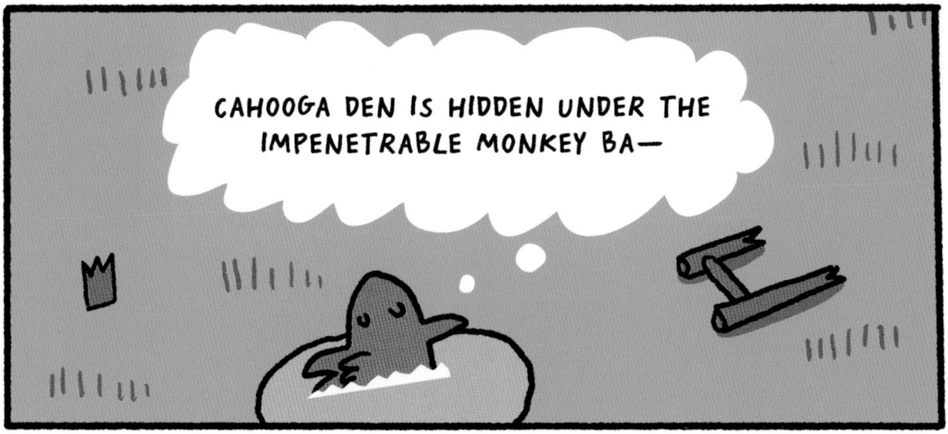
CAHOOGA DEN IS HIDDEN UNDER THE IMPENETRABLE MONKEY BA—

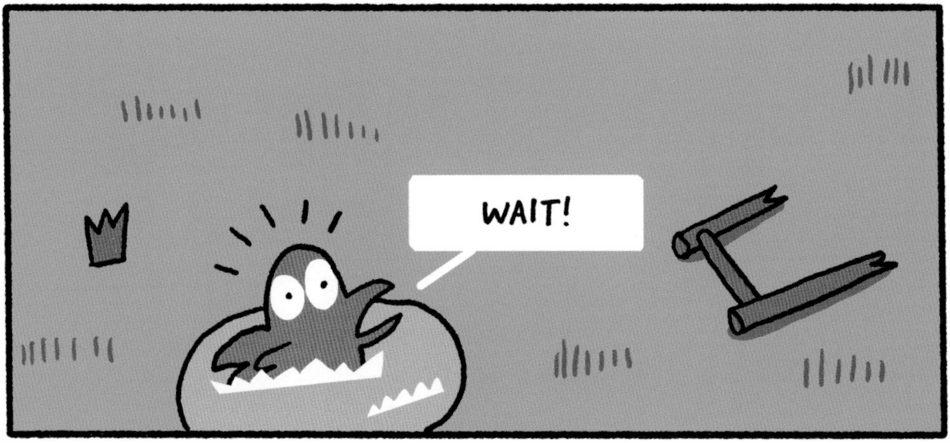
WAIT!

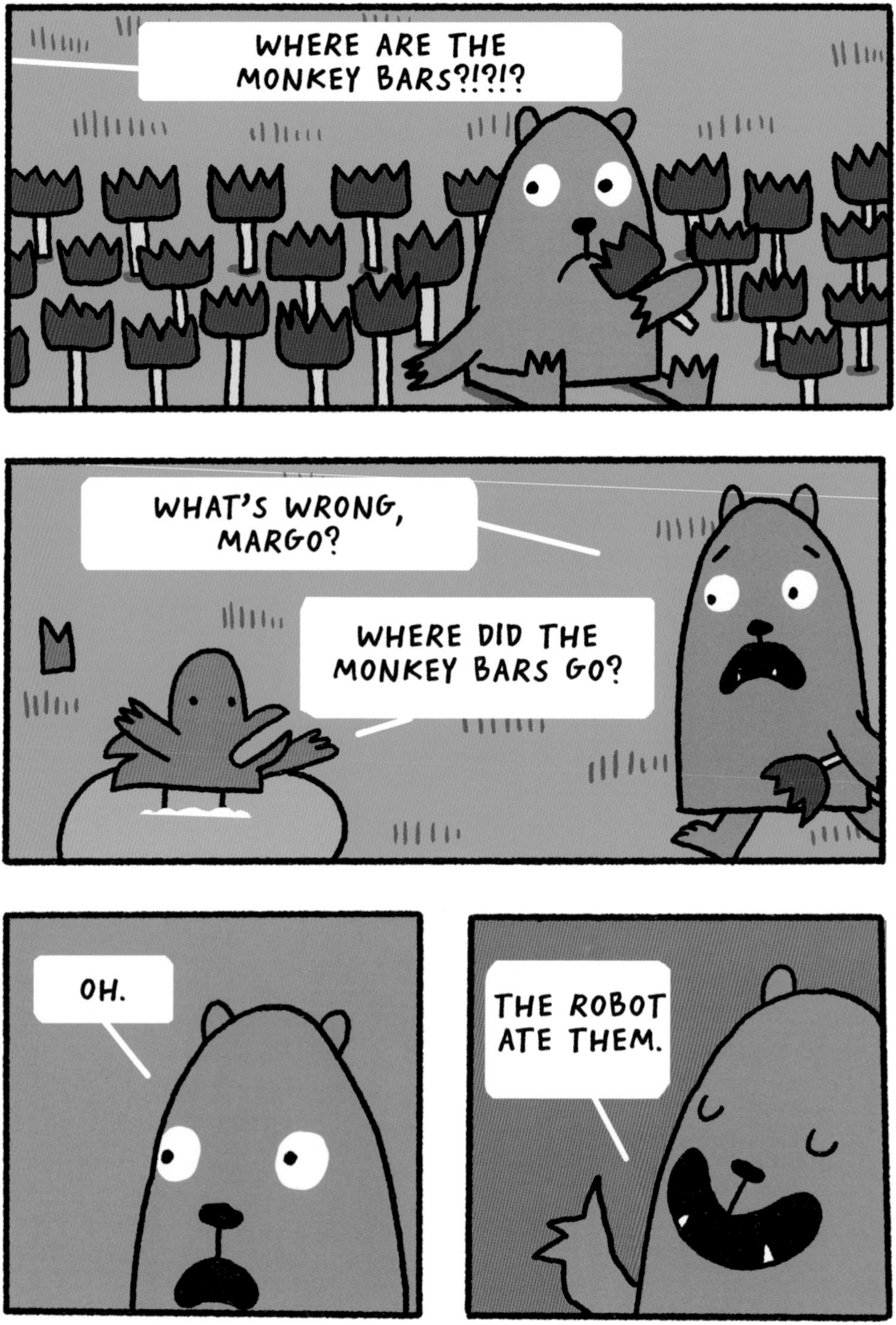
WHERE ARE THE MONKEY BARS?!?!?
WHAT'S WRONG, MARGO?
WHERE DID THE MONKEY BARS GO?
OH.
THE ROBOT ATE THEM.

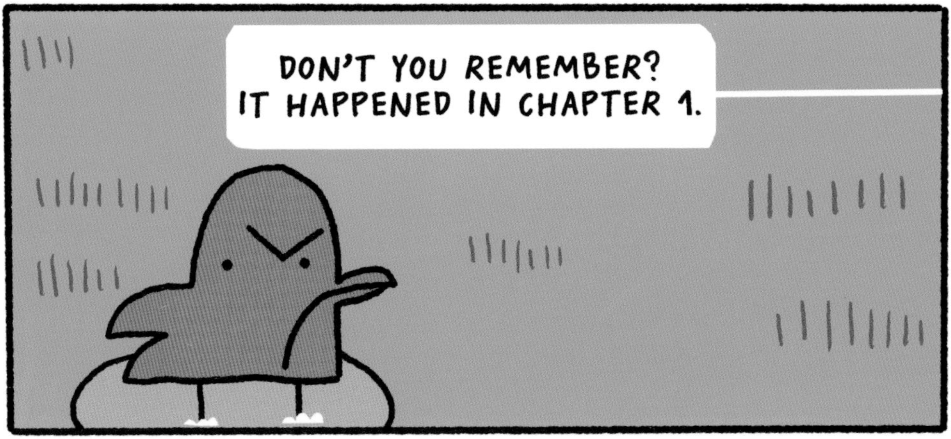
DON'T YOU REMEMBER?
IT HAPPENED IN CHAPTER 1.

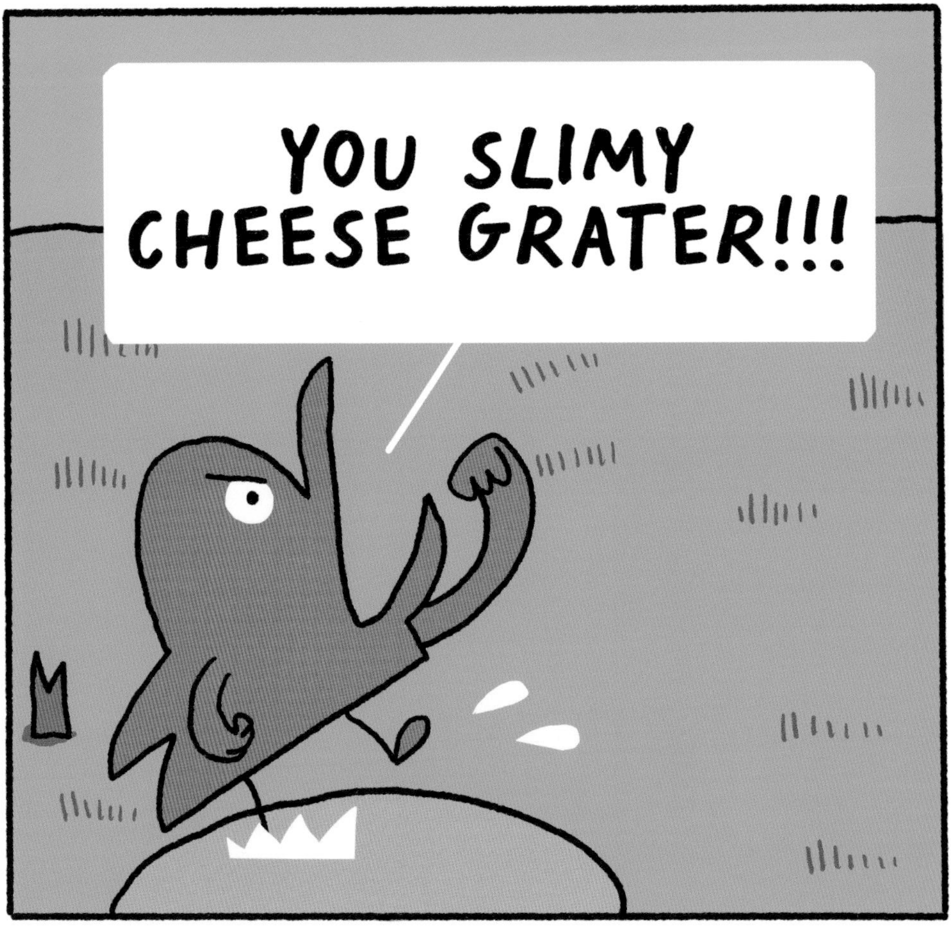
YOU SLIMY
CHEESE GRATER!!!

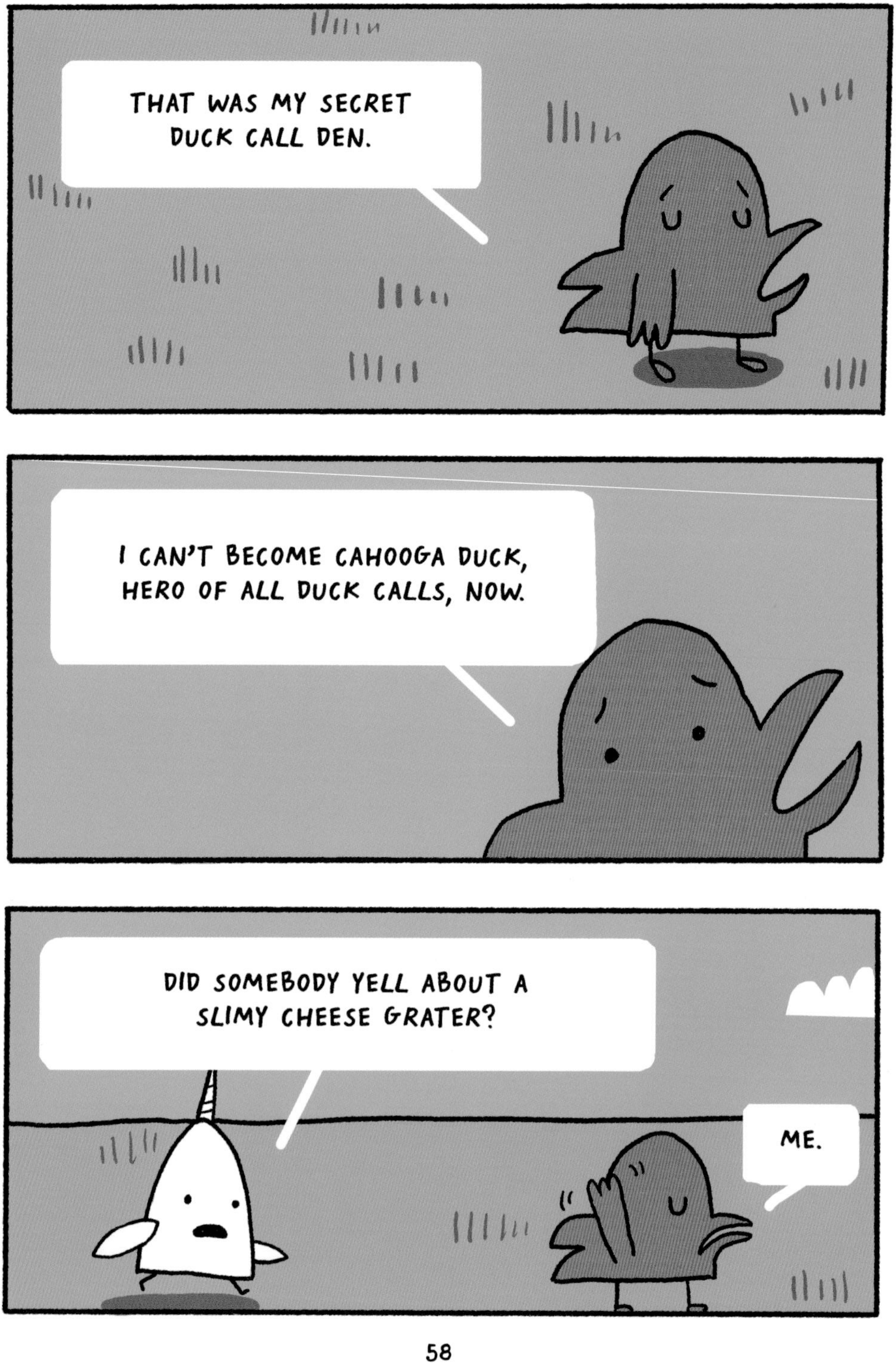
THAT WAS MY SECRET DUCK CALL DEN.
I CAN'T BECOME CAHOOGA DUCK, HERO OF ALL DUCK CALLS, NOW.
DID SOMEBODY YELL ABOUT A SLIMY CHEESE GRATER?
ME.

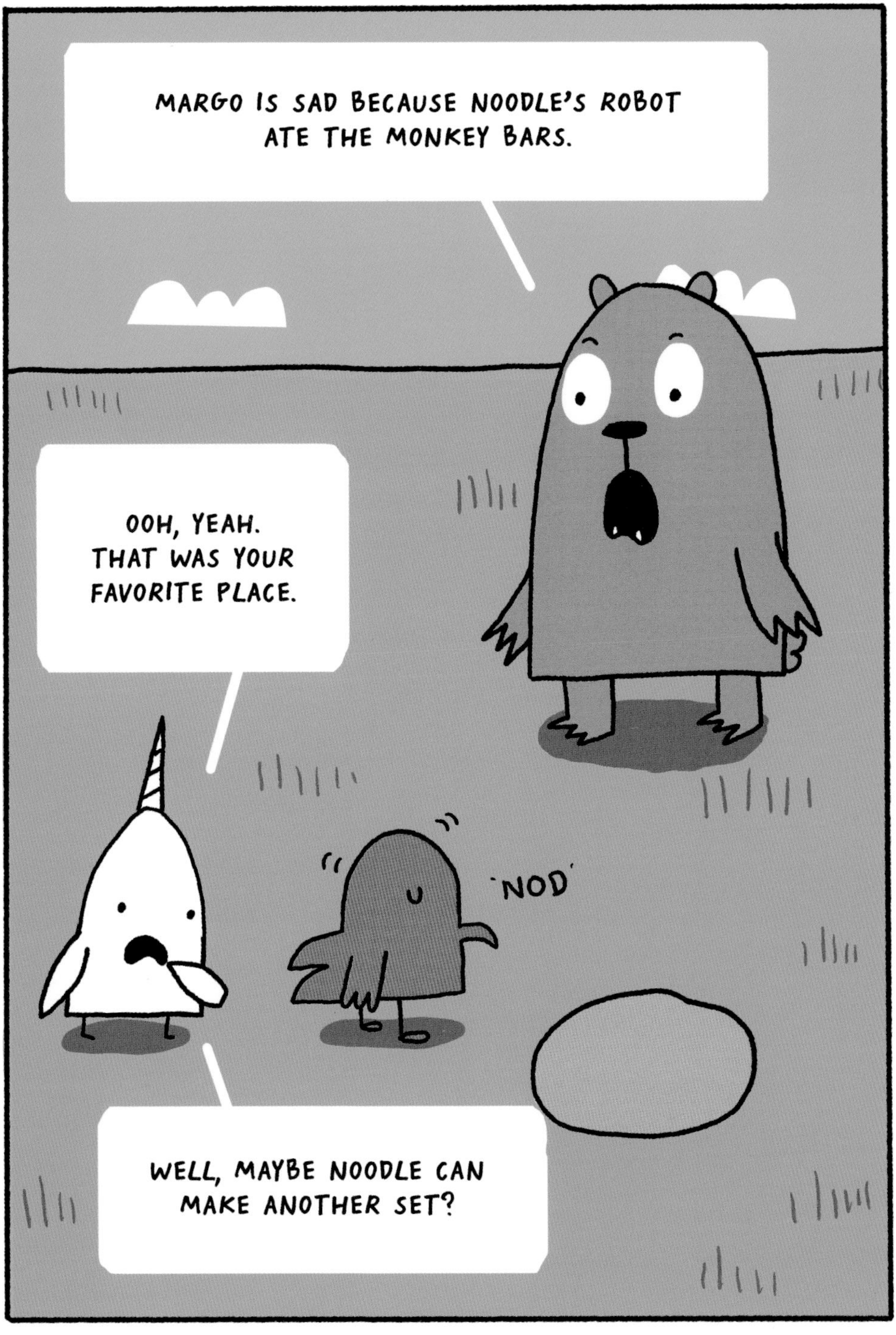
MARGO IS SAD BECAUSE NOODLE'S ROBOT ATE THE MONKEY BARS.
OOH, YEAH. THAT WAS YOUR FAVORITE PLACE.
NOD
WELL, MAYBE NOODLE CAN MAKE ANOTHER SET?

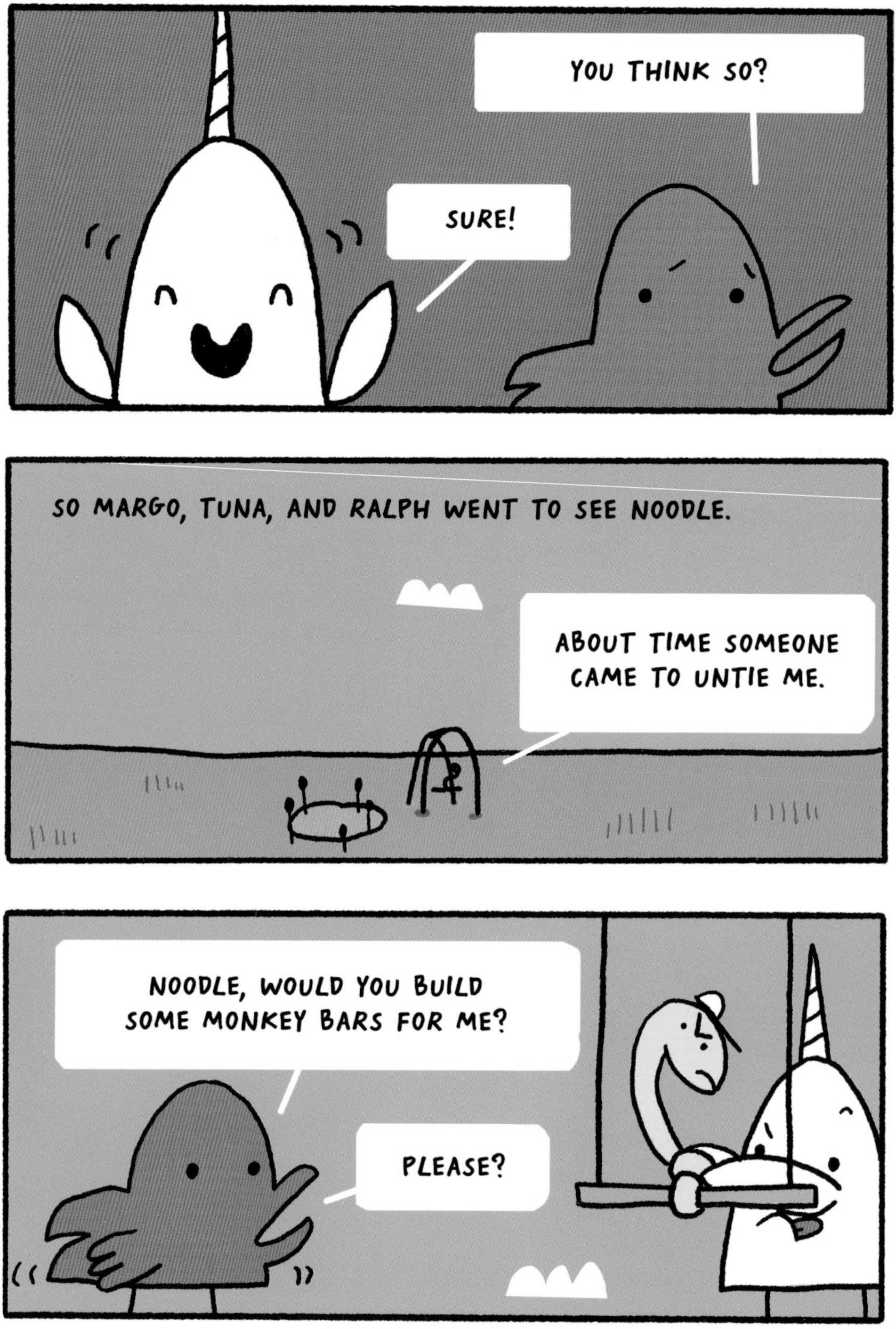
YOU THINK SO?
SURE!
SO MARGO, TUNA, AND RALPH WENT TO SEE NOODLE.
ABOUT TIME SOMEONE CAME TO UNTIE ME.
NOODLE, WOULD YOU BUILD SOME MONKEY BARS FOR ME?
PLEASE?

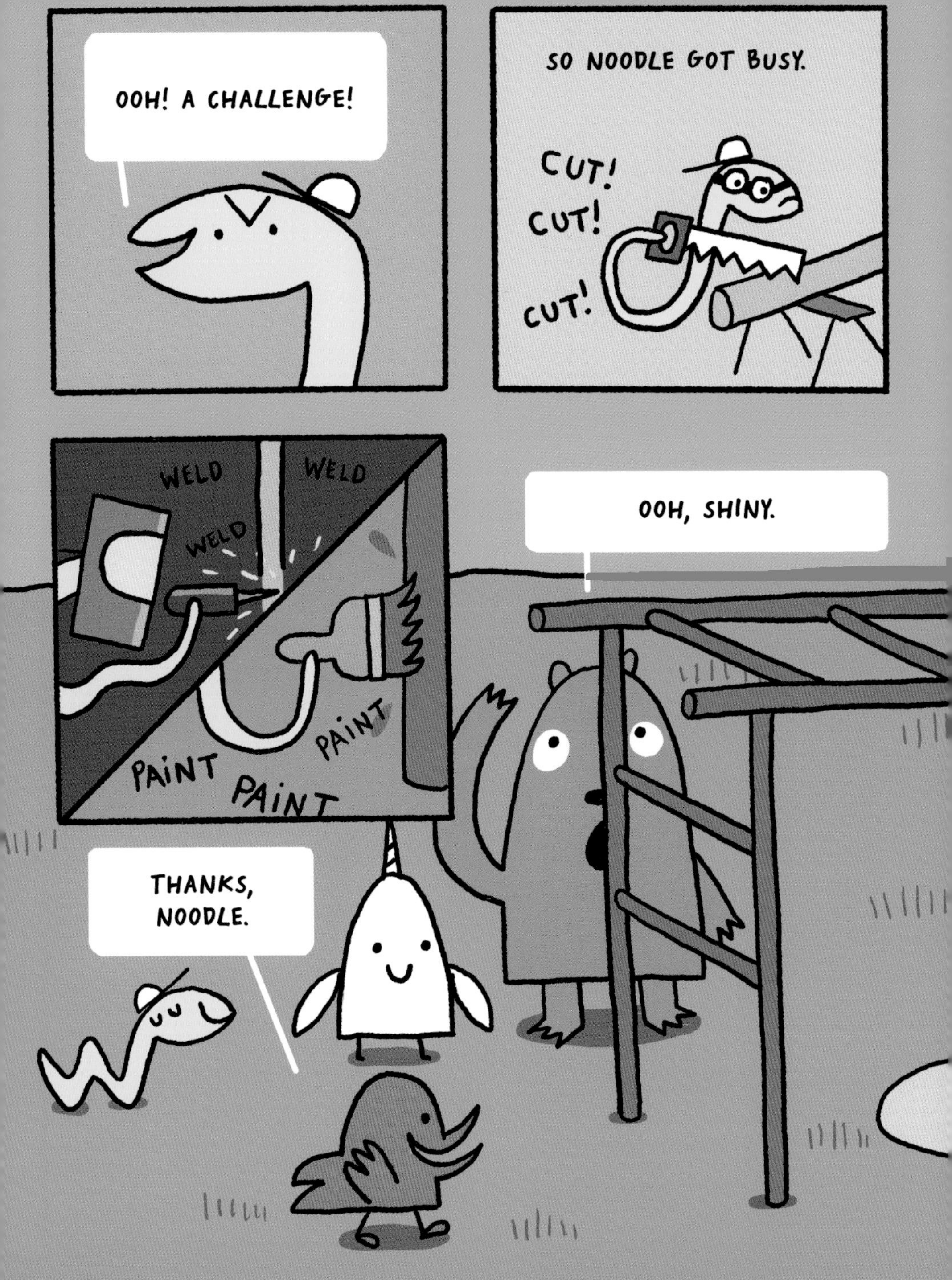
OOH! A CHALLENGE!
SO NOODLE GOT BUSY.
CUT!
CUT!
CUT!
WELD
WELD
WELD
PAINT
PAINT
PAINT
OOH, SHINY.
THANKS, NOODLE.

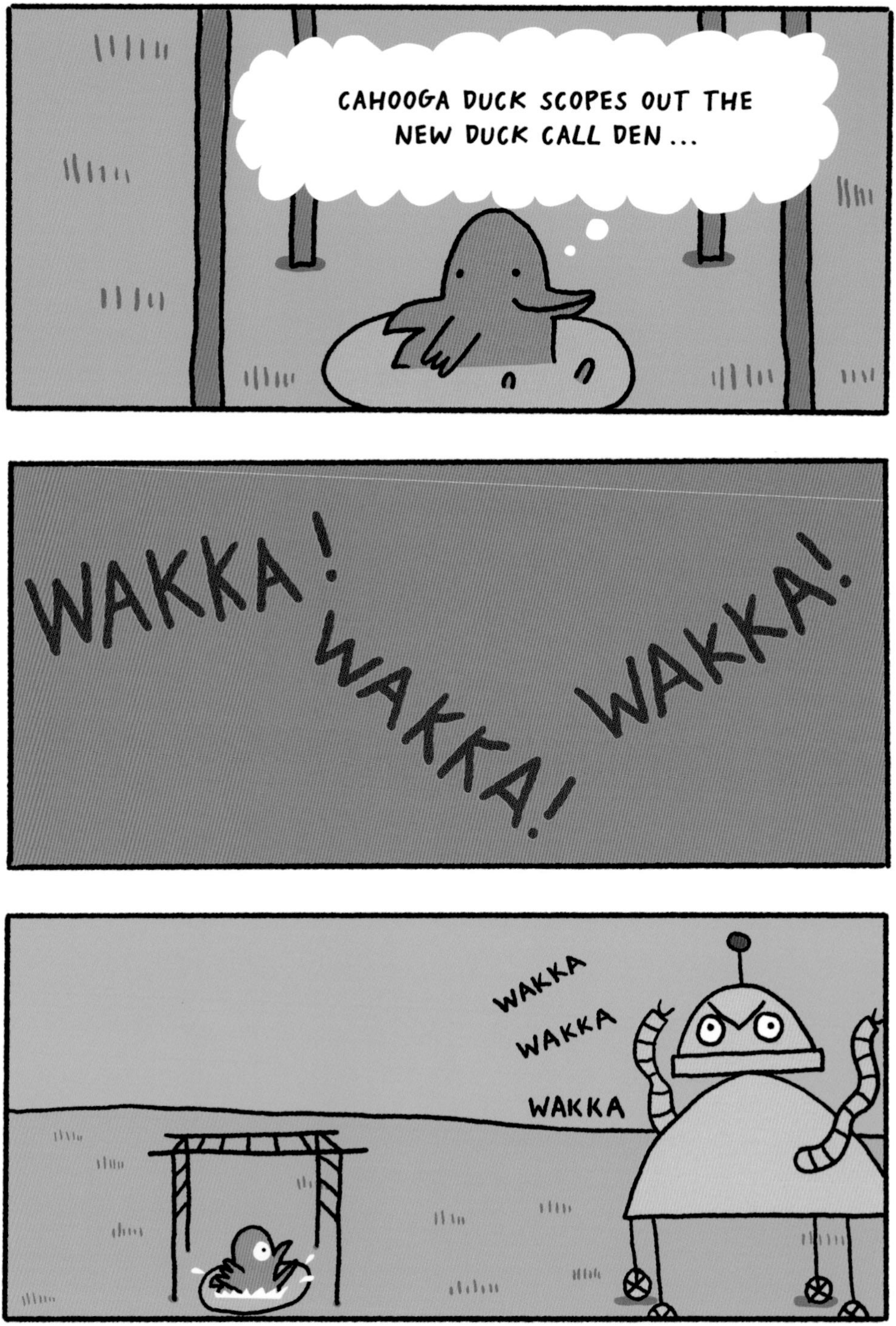
CAHOOGA DUCK SCOPES OUT THE NEW DUCK CALL DEN...
WAKKA!
WAKKA!
WAKKA!
WAKKA
WAKKA
WAKKA

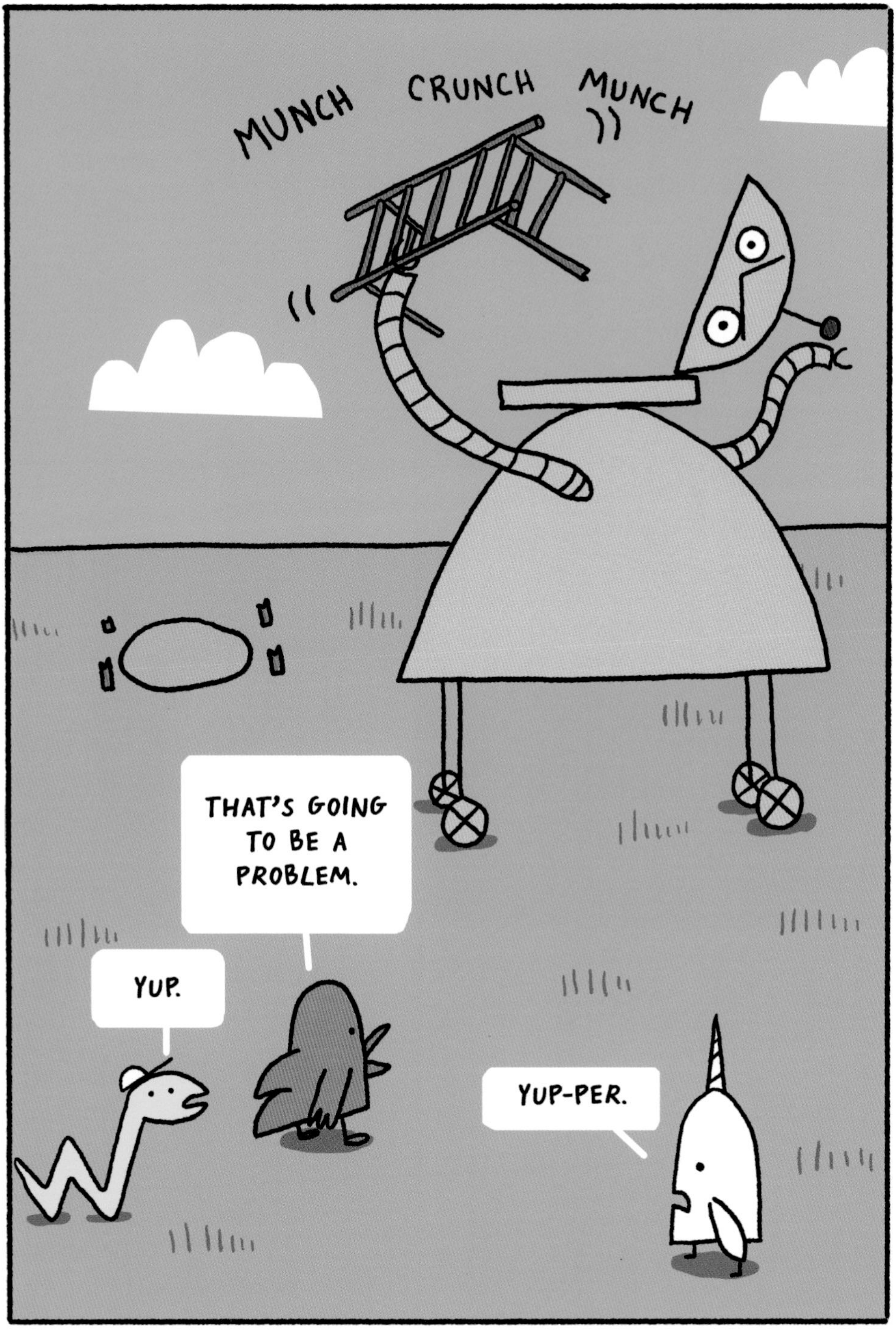
MUNCH CRUNCH MUNCH
THAT'S GOING TO BE A PROBLEM.
YUP.
YUP-PER.

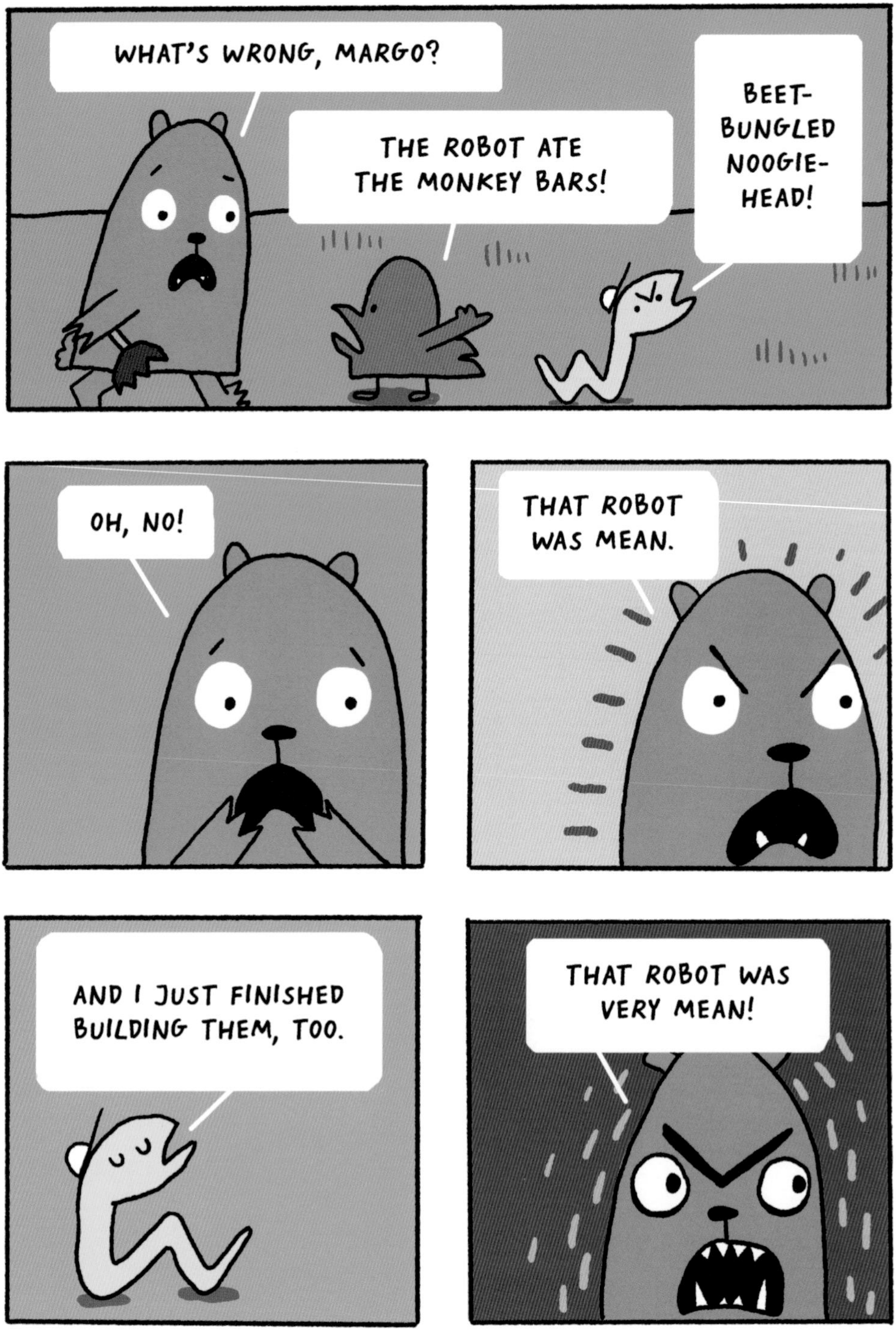
WHAT'S WRONG, MARGO?
THE ROBOT ATE THE MONKEY BARS!
BEET-BUNGLED NOOGIE-HEAD!
OH, NO!
THAT ROBOT WAS MEAN.
AND I JUST FINISHED BUILDING THEM, TOO.
THAT ROBOT WAS VERY MEAN!

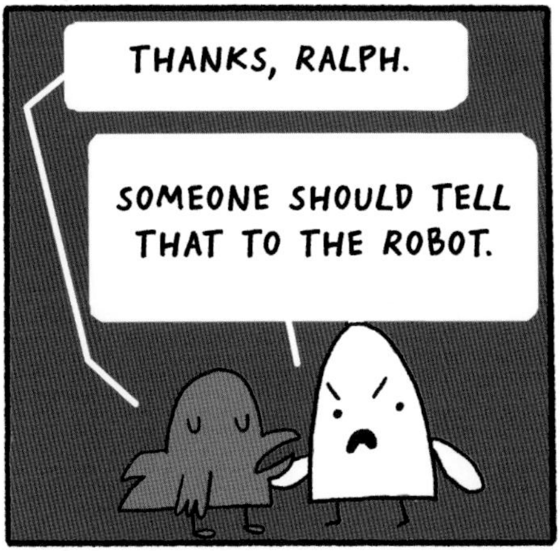
THANKS, RALPH.
SOMEONE SHOULD TELL THAT TO THE ROBOT.

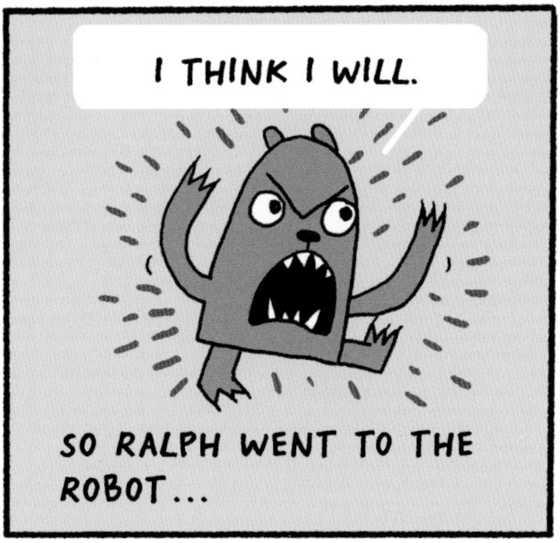
I THINK I WILL.
SO RALPH WENT TO THE ROBOT...

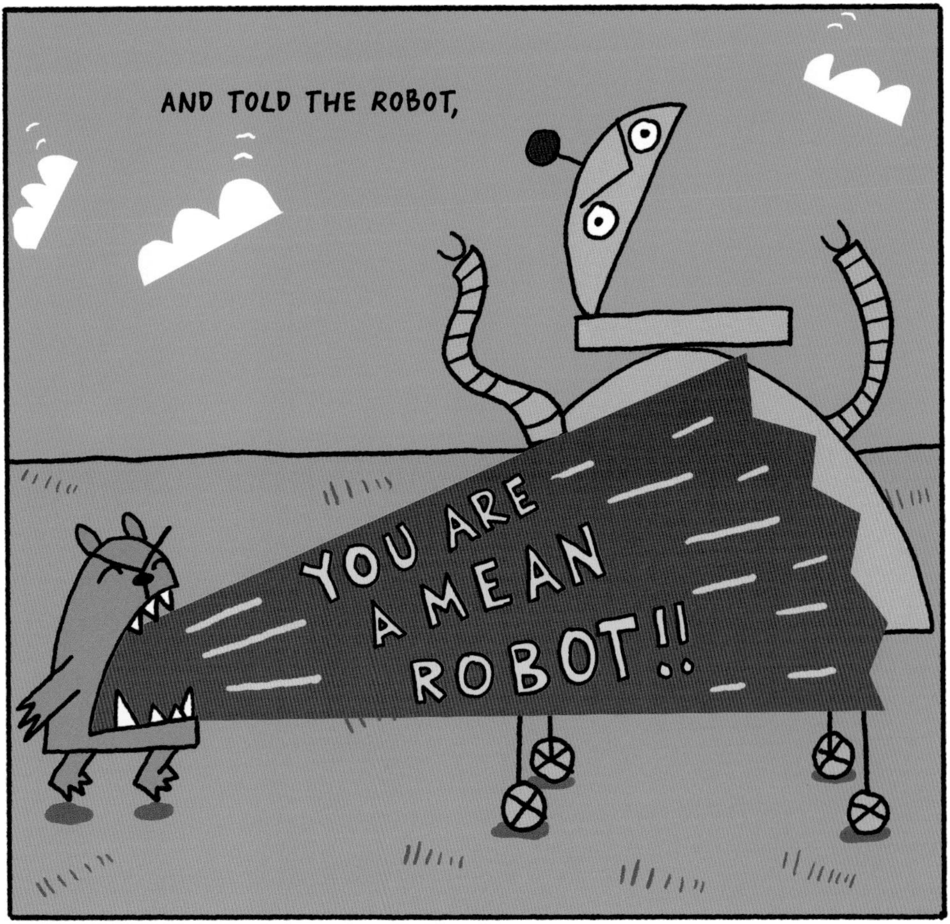
AND TOLD THE ROBOT,
YOU ARE A MEAN ROBOT!!

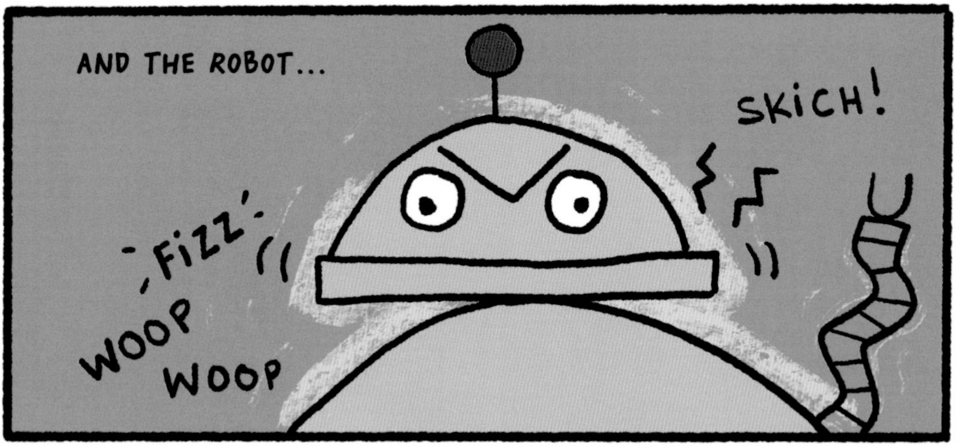
AND THE ROBOT...
SKICH!
FIZZ
WOOP
WOOP

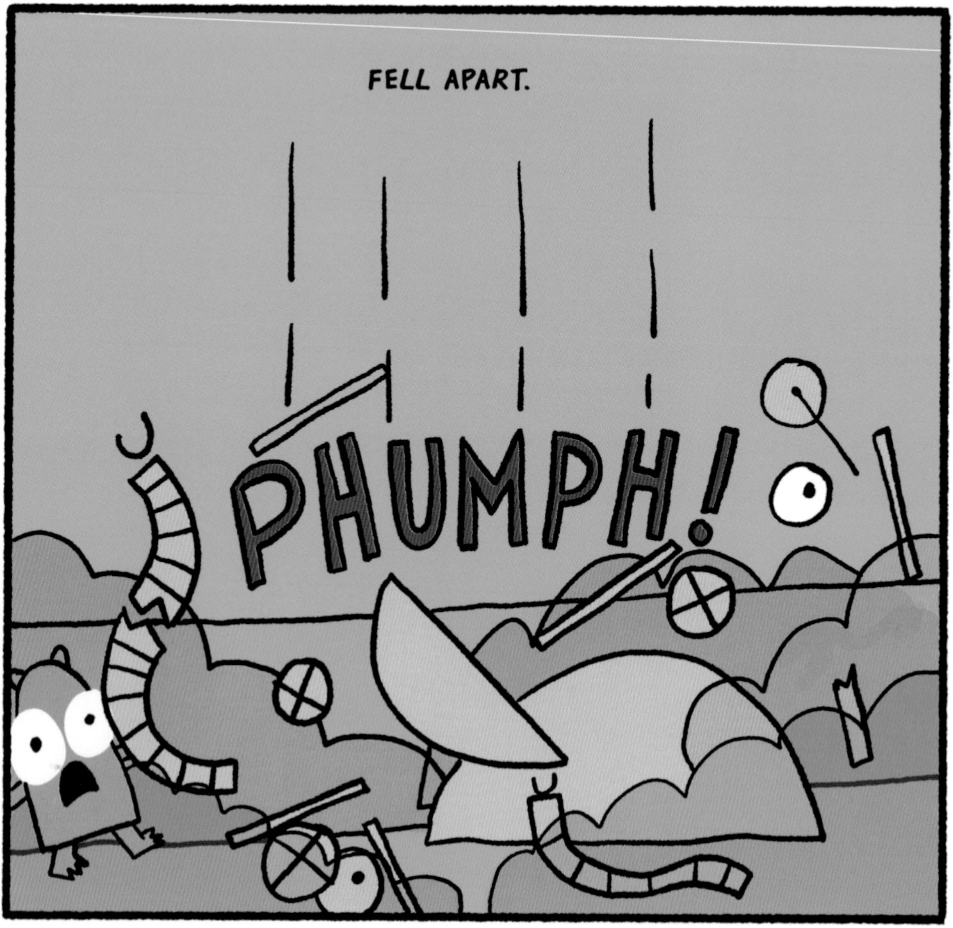
FELL APART.
PHUMPH!

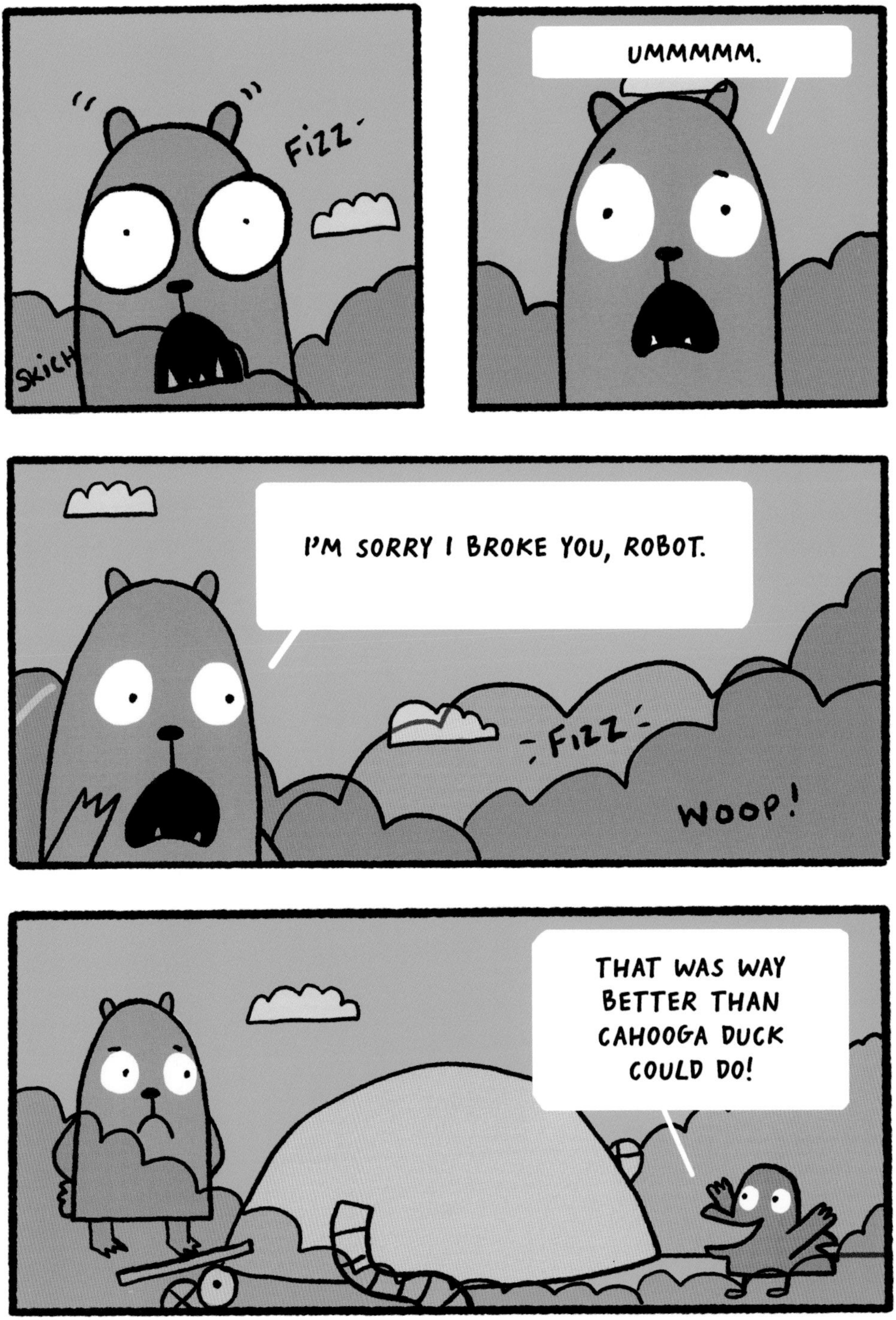

FIZZ
SKICH
UMMMMM.
I'M SORRY I BROKE YOU, ROBOT.
FIZZ
WOOP!
THAT WAS WAY BETTER THAN CAHOOGA DUCK COULD DO!

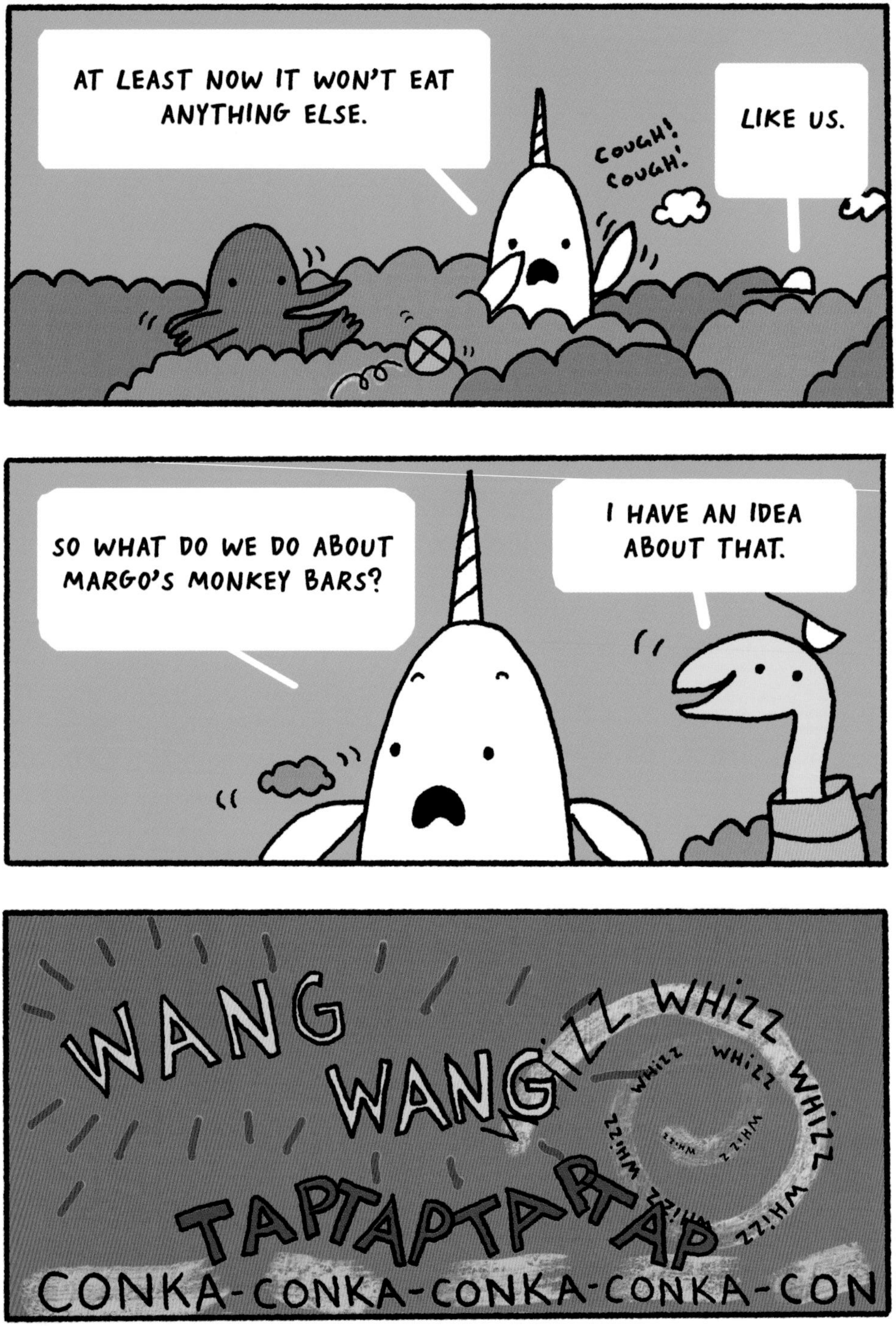
AT LEAST NOW IT WON'T EAT ANYTHING ELSE.
COUGH! COUGH!
LIKE US.
SO WHAT DO WE DO ABOUT MARGO'S MONKEY BARS?
I HAVE AN IDEA ABOUT THAT.
WANG
WANG
WHIZZ WHIZZ WHIZZ
WHIZZ WHIZZ
TAPTAPTAPTAP
CONKA-CONKA-CONKA-CONKA-CON

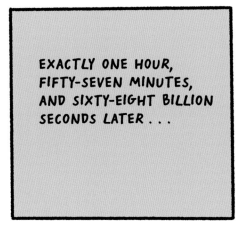

EXACTLY ONE HOUR, FIFTY-SEVEN MINUTES, AND SIXTY-EIGHT BILLION SECONDS LATER . . .

JUST A LITTLE FURTHER.

I STILL DON'T KNOW WHY WE CAN'T SEE WHERE WE'RE GOING!

SURPRISE!!!

WHAT?

OH!

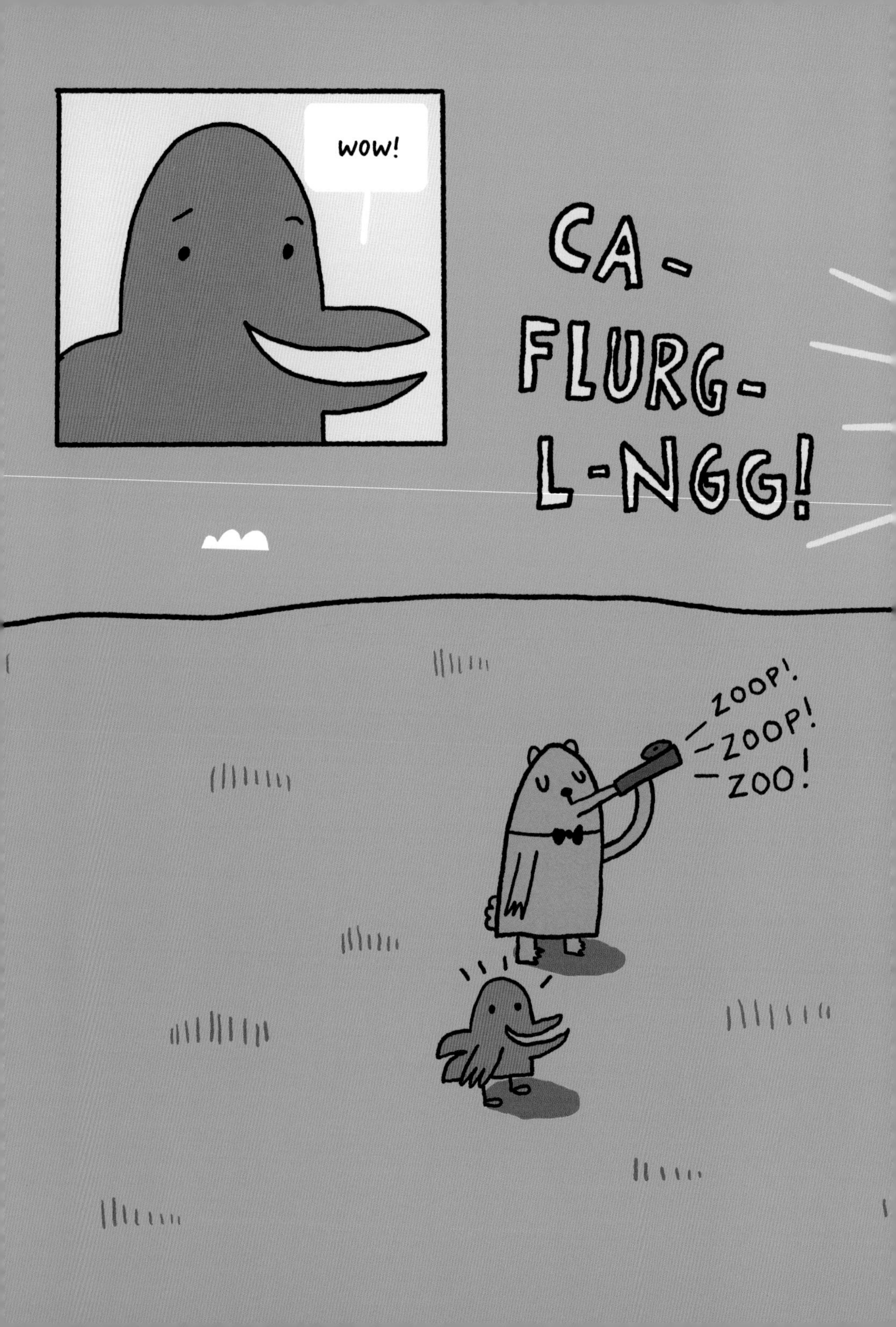
WOW!
CA-FLURG-L-NGG!
ZOOP!
ZOOP!
ZOO!

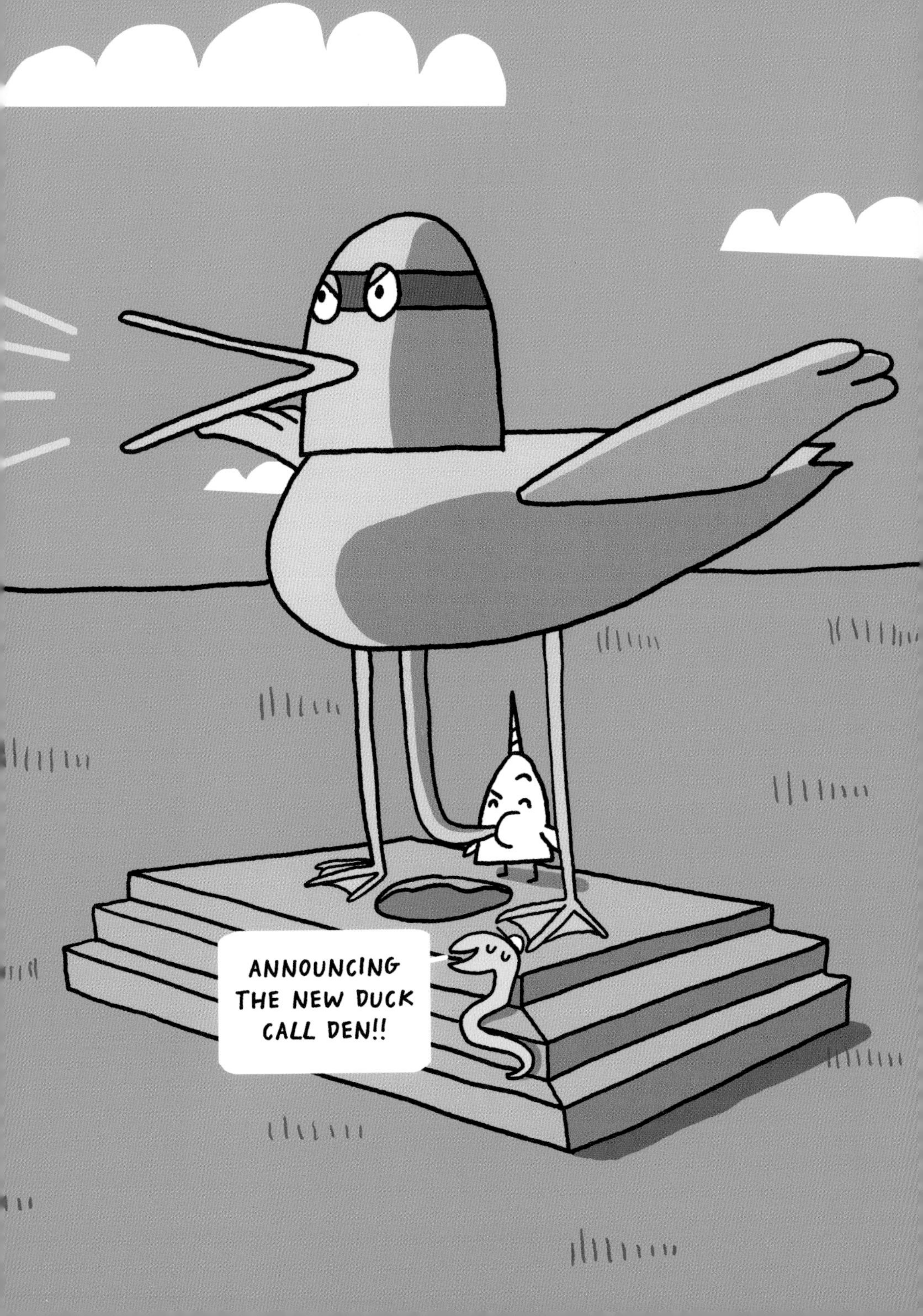
ANNOUNCING THE NEW DUCK CALL DEN!!

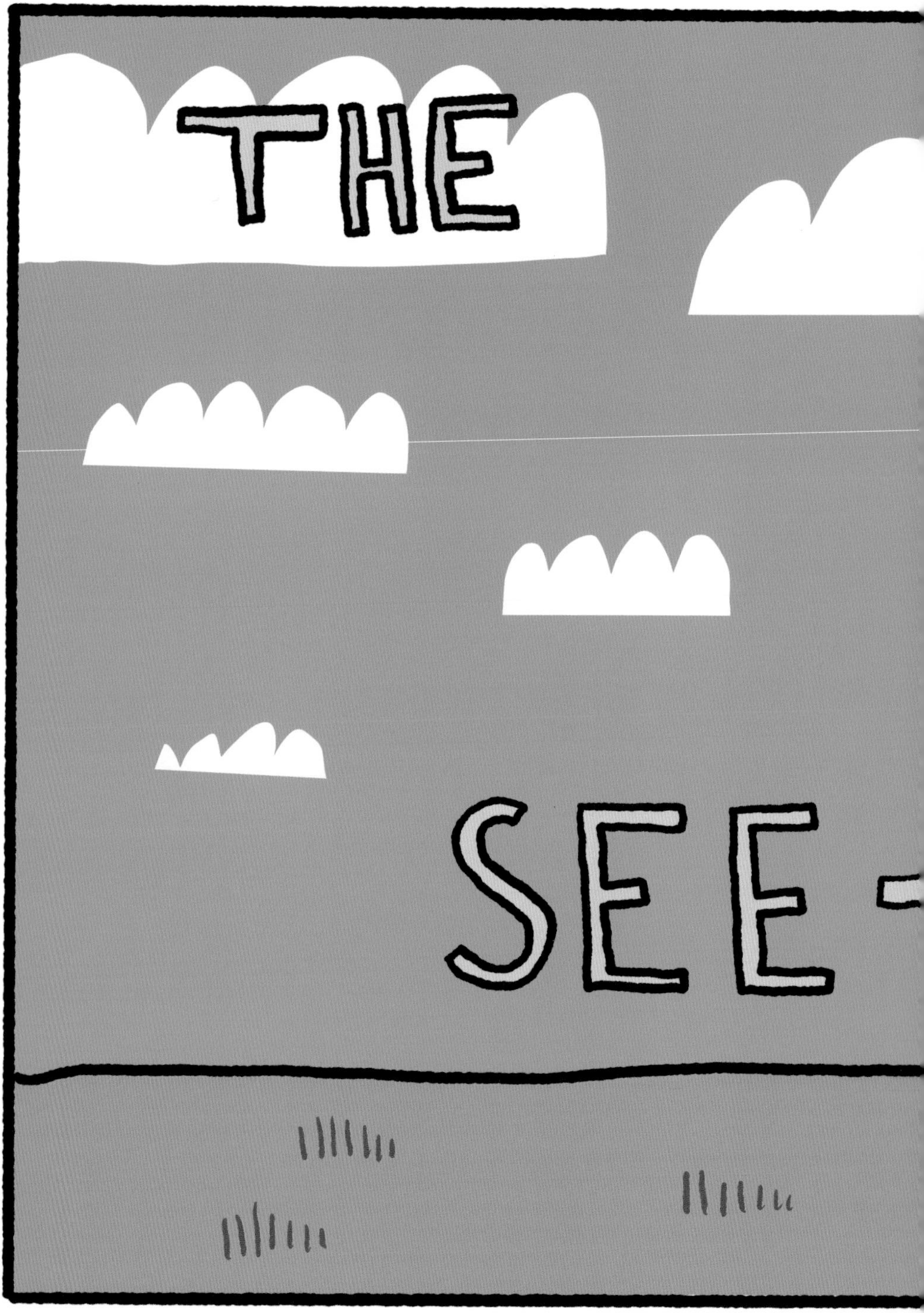
THE
SEE-

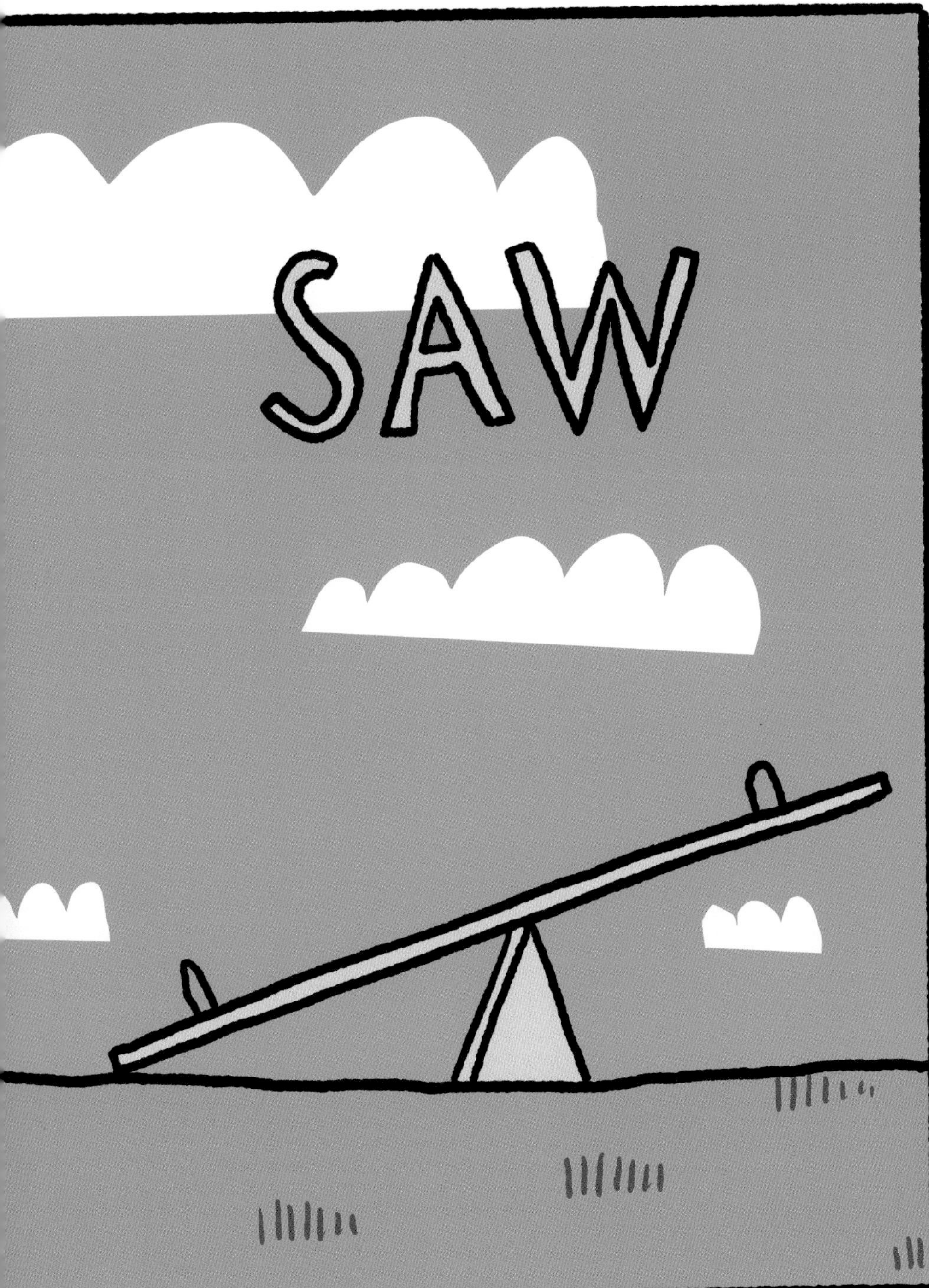
SAW

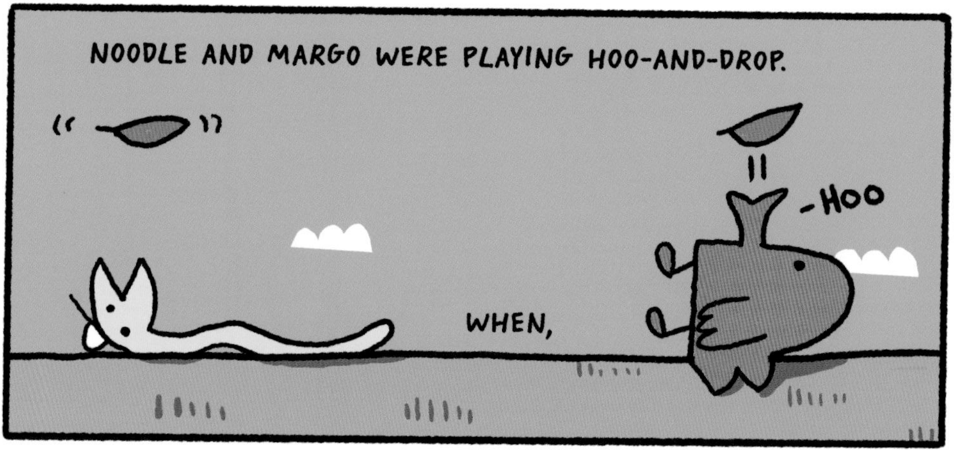
NOODLE AND MARGO WERE PLAYING HOO-AND-DROP.
-HOO
WHEN,

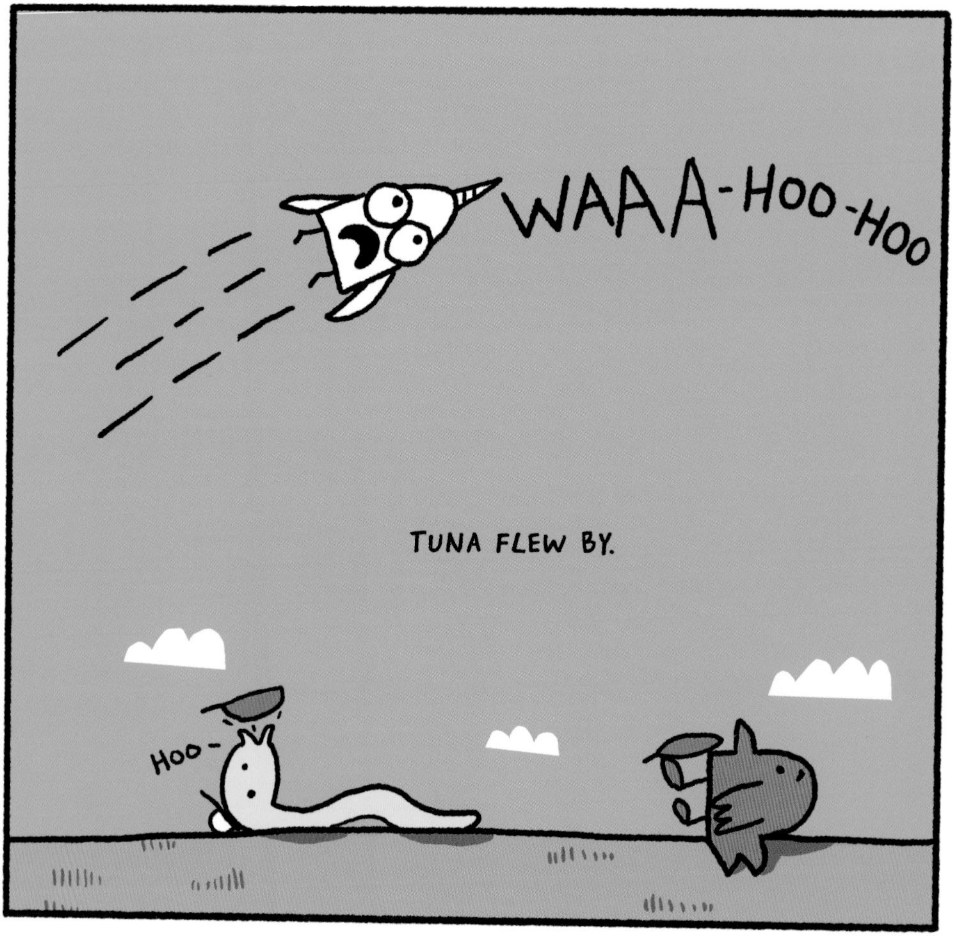
WAAA-HOO-HOO-HOO
TUNA FLEW BY.
HOO-

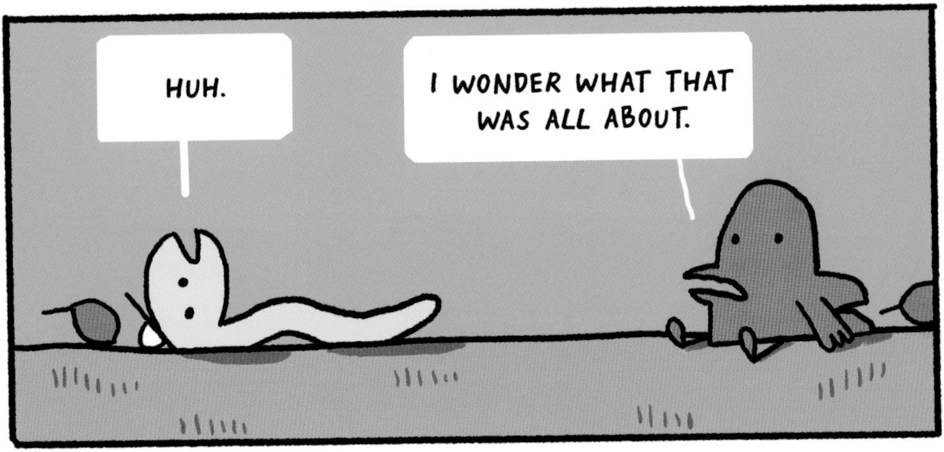
HUH.
I WONDER WHAT THAT WAS ALL ABOUT.

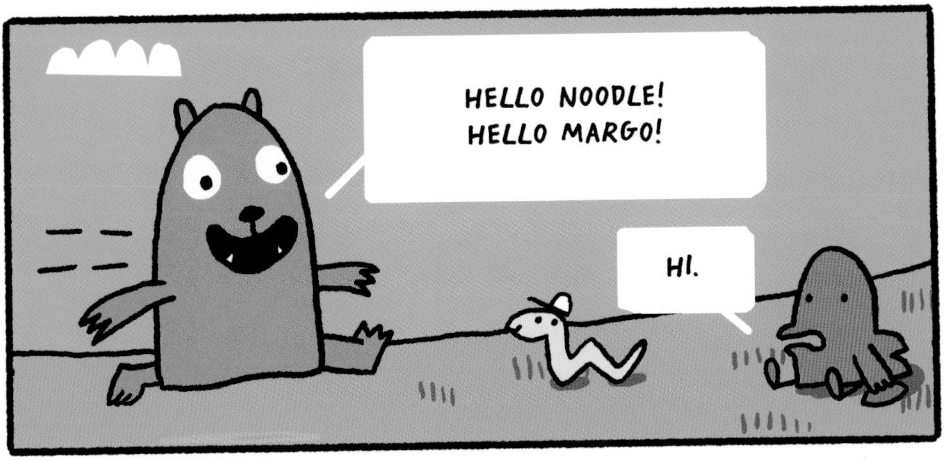
HELLO NOODLE! HELLO MARGO!
HI.

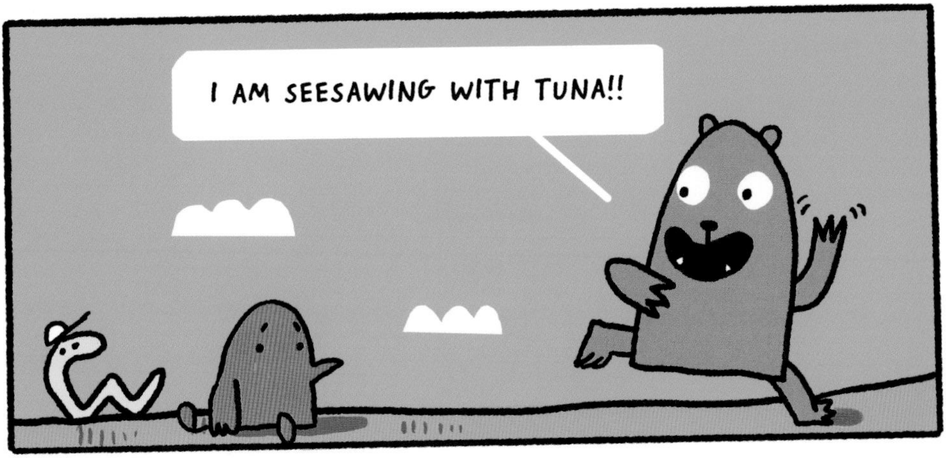
I AM SEESAWING WITH TUNA!!

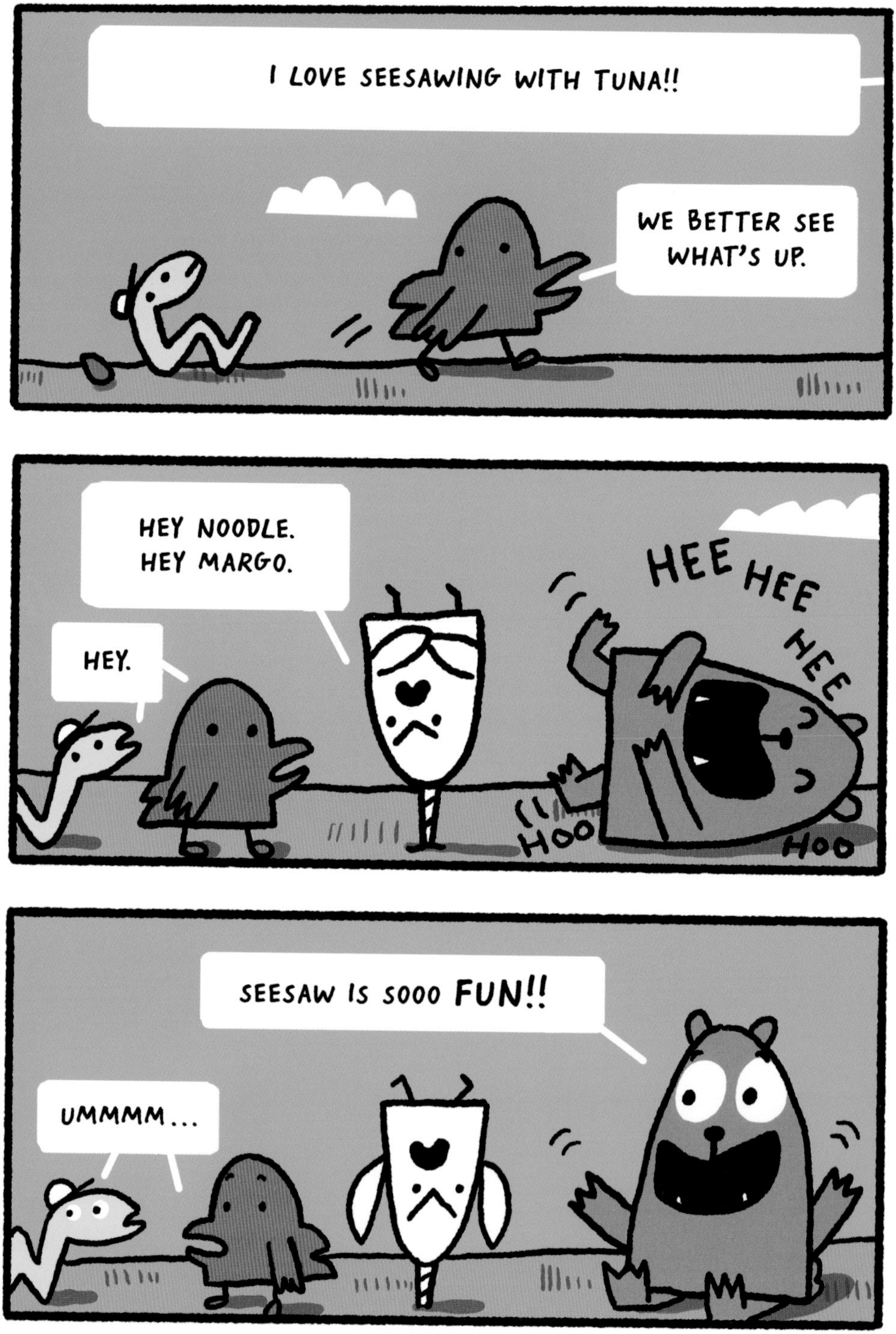
I LOVE SEESAWING WITH TUNA!!
WE BETTER SEE WHAT'S UP.
HEY NOODLE. HEY MARGO.
HEY.
HEE HEE HEE HEE
HOO
HOO
SEESAW IS SOOO FUN!!
UMMMM...

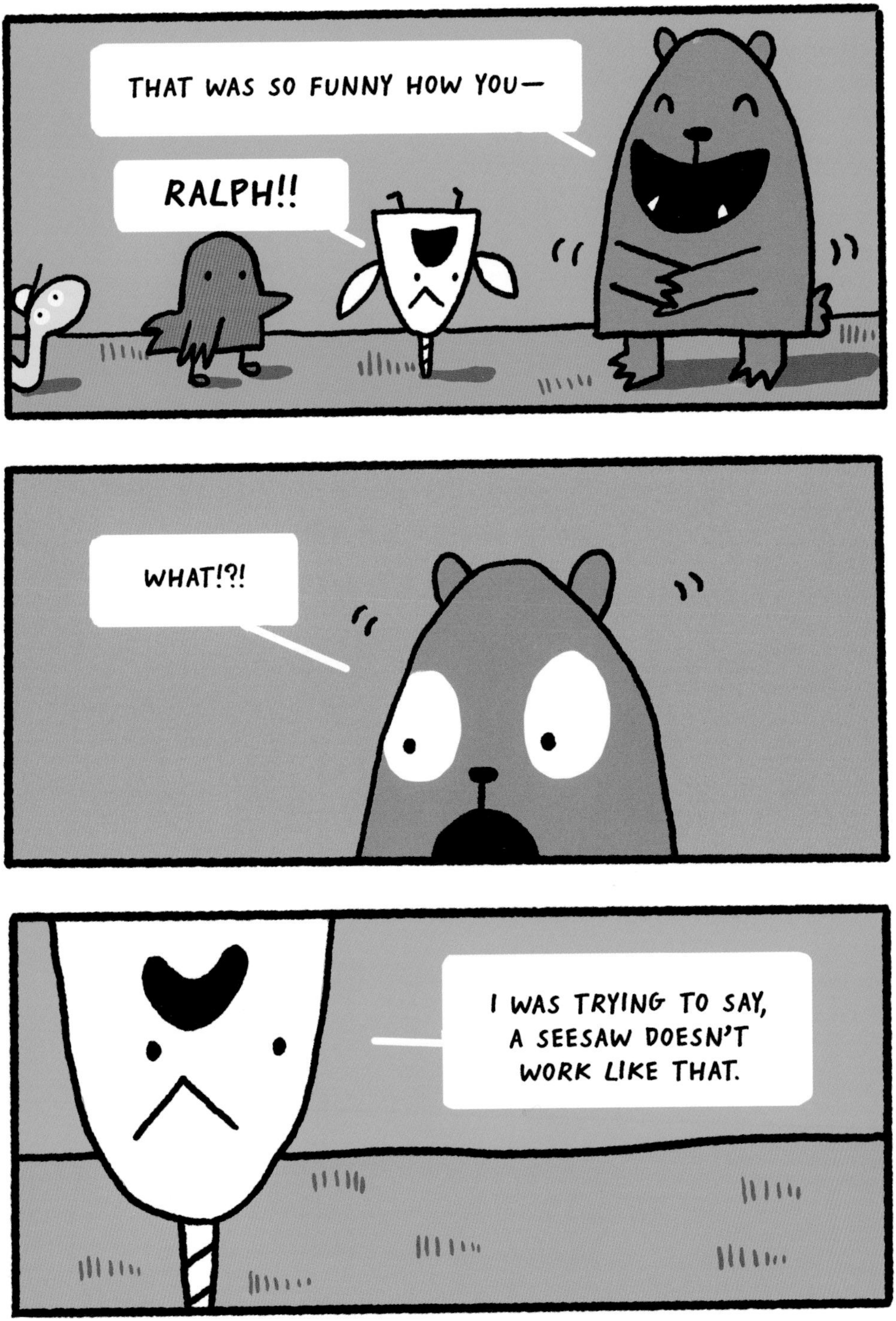
THAT WAS SO FUNNY HOW YOU—
RALPH!!
WHAT!?!
I WAS TRYING TO SAY, A SEESAW DOESN'T WORK LIKE THAT.

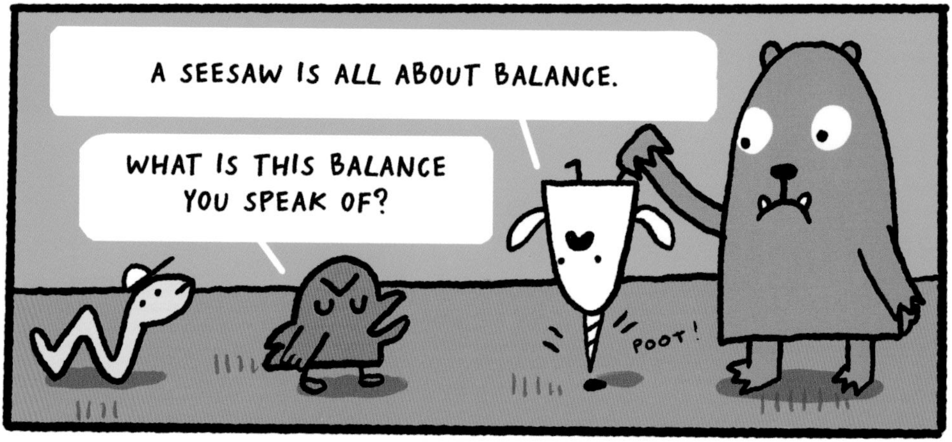
A SEESAW IS ALL ABOUT BALANCE.
WHAT IS THIS BALANCE YOU SPEAK OF?
POOT!

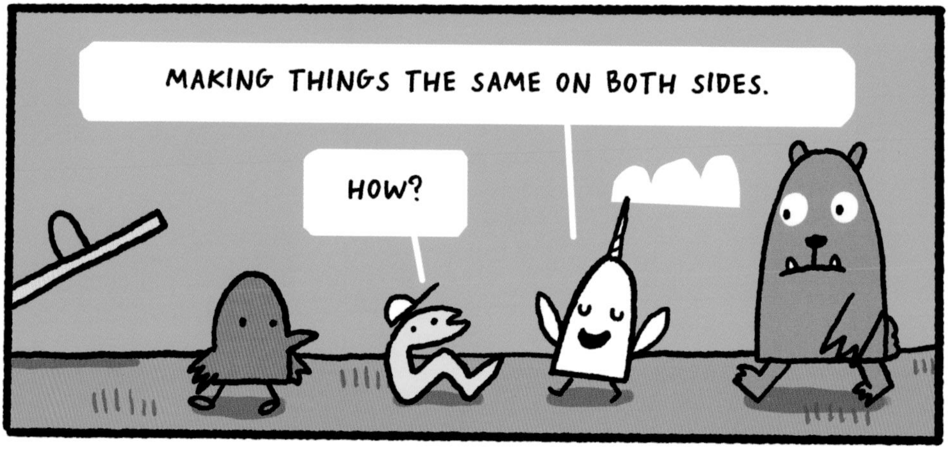
MAKING THINGS THE SAME ON BOTH SIDES.
HOW?

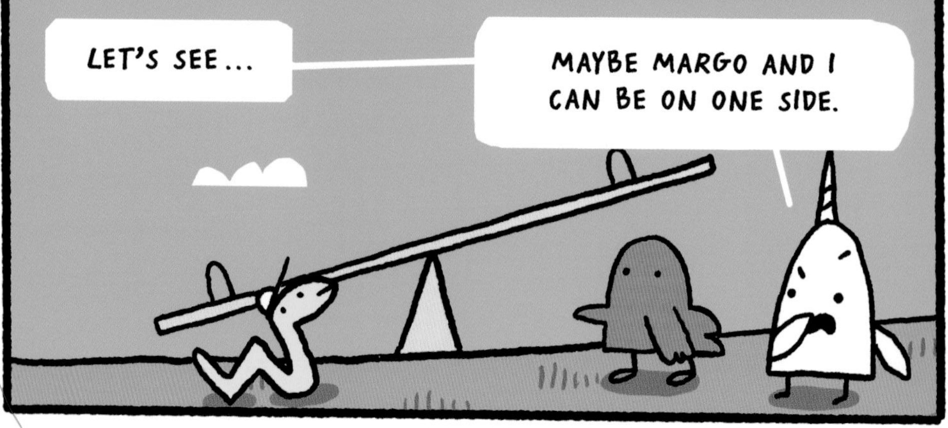
LET'S SEE...
MAYBE MARGO AND I CAN BE ON ONE SIDE.

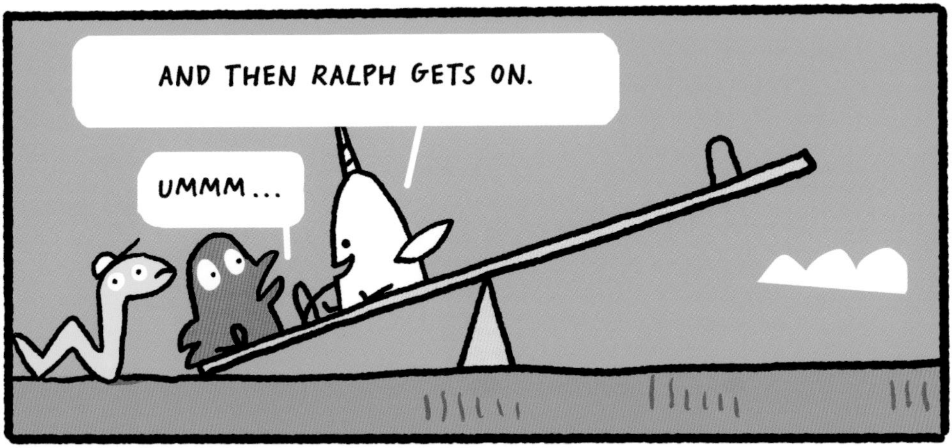
AND THEN RALPH GETS ON.
UMMM...

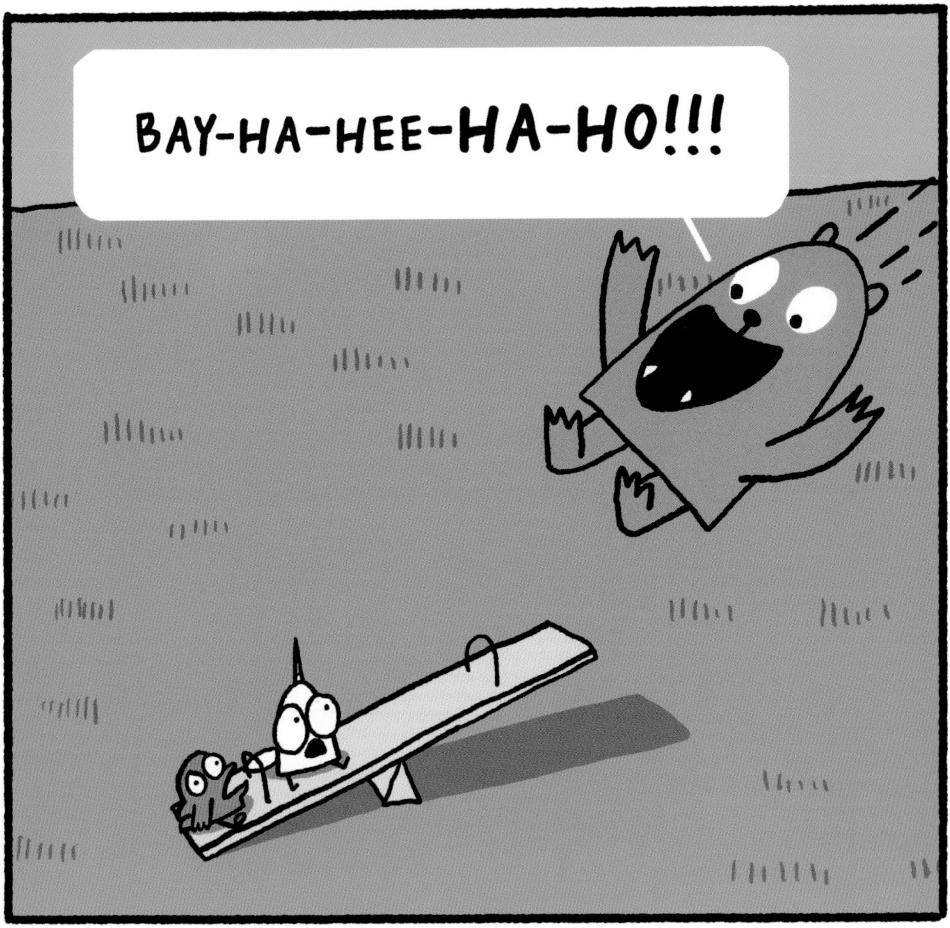
BAY-HA-HEE-HA-HO!!!

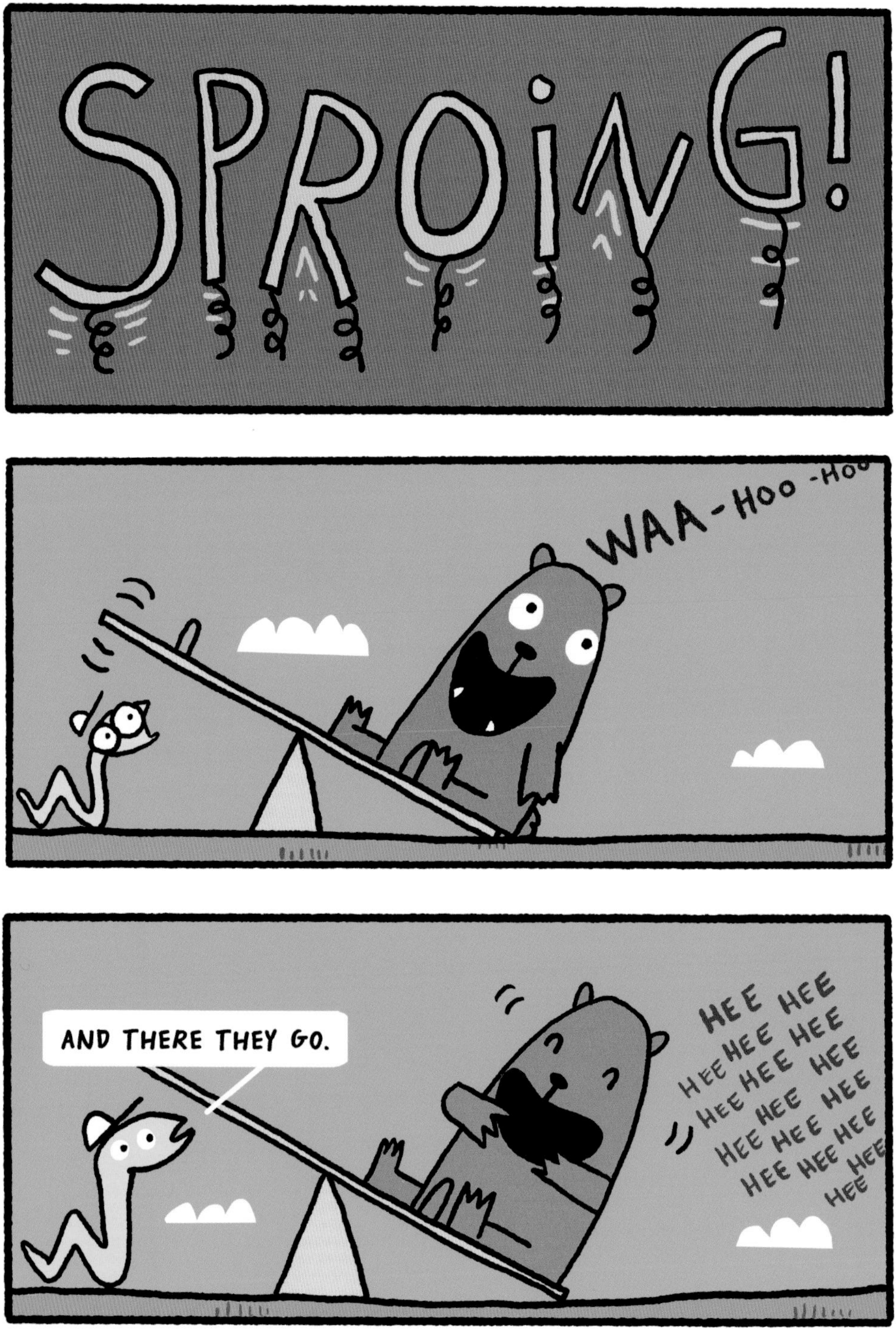
SPROING!
WAA-HOO-HOO
AND THERE THEY GO.
HEE HEE
HEE HEE HEE HEE
HEE HEE HEE HEE
HEE HEE HEE HEE
HEE HEE HEE HEE
HEE HEE HEE
HEE HEE HEE

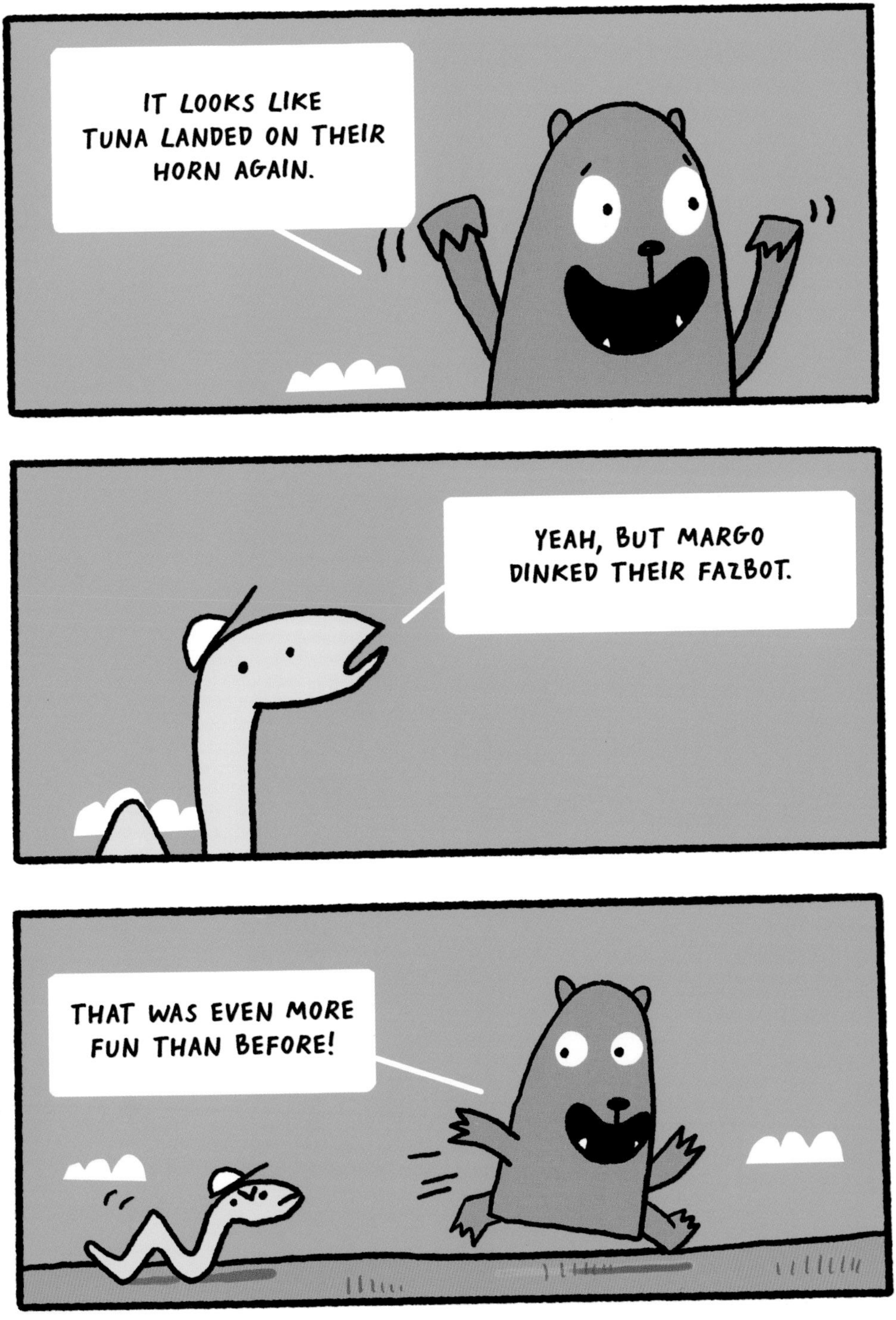
IT LOOKS LIKE TUNA LANDED ON THEIR HORN AGAIN.
YEAH, BUT MARGO DINKED THEIR FAZBOT.
THAT WAS EVEN MORE FUN THAN BEFORE!

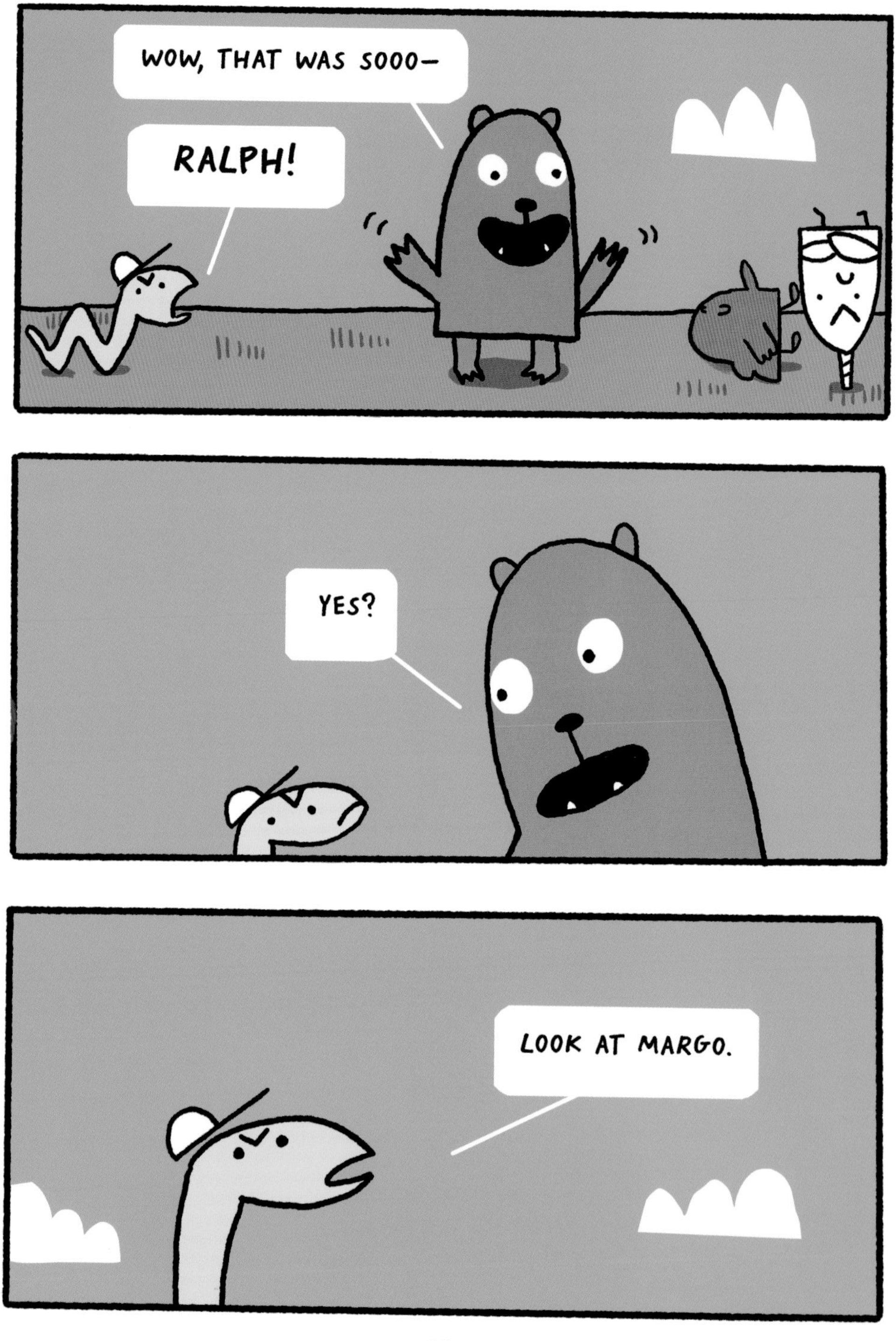
WOW, THAT WAS SOOO—
RALPH!
YES?
LOOK AT MARGO.

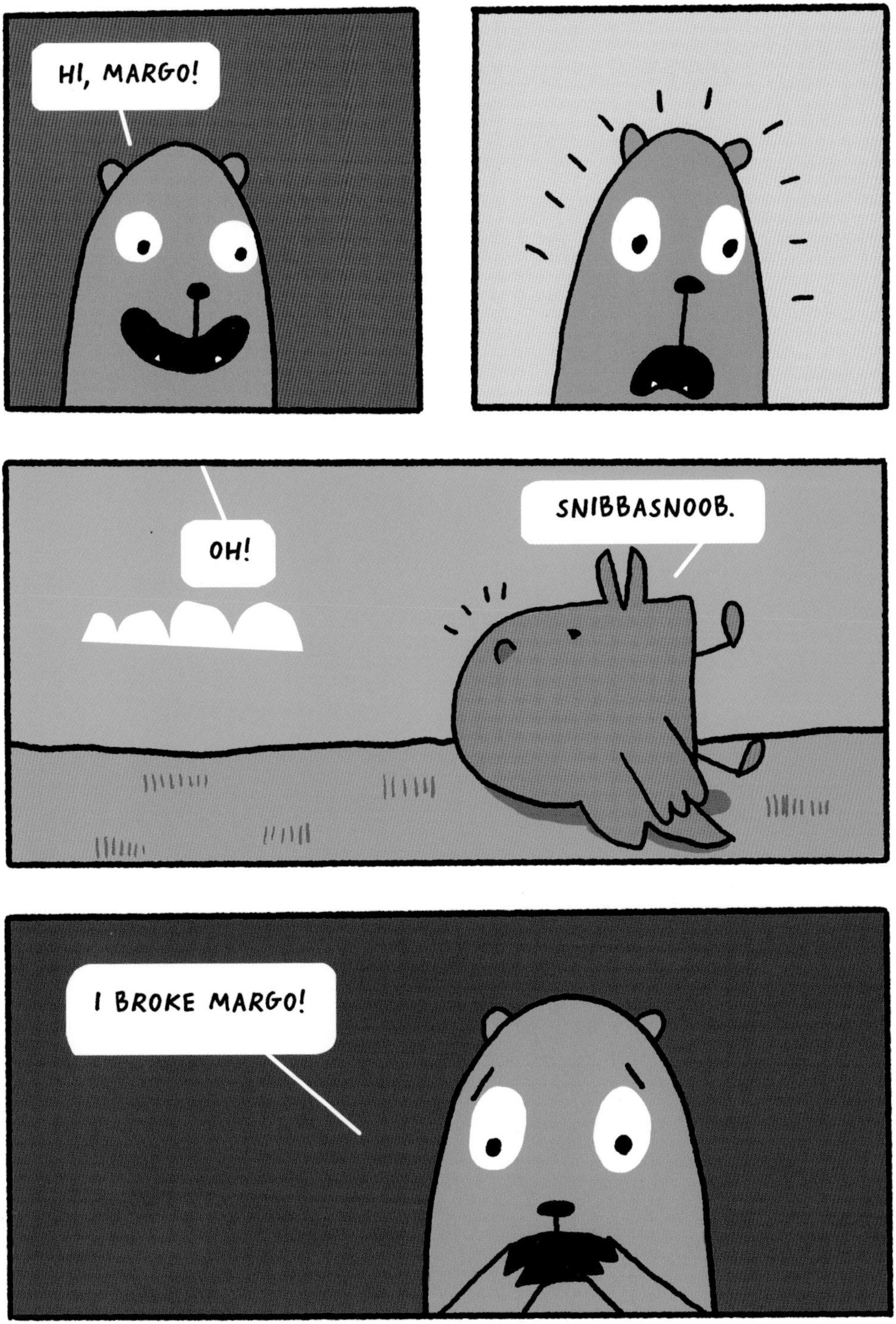
HI, MARGO!
OH!
SNIBBASNOOB.
I BROKE MARGO!

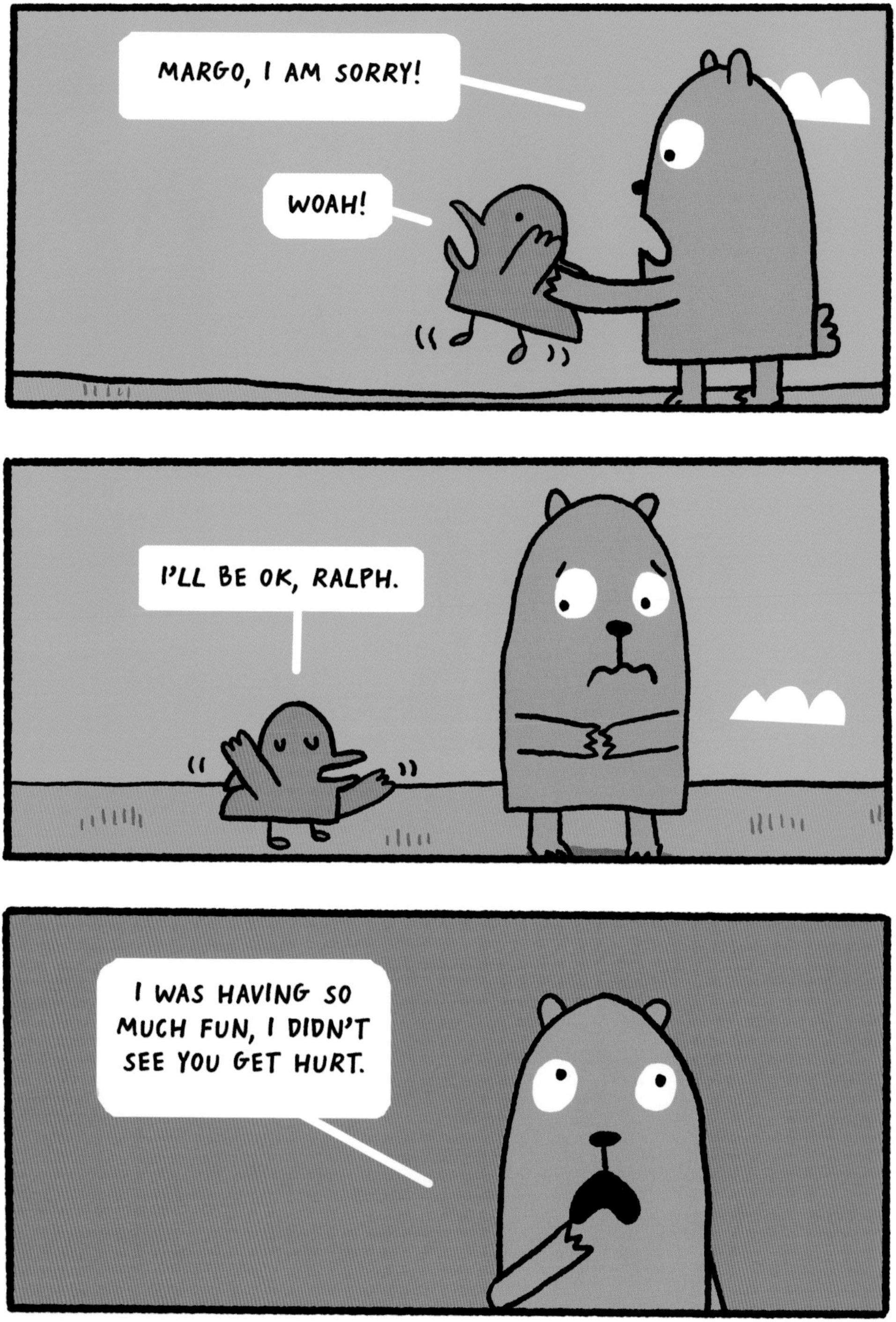
MARGO, I AM SORRY!
WOAH!
I'LL BE OK, RALPH.
I WAS HAVING SO MUCH FUN, I DIDN'T SEE YOU GET HURT.

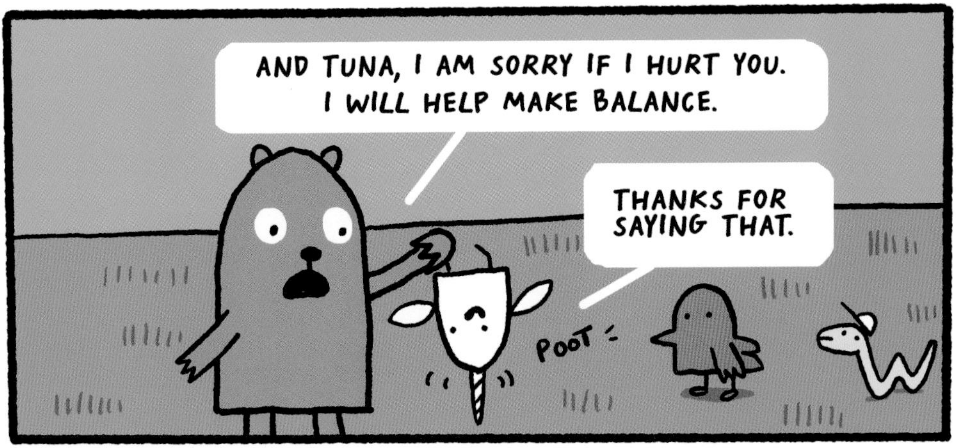
AND TUNA, I AM SORRY IF I HURT YOU. I WILL HELP MAKE BALANCE.
THANKS FOR SAYING THAT.
POOT

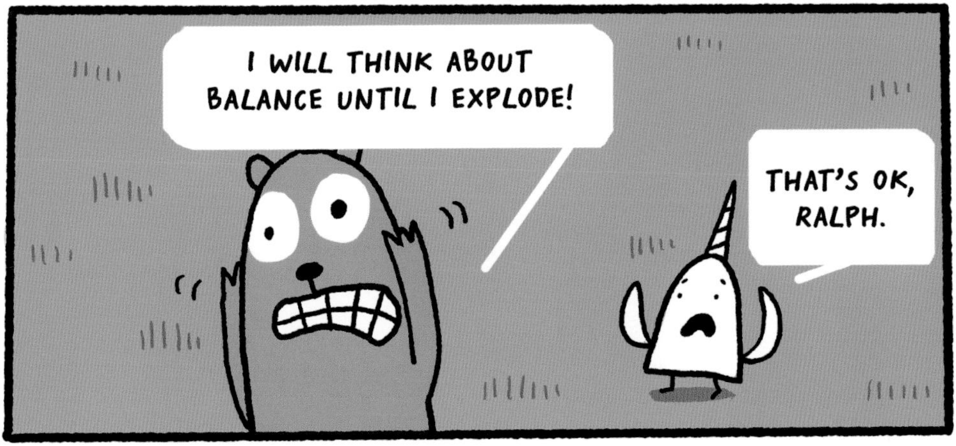
I WILL THINK ABOUT BALANCE UNTIL I EXPLODE!
THAT'S OK, RALPH.

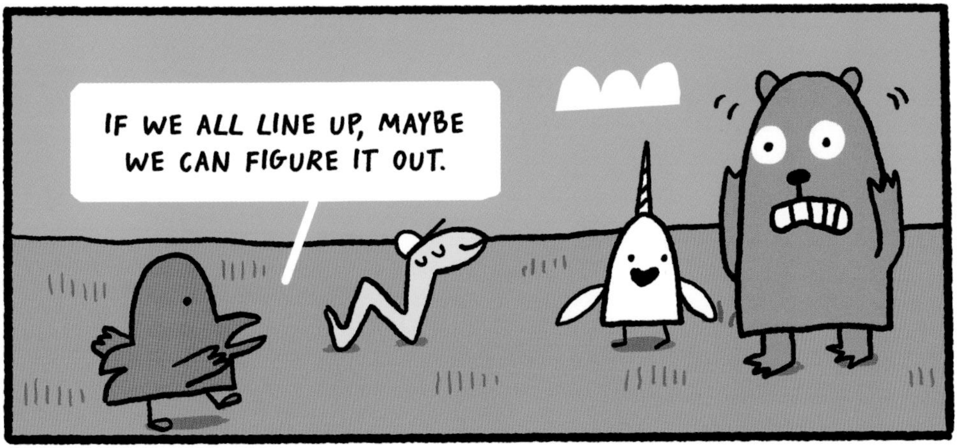
IF WE ALL LINE UP, MAYBE WE CAN FIGURE IT OUT.

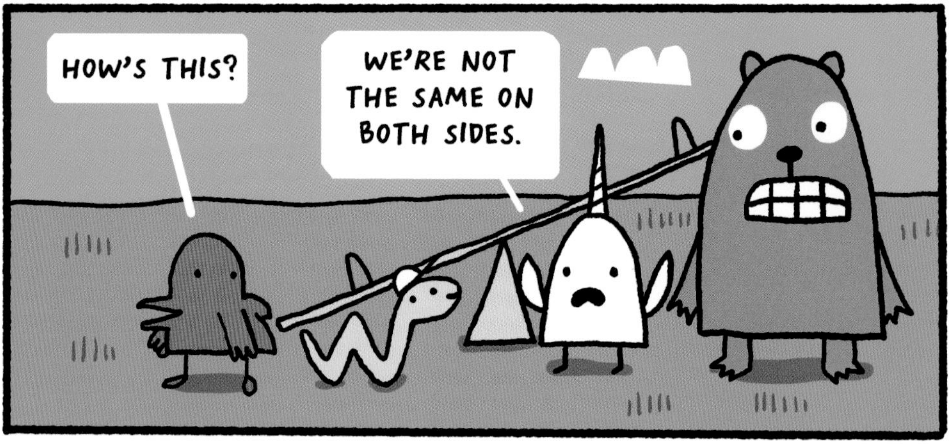
HOW'S THIS?
WE'RE NOT THE SAME ON BOTH SIDES.

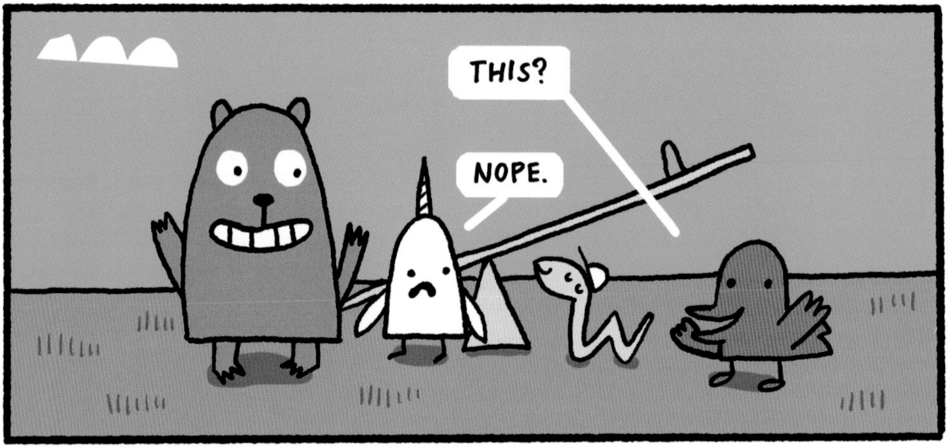
THIS?
NOPE.

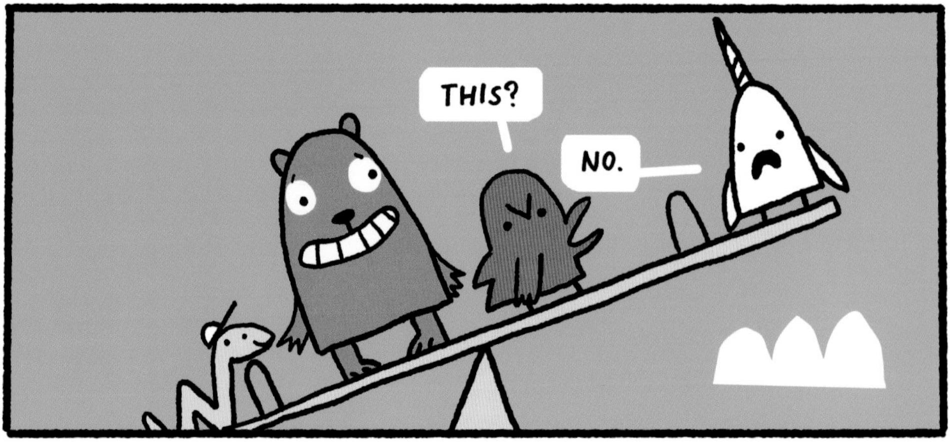
THIS?
NO.

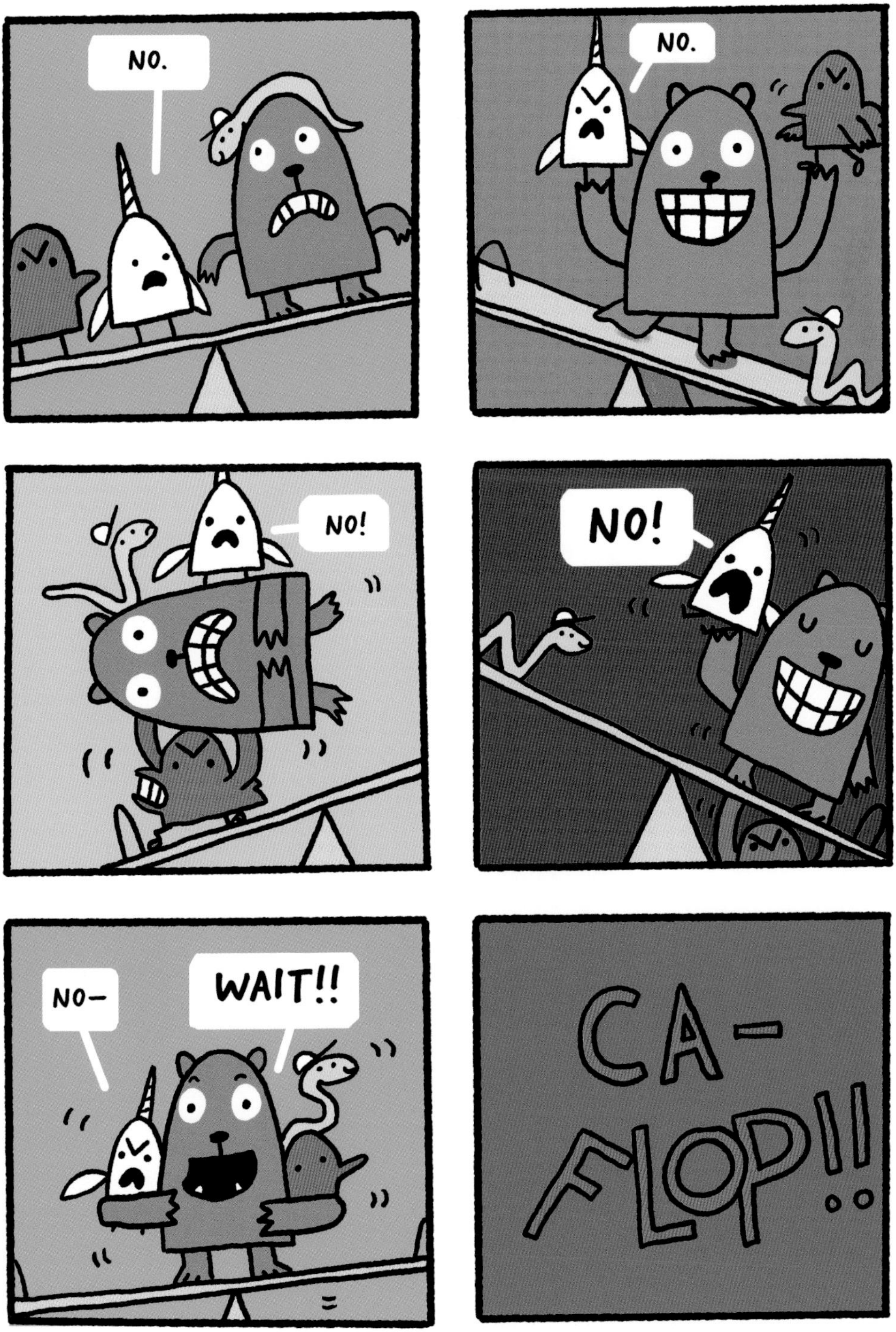
NO.
NO.
NO!
NO!
NO–
WAIT!!
CA-
FLOP!!

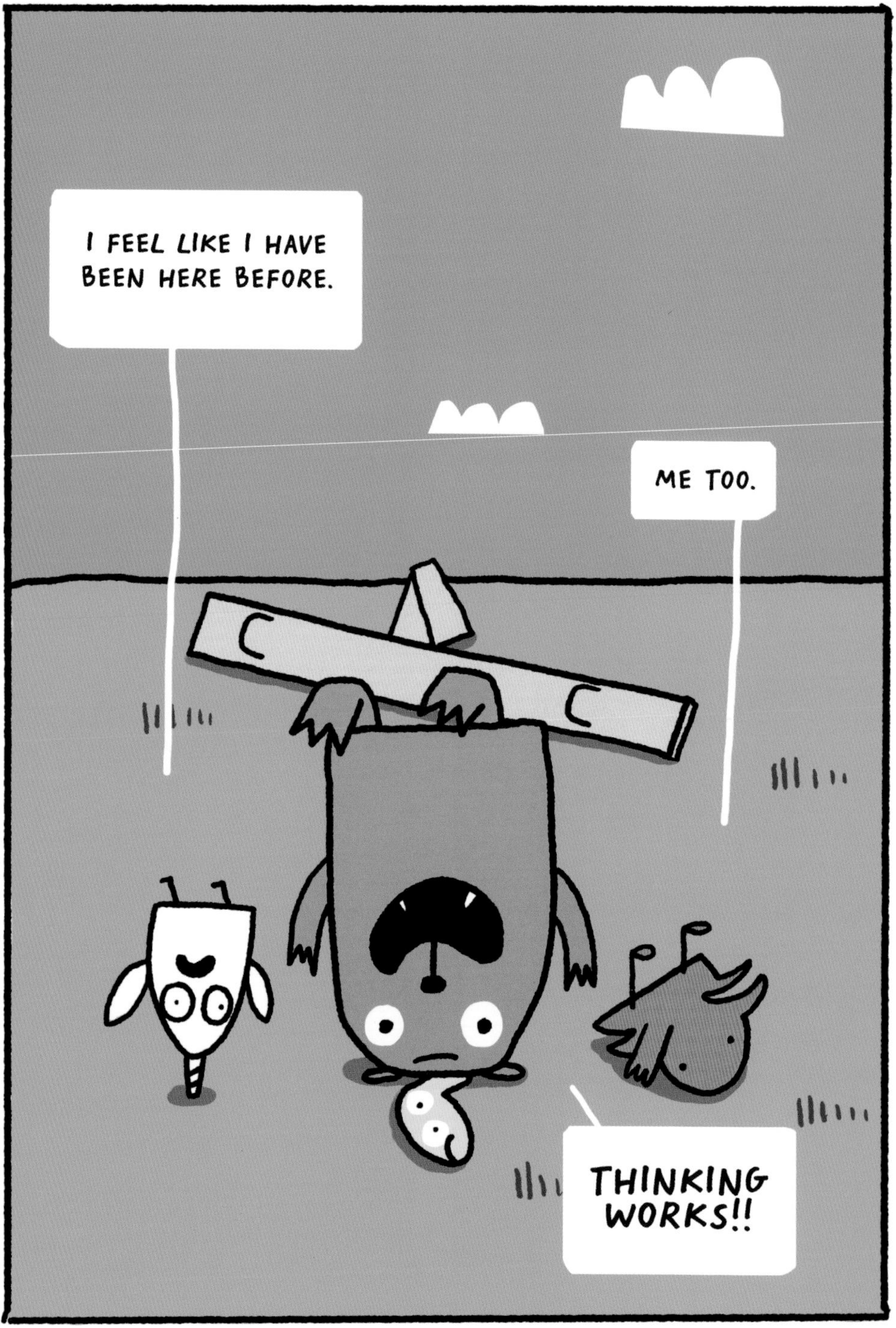
I FEEL LIKE I HAVE BEEN HERE BEFORE.
ME TOO.
THINKING WORKS!!

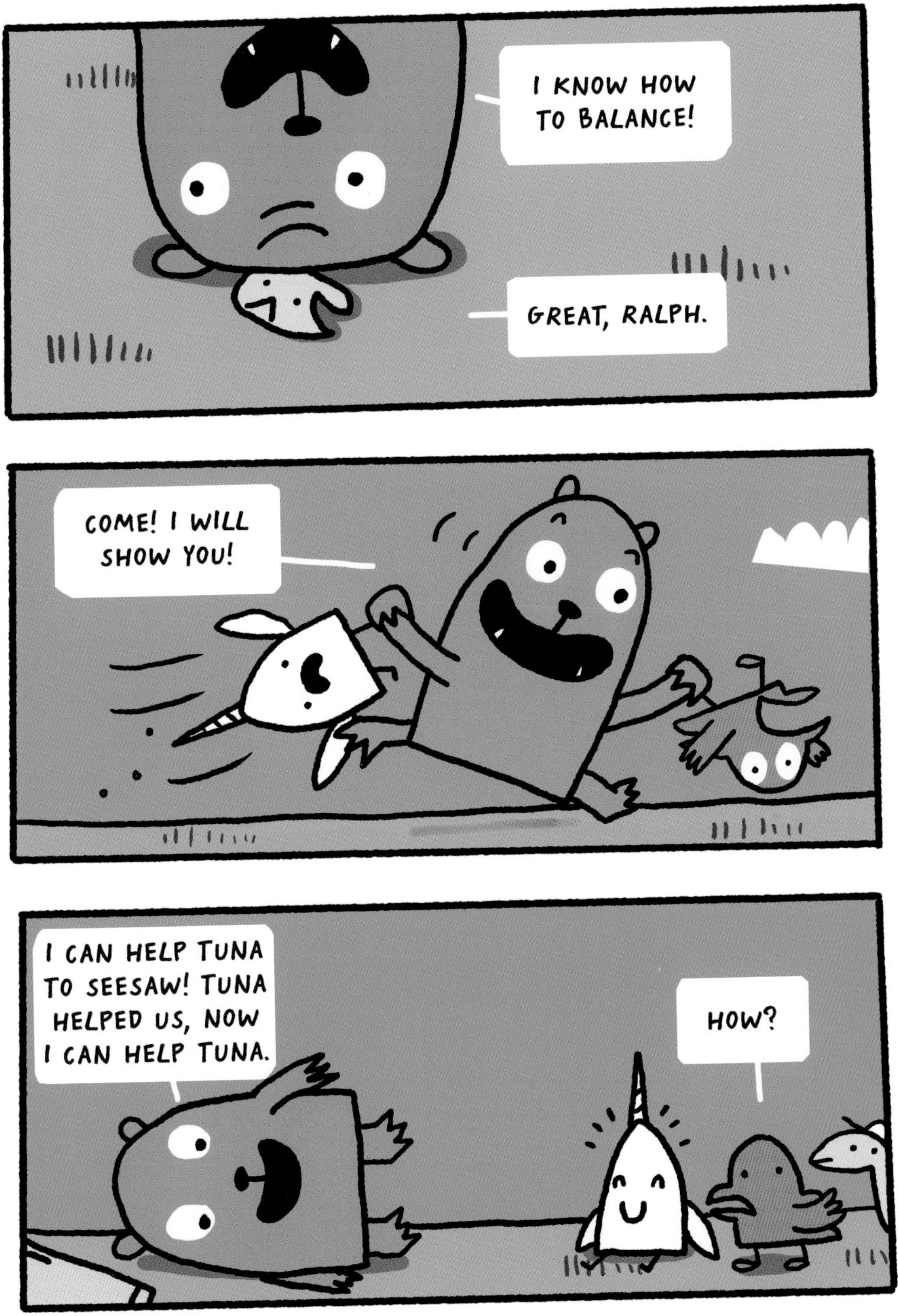
I KNOW HOW TO BALANCE!
GREAT, RALPH.
COME! I WILL SHOW YOU!
I CAN HELP TUNA TO SEESAW! TUNA HELPED US, NOW I CAN HELP TUNA.
HOW?

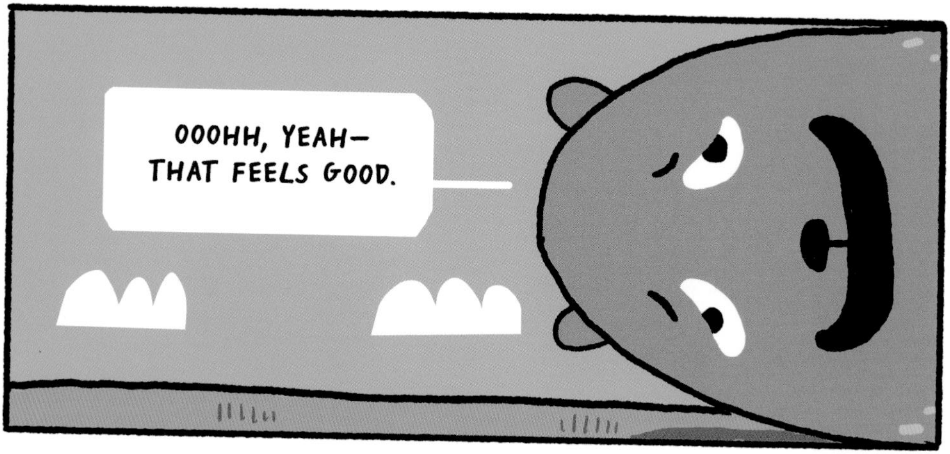
OOOHH, YEAH—
THAT FEELS GOOD.

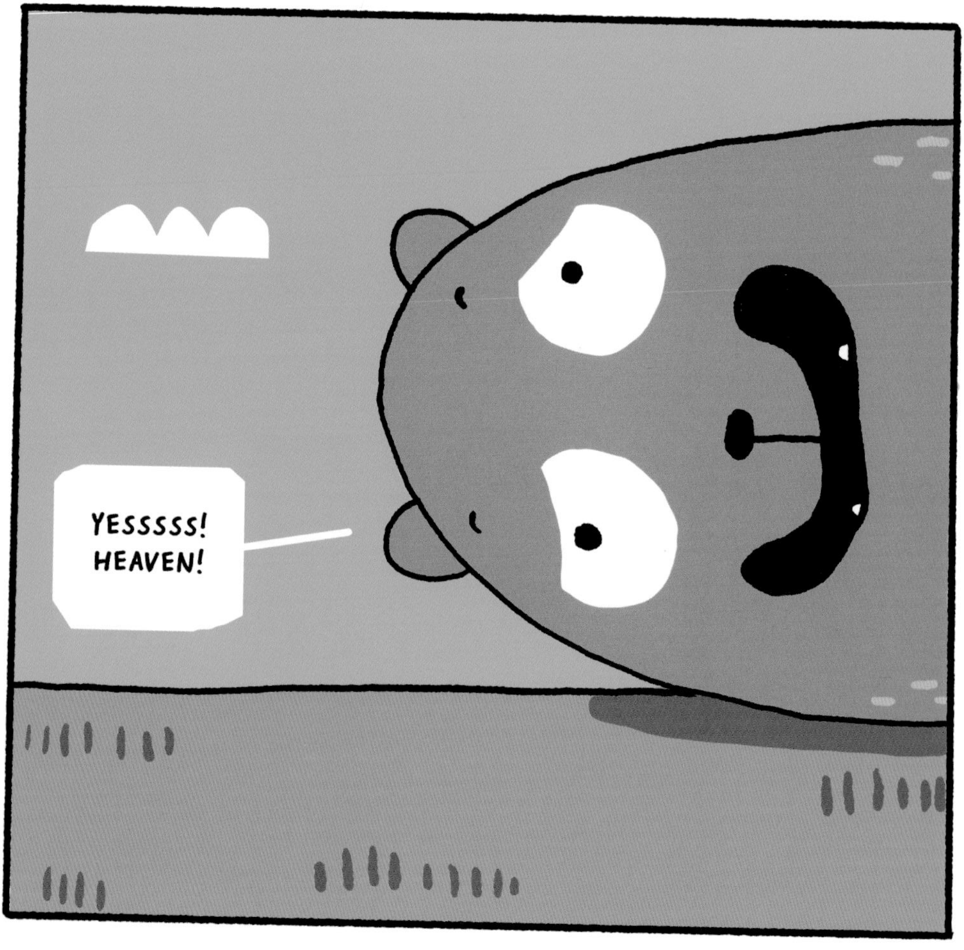
YESSSSS!
HEAVEN!

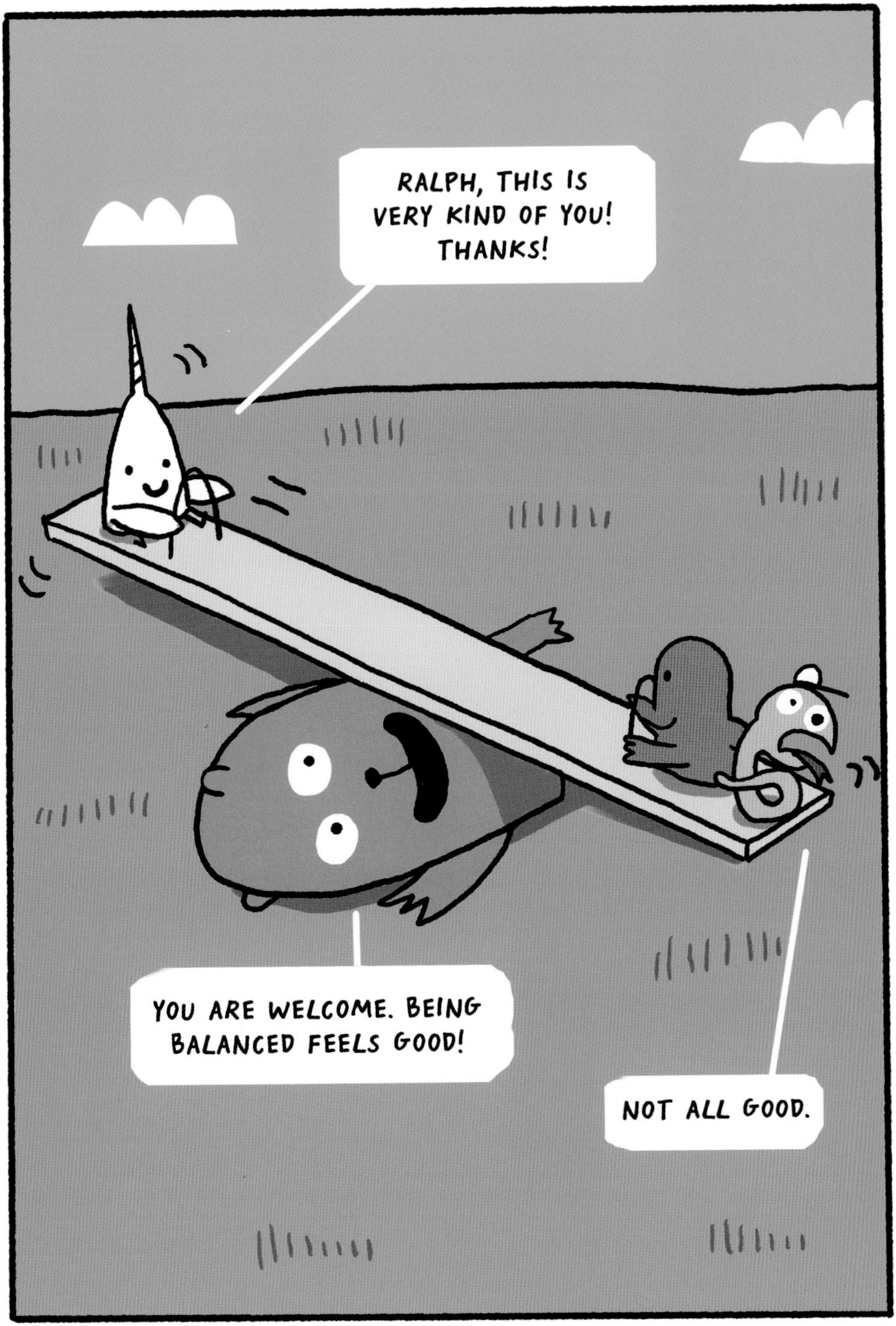
RALPH, THIS IS VERY KIND OF YOU! THANKS!
YOU ARE WELCOME. BEING BALANCED FEELS GOOD!
NOT ALL GOOD.

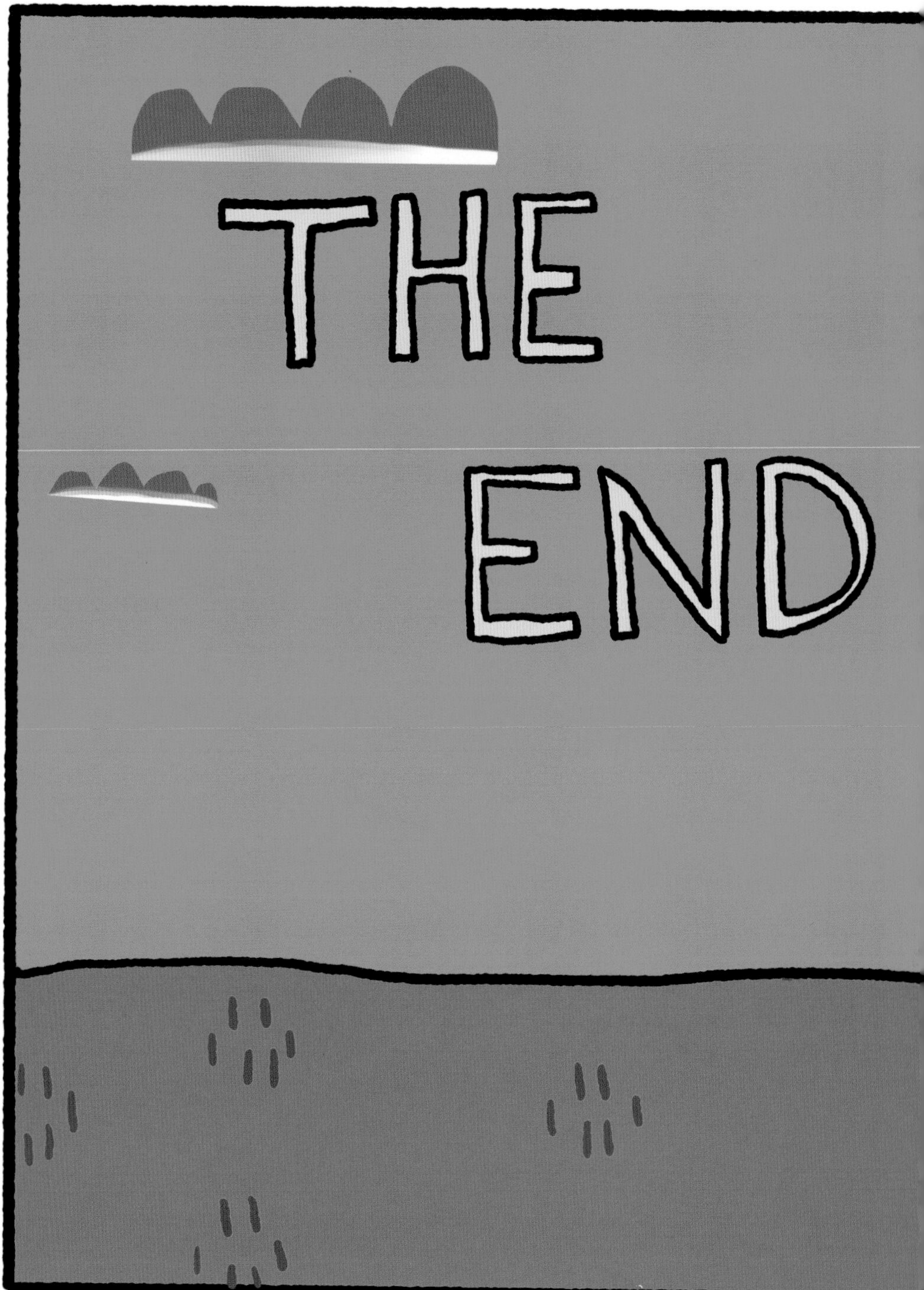
THE
END

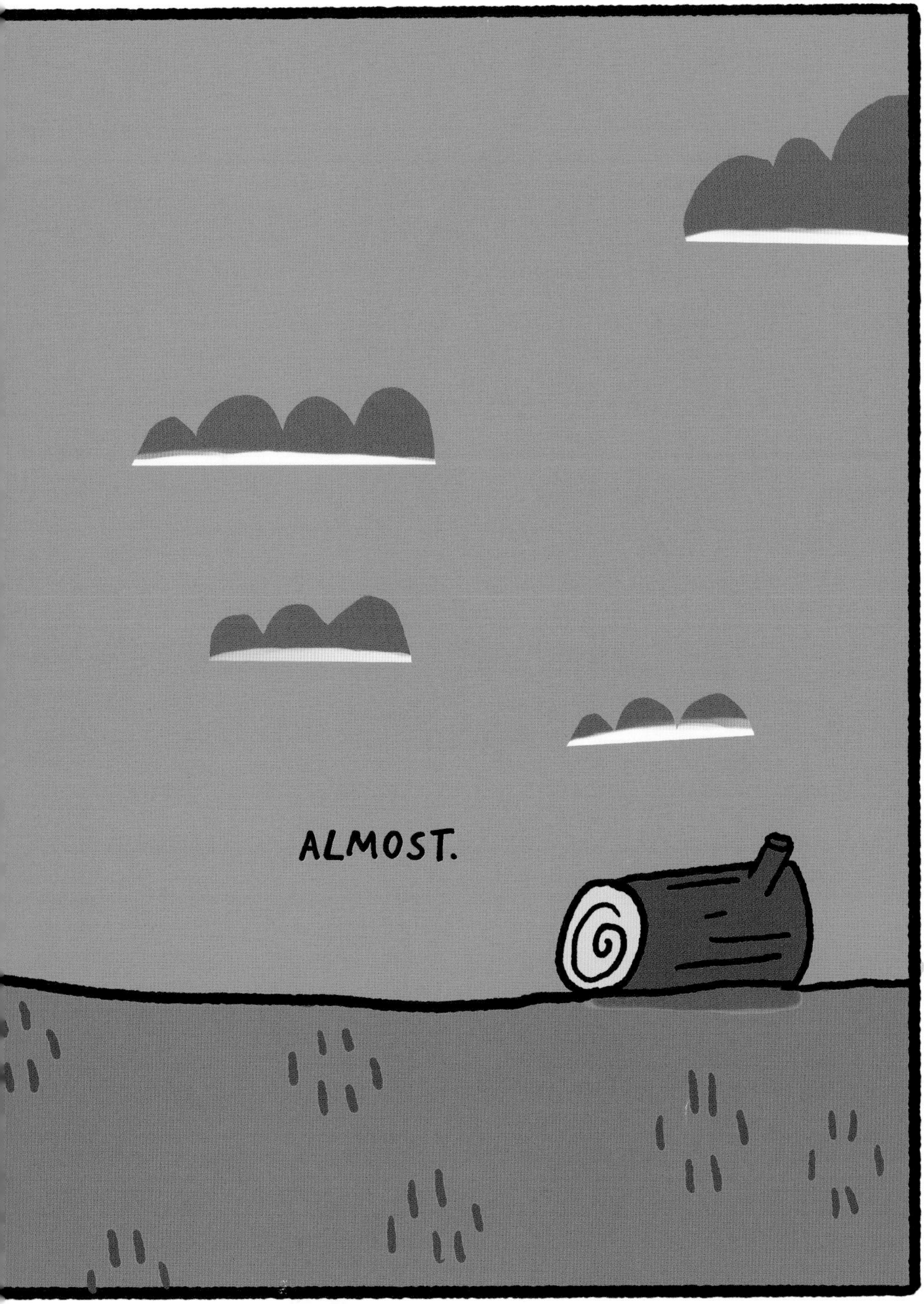
ALMOST.

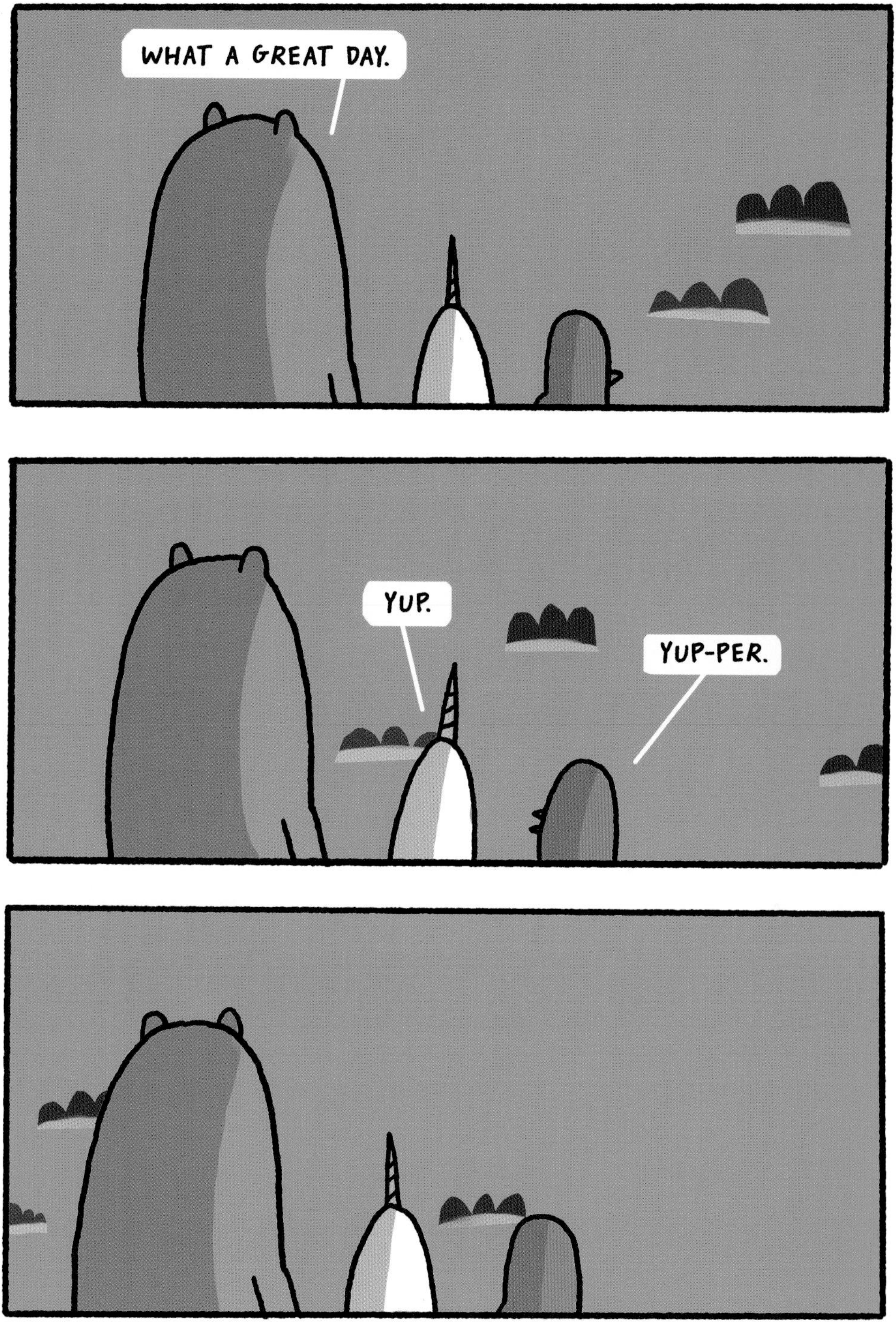
WHAT A GREAT DAY.
YUP.
YUP-PER.

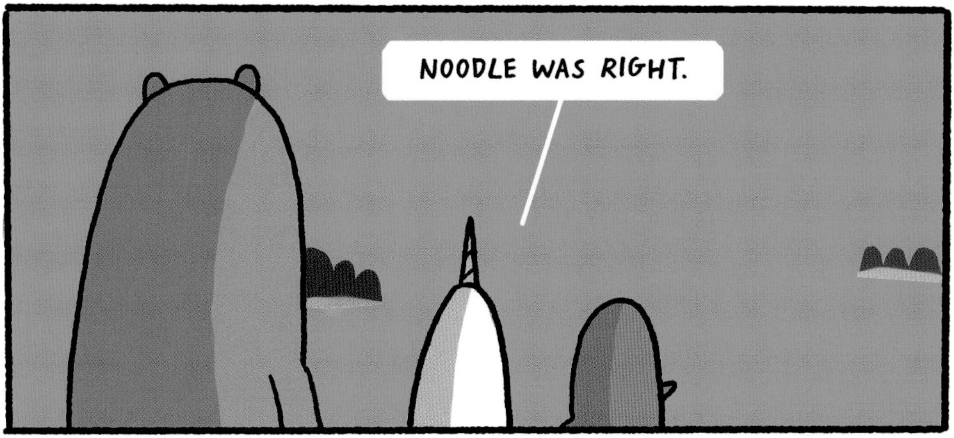
NOODLE WAS RIGHT.

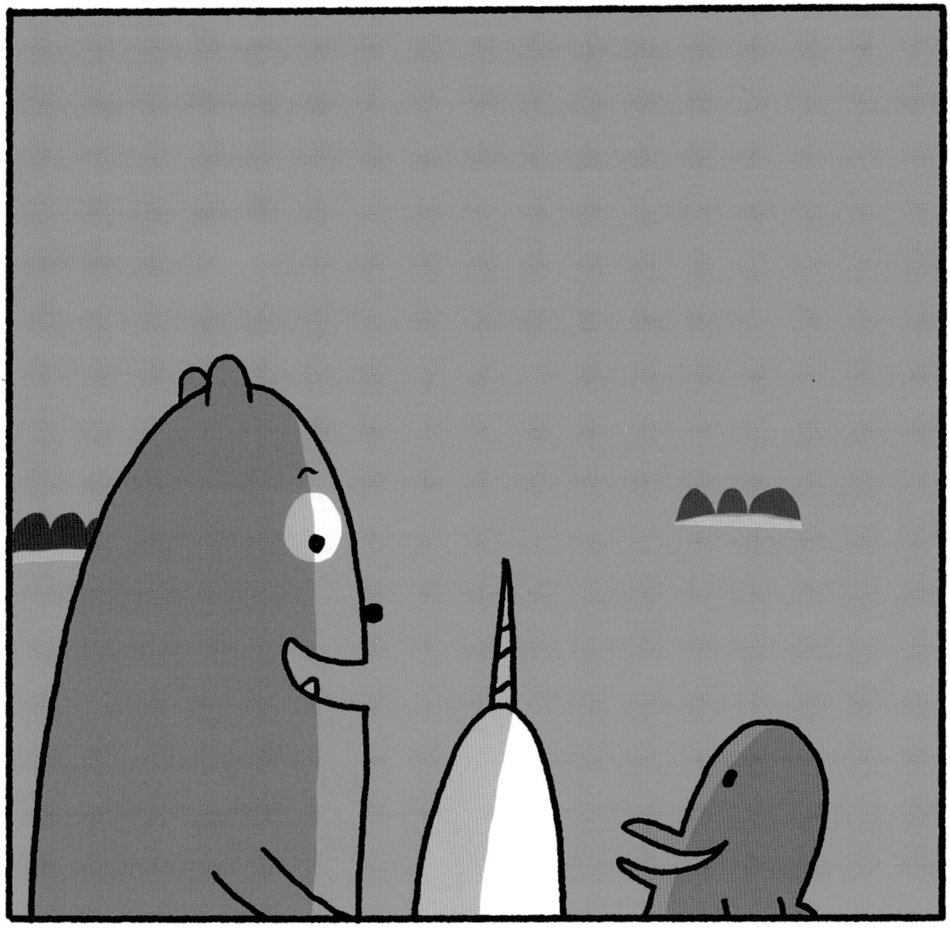

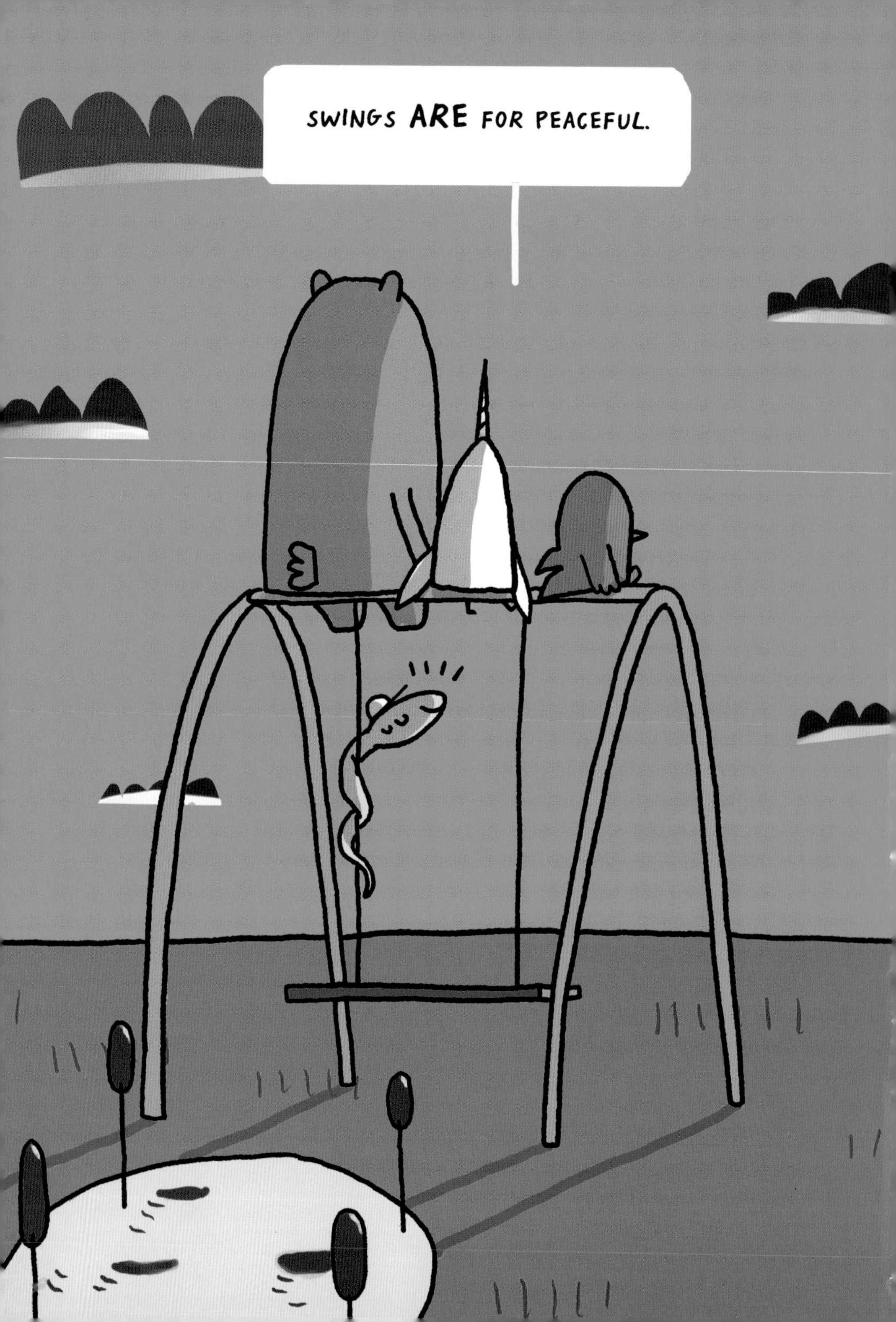
SWINGS ARE FOR PEACEFUL.